Death

of a

Master Chef

Also by Jean-Luc Bannalec

The Body by the Sea

The King Arthur Case

The Granite Coast Murders

The Killing Tide

The Missing Corpse

The Fleur de Sel Murders

Murder on Brittany Shores

Death in Brittany

Death

of a

Master Chef

—→❖ **A BRITTANY MYSTERY** ❖←—

Jean-Luc Bannalec

Translated by Jamie Lee Searle

MINOTAUR BOOKS
NEW YORK

First published in the United States by Minotaur Books, an imprint of St. Martin's Publishing Group

DEATH OF A MASTER CHEF. Copyright © 2020 by Verlag Kiepenheuer & Witsch. Translation copyright © 2024 Jamie Lee Searle. All rights reserved. Printed in the United States of America. For information, address St. Martin's Publishing Group, 120 Broadway, New York, NY 10271.

www.minotaurbooks.com

Designed by Devan Norman
Endpaper illustration © Shutterstock.com / Arsvik

Library of Congress Cataloging-in-Publication Data

Names: Bannalec, Jean-Luc, 1966- author. | Romanelli, Jamie Searle, translator.
Title: Death of a master chef / Jean-Luc Bannalec ; translated by Jamie Lee Searle.
Other titles: Bretonische Spezialitäten. English
Description: First U.S. edition. | New York : Minotaur Books, 2024. | Series: Brittany mystery series ; 9 |
Identifiers: LCCN 2023056207 | ISBN 9781250893055 (hardcover) | ISBN 9781250893079 (ebook)
Subjects: LCGFT: Detective and mystery fiction. | Novels.
Classification: LCC PT2662.A565 B73913 2024 | DDC 833/.92—dc23/eng/20231211
LC record available at https://lccn.loc.gov/2023056207

Our books may be purchased in bulk for promotional, educational, or business use. Please contact your local bookseller or the Macmillan Corporate and Premium Sales Department at 1-800-221-7945, extension 5442, or by email at MacmillanSpecialMarkets@macmillan.com.

Originally published in Germany
by Kiepenheuer & Witsch as *Bretonische Spezialitäten*

First U.S. Edition: 2024

10 9 8 7 6 5 4 3 2 1

À L.

À Stefan

Keuz a-raok ne vez ket
Keuz war-lerc'h ne dalv ket.
To regret—beforehand isn't done,
To regret after doesn't help.

—BRETON SAYING

Death

of a

Master Chef

The First Day

A piece of the Brillat-Savarin, please."

For a fraction of a second, he had hesitated. But Commissaire Georges Dupin from the Commissariat de Police Concarneau couldn't help it. He was salivating. It was one of his favorite cheeses. A rare, heavenly soft cheese. *Triple crème*. It tasted best on a fresh, crusty baguette, still warm from the oven.

To Dupin, cheese was a basic foodstuff—he could forgo many things, if it really came down to it, but not cheese. It probably ranked straight after coffee. And was followed by other unrelinquishable things, like baguettes and wine. Good charcuterie. And entrecôte, of course. Langoustines. On closer consideration, there was honestly so much that it made the definition of "unrelinquishable" seem absurd.

Dupin wandered up and down in front of the cheese stall in

the phenomenal market halls of Saint-Servan, a neighborhood to the west of Saint-Malo: "And a piece of the Langres too, please."

The market was lively but not hectic. It had that particular atmosphere of a week just beginning: the people had energy, and what lay ahead seemed conquerable. The Langres was another of Dupin's favorite cheeses, an orange-red-toned soft variety made from the raw milk of Champagne-Ardenne cows. It was refined with Calvados for several weeks and had an intense, spicily piquant taste.

"And also," he feigned hesitation, "a piece of the Rouelle du Tarn," a goat cheese from the south, aromatically well-balanced, with subtle notes of hazelnut.

Dozens of cheese varieties were displayed here, piled alongside and on top of one another. Cheese from goat, sheep, or cow milk, with a multitude of sizes, shapes, surfaces, and colors. Pure happiness.

The sign above the stand read *"Les Fromages de Sophie."* All kinds of cheese aromas hung in the air, mingling with the promising scents from the surrounding stands: fresh herbs, local and exotic spices, hard-cured sausage and pâtés, thick-bellied *cœur-de-bœuf* tomatoes, raspberries and strawberries, dried and candied fruits, irresistible pastries. An aromatic orchestra of savory and sweet. It made one hungry—for everything.

"Try some of this, monsieur: the Ferme de la Moltais, a Breton Tomme. It's from the Rennes region, also a cow milk cheese, with astonishingly fruity nuances. It has a slightly firmer, gorgeous texture. You'll see."

The friendly young woman with short dark hair, glasses, and a sky-blue scarf knotted around her neck proffered a piece of the cheese. Dupin had wanted to try it even before the cheesemonger's persuasive efforts—the sight of it alone was enough—but her description made it all the more enticing.

"Take it," commanded an elderly, impressively white-haired woman who stood behind him in the queue, raising her eyebrows. "You're standing at one of the best cheese stands in town, young man! And we have a lot of them! Obviously you're not from around here." It sounded like an accusation.

The woman had accurately identified Dupin as an outsider, even though the commissaire didn't have the faintest idea why. Admittedly he was "far up north" here, to the east of the Canal d'Ille-et-Rance, not far from the Normandy border; but Saint-Malo in its entirety belonged to Brittany. However, he had already noted from Nolwenn's and Riwal's initial reaction to the news he would be attending a police seminar in Saint-Malo for a few days that the matter was apparently more complicated. The city must have some kind of special status, because both of them—his wonderful assistant and his first inspector—had only visited once, while they'd been to every other place in Brittany, or so it seemed to Dupin, countless times.

In addition, and this was also rather suspicious, the encyclopedic instructions they usually inflicted on him as soon as he had to leave Concarneau for any other location in Brittany had never appeared. Instead, Nolwenn and Riwal had instantly begun to talk about the Creed of Saint-Malo, which had shaped the self-assured city for centuries. *Ni Français, ni Breton: Malouin suis!* Neither Frenchman nor Breton; inhabitant of Saint-Malo am I!

Malouin. Riwal had briefly explained that the city had been bestowed with fairy-tale wealth between the sixteenth and nineteenth centuries, initially through the textile trade, and then predominantly through piracy—the corsairs, who were legalized by the French kings. Rich, powerful, and independent. The small city had become a bold maritime power that acted on an equal footing with the other maritime powers of the era. And so the *malouinière* character had formed: victory-assured, sovereign, proud. To some—like Nolwenn and Riwal—it was more like: arrogant, superior, cocky. What's more, the willful—scandalous, even—claim of not being Breton was deeply provocative. And yet the flip side, not belonging to the French, prompted the warmest Breton sympathies. The rebellion against all "foreign rule," the unconditional love of freedom and the defiant will to risk life and limb protecting it, all of this was, of course, deeply ingrained in the Breton spirit, with the result that Riwal, by the end of his uncharacteristically short explanation, had arrived at a bold paradox: that Saint-Malo, precisely because it didn't want to be Breton, was a "uniquely Breton, downright ur-Breton city." He had even expressed considerable praise: that the region was—"one has to give it fair recognition"—the culinary heart of Brittany. "A singular epicurean feast! The whole region, that is, including Dinard and Cancale, not just Saint-Malo."

"This Tomme is aged for ten weeks with secret ingredients!" The cheesemonger interrupted Dupin's train of thought. "Breton cheese has swiftly gained popularity over the last few years, monsieur. The young *affineurs* in particular are producing some fantastic creations."

Dupin really liked trying the offerings at market stands. It was an essential part of visiting the market. By the time he left the Concarneau halls on Saturday mornings, he was always full. Dupin loved markets in general—culinary paradises, which, through the sheer variety of their offerings, the abundance and overabundance, were capable of unleashing a sweet rapture.

Stands with kitchen utensils, especially pots and knives, were also an integral component of the rich market culture; Dupin had a penchant for good knives.

The Marché de Saint-Servan in Saint-Malo was a particularly noteworthy market. Not just for its location in the heart of this atmospheric part of the town, but also the exceptionally beautiful building. Dating from the 1920s, Dupin presumed. The floor was laid with large beige tiles, the walkways lined with rust-colored columns. The most impressive feature was that glass had been integrated wherever possible, letting light flood in from all around. The window and door frames were a maritime turquoise green, and there were decorative metal arches in the aisles, including above Sophie's cheese stall.

"I'll take a big piece, please." Dupin was blown away by it.

"Anything else, monsieur?" The saleswoman smiled expectantly. "I also have a . . ."

Now it was time for the voice of reason.

"No, thank you. That's it for today."

She weighed the pieces at an impressive speed and packed them, no less swiftly, into a light blue paper bag with the inscription *"Les Fromages de Sophie,"* which Dupin took from her contentedly.

He was fully aware it hadn't been a good idea to buy so much cheese, or to buy any cheese at all, for that matter. They would undoubtedly be given plenty to eat over the coming days. The packed seminar schedule—four pages in landscape format—included a restaurant visit every evening.

Dupin's mood had brightened significantly while he was in the market; he had begun with two *petits cafés* in the Café du Théâtre, on the corner of the tree-lined square in front of the market halls. On his arrival at the police school campus at 7:58 that morning, his mood had seemed low, only to sink even further, all the way through to lunch. Still: it was a beautiful summer's day. Everyone in Concarneau had warned the commissaire of the cold and rain "up north," even now, in early June, but currently it was twenty-eight degrees, the sun was blazing, and the sky a brilliant, shining blue.

His good mood unfortunately wouldn't last long. In twenty minutes, he had to be back in the police school. While conferences of this kind were essentially a nightmare for Dupin, this one was sure to be even worse than any that had preceded it. A month before, the prefect had turned up unannounced in Concarneau, and with a beaming smile, had declared to Dupin: "I have news, a great honor for you, Commissaire." Dupin hadn't been able to imagine—hadn't *wanted* to imagine—what the prefect meant, but had instantly feared the worst. And of course, he'd been right to. In the first week of June, at the École de Police de Saint-Malo, one of the most revered police schools in the country, there would be a "unique seminar." Every prefect from the four Breton *départements*—three women and one man—had been asked to select a commissaire to participate alongside them. It really couldn't get any worse. The unbearable thought of he and Locmariaquer, together, for four whole days, Monday morning to Thursday evening. That was many, many hours. Longer than ever before. Dupin usually managed to keep his encounters with the prefect drastically short. The comfortable special status that Dupin had commanded for a long time, due to an attractive job offer from Paris, had been forfeited last autumn when he'd definitively turned it down—ending, in the process, the prefect's moratorium on attacks. Their exhausting feud had long since resumed. Locmariaquer's final sentence sealed the deal: "You should know that this extraordinary seminar is also a recognition of your team's untiring engagement. Our colleagues in Saint-Malo have created an incredibly appealing accompanying program, you'll see."

For the purposes of "intensive team building," the idea had been to have shared accommodation in the police school. A horror scenario had shot into Dupin's mind: prefects and commissaires in double rooms or dormitories, certainly with shared bathrooms. After first pondering falling victim to a severe flu-like infection in the coming month—which would have meant house arrest—he had taken immediate action, searching online for a nice, small hotel. It hadn't taken him long to find one: the Villa Saint Raphaël, a pretty *maison d'hôtes* in the center of Saint-Servan. Sure, Locmariaquer had been far from happy when he got wind of it, but Dupin accepted that.

He had arrived in Saint-Malo the previous evening, after a relaxing drive through the deserted Breton inland, and had established he couldn't have chosen better lodgings; his room—directly below the roof—was wonderful, just like the entire Villa Saint Raphaël and its expansive garden. Dupin still wasn't sure what the "unique seminar" was actually about. Neither the documents sent out in advance nor the truly impassioned introductory words from the host prefect of Département Ille-et-Vilaine that morning had been able to shed any light. The prefect had said something about "improving operative, practical working alliances" between the four *départements*, adding with a smile that "the most important thing, however, was to get to know one another better in the relaxed atmosphere of Saint-Malo" and to "spend a few enjoyable and constructive days together." She had meant it seriously. And it fit the genuinely impressive accompanying program, from which Nolwenn and Riwal had surmised that a large part of this, for the proud Malouins, was self-promotion. "They even make a police seminar into a PR show . . ." A malicious interpretation, in Dupin's opinion. If Concarneau were the host location, they too would call upon everything the region had to offer. The eternal battle of the Breton tribes: Who was the best, the most Breton of them all? An ancient tradition.

Either way, it was a curious concept: all the prefects and commissaires crowded together in one place. Dupin couldn't help but think of the Druids' gathering in *Asterix and Obelix*.

Sighing deeply, Dupin made his way toward the market exit. "We'll recommence at two o'clock on the dot!" Locmariaquer had warned him as he left the seminar room. At least it wasn't far to the police school, whose grounds were as sprawling as a small village. Four hectares, the prefect had explained, in the best of locations, not far from the world-famous old town of Saint-Malo—*intra muros*—and its equally famous beach.

Dupin's gaze rested on a stall selling delectable-looking sausage meats. Breton sausages, entire hams, raw, cooked, smoked.

"How can I help you?" asked the tall stall owner.

"I . . ."

Dupin was interrupted by high, shrill screaming.

It came from nearby, perhaps just a few meters away.

Terrible screams. Screams of pain. Dupin whipped around to look. To his right was an imposing spice stall.

Something was happening toward the back of the stall, next to one of the columns.

The screams of pain stopped suddenly, but were replaced by different ones, of panic. And agitated voices.

Dupin darted toward the scene, ready to intervene. His muscles tensed.

The panicked cries came from two women who had terror etched on their faces. Other market visitors backed away in shock or began to run. Chaos broke out.

All at once, the screams stopped.

On the sparkling tiles—Dupin only saw her now—a woman lay on her right side, contorted, unmoving. Her white linen shirt was stained a deep red at chest height. There were several punctures in the fabric. And the most macabre detail: plunged right into where her heart was, there was a knife.

Dupin was beside her in a flash, crouching down, putting his ear to her mouth, checking her wrist, then her neck, for a pulse.

He pulled his cell phone out of his jeans pocket.

"Commissaire Dupin. I need an ambulance right away, Marché de Saint-Servan, by the big spice stall, close to the exit. A woman's been stabbed, she's unresponsive," he said professionally, "stabbed in the heart." He glanced around and noticed the stand selling knives, which he had just walked past, right next to the spice stall. "A kitchen knife, it's still in her body. And," he hesitated briefly, "send the police."

Dupin had great difficulty finding a pulse—it was incredibly weak.

"A doctor? Is there a doctor here?" called Dupin—still crouched down—as loudly as he could. "I'm a policeman. This woman is seriously injured."

A few of the market visitors had gathered curiously around him, but no one made any move to help.

Dupin had an ominous feeling. The woman was in critical condition. She wasn't making a sound.

"She ran out over there. The woman who did it." A girl, perhaps twelve or thirteen years old, had come over to Dupin and was pointing toward the exit. "She went out there, just now. Then she turned left."

Dupin quickly got to his feet.

"That's right." A short-haired woman appeared next to the girl, perhaps in her forties, presumably the mother. "Two women were yelling at each other. Then one suddenly stabbed the other one. It happened so quickly. She just grabbed a knife from that stall. They were standing here by the column, I saw it out of the corner of my eye. What're you waiting for, follow them!"

Dupin hesitated; he couldn't just leave the severely injured victim lying here.

"I'll take care of her. I'm a teacher and a first-aid helper at our school."

She was already leaning over the woman.

Dupin rushed off. The police and paramedics were sure to arrive any moment.

He didn't have a gun. A mistake, but he ran on regardless.

Reaching the exit, he headed left along Rue Georges Clemenceau.

And there, up ahead—a woman, running away frantically.

Dupin quickened his pace.

By the end of the street, he had already gained a few meters on her.

Once again, the woman turned left. Rue de Siam.

Annoyingly Dupin had only a rough orientation of the town, but his gut told him they weren't far from the sea; the *port de plaisance* had to be nearby, he had driven past it the previous evening.

The fugitive switched sides of the street. She had noticed her pursuer, and was glancing over her shoulder at regular intervals, all without slowing down.

Now she turned in to a long, straight road.

The distance between them continued to shrink. Dupin had a good chance. He mobilized all his strength. Suddenly, a gap appeared between the rows of houses, giving a broad view of the ocean and marina.

Now Dupin realized what she was heading toward. A parking lot. The road forked and created a long, drawn-out strip, big enough for two lanes of traffic.

The woman ran another few meters, then squeezed into a gap between two cars. The taillights of one of the vehicles briefly illuminated twice.

Another twenty meters. Dupin would have to hurry.

She was in her car already. The engine roared into life.

Ten meters.

The car reversed abruptly. The woman steered sharply to the right. Braked violently. Within seconds, she would switch into first gear.

Dupin had reached the car, a smaller-model Land Rover, dark blue. He knew he only had a fraction of a second. Without hesitating, Dupin reached for the handle of the left rear door.

At that moment, the car lurched forward. Dupin lost his balance and had to let go of the handle; the force of the acceleration pulled him to the ground. As he rolled away to the left, the car tore along the row of parked vehicles.

Dupin immediately got back on his feet, sprinting after it.

At the end of the parking lot, the fugitive would file left into the traffic—and perhaps have to slow down, he hoped.

But it was in vain. The blue Land Rover accelerated and drove straight out onto the street. Now the parked cars blocked his view. He heard a revving engine and, a moment later, loud beeping accompanied by a deafening metallic bang, swiftly followed by another.

Dupin had reached the end of the parking lot and ran onto the street.

All that could be seen of the Land Rover were the taillights. It turned sharply left at the end of the street.

He looked around: there had been a serious crash. One car had clearly tried to swerve around the Land Rover and had driven into the side of the parked cars; another vehicle—this collision didn't look as bad—had gone into the back of it.

Dupin ran toward the first car. The driver, a man in his mid-thirties, opened the door.

"Are you injured?"

"I—yes—I mean, no. Not injured."

The man seemed shaken, but unharmed.

A pedestrian, who must've seen the whole thing, hurried over and pulled out his cell phone.

"I'll call an ambulance."

The cars coming from the opposite direction had stopped too; a few of the drivers got out, ready to help.

Dupin headed straight toward a small Peugeot with promising rally stripes on its side. A young man with closely shaven hair, who had stayed in his car and now rolled down the window, stared up at him.

"Commissaire Georges Dupin," Dupin informed him without any further explanation. "I need to borrow your car briefly."

It took the driver a moment to grasp what he was saying. The commissaire's posture, expression, and tone made it abundantly clear that this wasn't a joke.

"I . . ."

"Please get out." A command, not a request.

The young man looked hesitant, but then did as he was told. Dupin pushed past him into the Peugeot.

"And how do I get my car back?"

Dupin was already at the wheel.

"Pick it up later from the police school."

He slammed the door shut, started the engine, and floored the gas pedal. A deafening screech pounded his eardrums as the car leaped forward. The police didn't call these cars "boy racers" for nothing.

The commissaire sped off, turning left at the end of the street. A tangle of streets and alleys appeared, and the Land Rover was nowhere to be seen. Dupin presumed the fugitive would head for the main roads. He followed the widest one. After about a hundred meters, it veered to the left, then continued straight. There were two other cars in front of him, which he decisively overtook in one go; the light, compact Peugeot was unbelievably nimble. Soon Dupin emerged onto one of the larger boulevards and made a split-second decision to head away from the town.

In all probability, what he was doing was pointless, but to stop now would have felt like giving up without a fight.

He steered toward a large roundabout with tall trees in its

center. Further daring overtaking maneuvers followed, one of which was a very close call.

Beyond the roundabout, the road widened even more. Dupin had to brake sharply—a traffic jam.

"Wonderful!" he exclaimed. There was still no sign of the dark blue Land Rover—which, admittedly, could be down to the large school bus a few cars in front of Dupin. The traffic moved slowly; then there was another roundabout. Eventually, a large sign indicated the N176, the "four-laner"—the Breton highway.

For no discernible reason, the traffic jam suddenly cleared. In next to no time, the Peugeot's speedometer was showing 120 kilometers per hour. In a few moments Dupin would have to decide: Was he heading toward Mont Saint-Michel and into Normandy, in other words, eastward, or toward Saint-Brieuc, westward?

"Damn it!"

As soon as the expletive left his mouth, he thought he saw a higher, dark-toned car some way ahead of him driving along the N176 toward Saint-Brieuc. Dupin kept to the right. All of a sudden, his telephone rang. Not the best timing.

Dupin floored the accelerator, and the engine responded noisily.

The road ran in a gentle curve, and now Dupin could see the car in more detail.

It was the one. Unmistakably. A Land Rover. This time he wouldn't lose it.

Or would he? As hard as he pushed his foot on the gas pedal, he couldn't get past 170 kilometers per hour. Little by little, the distance between them increased, and Dupin wasn't able to do the slightest thing about it.

He had no choice but to watch as the woman in the Land Rover raced away.

"I don't believe this!" Dupin pounded the steering wheel.

The game was lost. She'd escaped him yet again.

"God damn it!"

The penetrating tone of his cell phone started up again. He rummaged around for it with his right hand. He was still driving at top speed in the fast lane, not wanting to fully admit defeat.

"Yes?" he barked angrily into the phone.

"It's Locmariaquer." A markedly displeased tone. "We've been waiting for you for eighteen minutes. Group work in twos is planned for this afternoon. When can we expect you to grace us with your presence?"

"I'm . . ." Dupin contemplated simply hanging up. But that wouldn't be the smartest move. There was no getting around this conversation; he would have to report what had happened.

"Dupin—your behavior is disgraceful, you—"

"There's been a serious knife attack. At the Marché de Saint-Servan. Just now. I was"—Dupin had to make it abundantly clear he'd had no choice but to intervene—"sort of a witness to the attack." But on the other hand, of course, he couldn't let it seem as though he'd somehow been involved. "But I was there entirely by chance. A woman stabbed another woman. She fled, and I had to give chase, in the line of—"

"Aha!" the prefect interrupted him, his tone now altered, "that must be the incident that called our host and her commissaire away so suddenly. What exactly happened, Dupin?"

"That's all I know, Monsieur le Préfet," was Dupin's honest answer. It always helped a little, bringing the title into play;

also, even after nine years, Dupin still couldn't pronounce the prefect's name correctly.

"Where are you now?"

"I'm on the N176 toward Saint-Brieuc, Monsieur le Préfet, I took up the chase, but unfortunately," he had no choice but to let on, "unfortunately I lost the car."

"You *lost* it? How?"

Dupin had switched into the right-hand lane and was looking for the next exit. As frustrating as it was, there was only one thing he could do now: drive back.

"I'm in a very small car. It won't go faster than one seventy."

"But why? Why are you driving a very sma—"

"I'll tell you later, Monsieur le Préfet. I don't have hands-free, I need to concentrate on the road."

"Right, okay. I'll see you here shortly then. I—"

Dupin hung up.

He had just thrown the phone on the passenger seat in frustration when it rang again.

An unknown number.

"Yes?"

"This is Commissaire Louane Huppert"—a thoroughly no-nonsense tone—"your colleague from the seminar."

The commissaire from Saint-Malo.

"I'm listening."

"I'm at the scene, Commissaire. Where the murder that you just—"

"She's dead?"

"Unfortunately yes. Blanche Trouin died at the scene. A teacher here says that a commissaire from Concarneau left the severely injured victim in her care and—"

"Was she dead when the paramedics arrived?"

The commissaire didn't answer his question.

"—and took off in pursuit of the murderer. During which there was a collision between two vehicles. The witnesses reported to my colleagues that it was like something from a movie. The entire neighborhood is in chaos. It—"

"So you already know the victim's identity?"

"We do, yes. And not only that. We also know who the murderer is."

Dupin couldn't believe it. "You know who I was just pursuing in the dark blue Land Rover on the N176?"

"You were what?"

"Who is it?"

"So the story about the 'borrowed' car is true? A Peugeot 208?"

"I had a real chance of catching her . . ." Dupin needed to make the argument for borrowing the car as convincing as possible, of course. But if he portrayed the chance of catching her as too realistic, it would be all the more embarrassing for him. "But then she escaped, after all. Who is it?"

"You let her get away?"

"The car I'm in won't go above one seventy. You know the victim *and* the murderer?"

"Toward Saint-Brieuc or Normandy?"

"Saint-Brieuc."

"Where did you lose her—roughly?"

"By the exit to Quévert."

"Okay. The victim, Blanche Trouin," the commissaire at last answered Dupin's question, "is a well-known chef, she owns a restaurant in Dinard. Le Désir. One Michelin star. She was forty-four years old."

"And the perpetrator?"

"Lucille Trouin."

Dupin must have misheard.

"What?"

"Her sister. Two years younger, also a chef, also successful. Her restaurant is in Saint-Malo. No Michelin star yet, but on the brink of getting one."

Dupin paused. The story sounded too peculiar. He had left the highway by now.

"You realize you had no authority to do what you did."

It wasn't even a rhetorical question, but a simple statement of fact.

"I'm thoroughly aware"—in these circumstances, it couldn't hurt to be especially friendly—"but I wanted to help. I happened to be at the scene. And"—the argument occurred to him only at that moment—"isn't our whole seminar about intensifying collaborative work? That's the spirit in which I understood my actions."

Now he had overdone it.

"So do you know," he quickly changed the subject, "what happened at the market? Are there clues as to why the sister did it?"

"Dupin"—no *Commissaire,* no *monsieur,* nothing—"I'd like you to return to the market immediately. To Blanche Trouin's spice stall. I'll see you there in a few minutes."

"The stall where it happened belonged to the victim?"

The commissaire had already hung up.

Even so: in view of his "unauthorized" actions, the conversation hadn't gone too badly.

He reached a large roundabout—there seemed to be hundreds of them here—and tried to get his bearings. He needed the fastest route back to Saint-Servan.

The best plan would be to leave the car where the fugitive had parked. Lucille Trouin. Who had stabbed her older sister amidst the hustle and bustle of the market.

What was this? On a purely statistical level, murder within families was admittedly the most common. But what had happened between the two sisters? What terrible tragedy lay behind it?

Less than ten minutes later, Dupin parked the car in the lot by the *port de plaisance*. The dark blue Land Rover had been right here. Dupin had counted five police cars with their blue lights flashing race past him on the access road, to take up pursuit of the younger sister, even though her head start was surely too much to make up by now.

The market halls were already coming into view.

Dupin reached the spice stall. There was an intense aroma of coriander, ginger, cardamom, caraway seeds, like an especially wildly mixed curry. Everything around was cordoned off; the traders had had to leave their stalls.

The group gathered around the crime scene was impressively large. At least a dozen police officers, the forensics team, paramedics with two ambulances that had stopped right in front of the entrance, and the medical examiner, who seemed a little lost as he waited next to the body. On the very edge of the crowd, Dupin saw the first-aider with her daughter; a policewoman was looking after them.

Commissaire Huppert was standing slightly off to the side,

in conversation with a paramedic. She was very tall, almost as tall as Dupin, slim, with dark blond hair tied into a ponytail and highly vigilant, alert green eyes.

"Good, okay. Take the body to the forensics lab."

The paramedic went over to the medical examiner, and Huppert turned to Dupin: "There's actually nothing for Forensics to do. We already know everything. The victim. The cause of death, the time of death. Even the murderer. The only things we're missing"—she took her time formulating her words, utterly prosaic—"are the motive and escaped perpetrator. It's common knowledge that the sisters couldn't stand each other. But . . ." She broke off and looked at Dupin, her expression serious.

"So, Dupin, what did you see? And hear? What can you tell me about the incident?"

"I only heard the screams. I didn't see the confrontation or the murder itself."

Dupin concisely recounted what had happened, from the first cries of pain to his pursuit on foot and then in the car. Commissaire Huppert listened attentively.

"The first responder took over here at the scene." Dupin nodded his head toward her.

"I know. There was nothing she could do. By the time the paramedics arrived, Blanche Trouin was already dead."

With that final syllable, Dupin's phone rang. He quickly pulled it out of his trouser pocket.

It wasn't a good time—but it was Nolwenn.

"Just a moment, I'll be right back."

Before Commissaire Huppert could respond, he took a few steps to the side. He spoke in a hushed tone:

"This isn't the best time . . ."

"Was that you?"

"What?"

"The chase on the N176?"

"I was only . . ."

Presumably she had heard about it via the internal police radio—an alert had been put out on the Land Rover, and by now police all across Brittany would know.

"You let her escape?"

Nolwenn had a tendency to criticize Dupin's actions—but this question sounded unusually sharp.

"I can only tell you one thing," she said firmly. "Stay out of it, Monsieur le Commissaire! It's Saint-Malo's responsibility. They always seem to know better anyway. And they march to a different beat."

His phenomenal assistant had never demanded he keep out of an investigation before; her feelings toward Saint-Malo seemed more complicated than he'd realized.

"I'm in the middle of speaking with the commissaire, Nolwenn. At the crime scene."

"Don't get involved, Monsieur le Commissaire. It'll be nothing but trouble. Concentrate on the seminar, and then come home." In a more conciliatory tone, she added: "Or concentrate on the culinary side. The accompanying program includes a few wonderful dinners."

"I have to get back to this, Nolwenn."

He waited a moment before hanging up, not wanting to seem too abrupt.

"Talk later, Monsieur le Commissaire."

Dupin put his cell phone back in his pocket.

Nolwenn was right, naturally. He could get himself into all

kinds of trouble if he got involved. During the phone call, he'd been discreetly looking around for the light blue paper bag containing the cheese that he'd left lying around somewhere. But it was nowhere to be seen.

He went back over to Huppert, who had kept him in view the whole time.

"My colleague from Concarneau . . ."

"Nolwenn."

A glimmer of pride appeared on Dupin's face—evidently, Nolwenn's fame extended all across Brittany.

"What were you saying just then? That everyone knows the sisters couldn't stand each other?" asked Dupin.

"Let's just say they were in constant competition. In public, too. It was an unconcealed rivalry."

"But it must have been much more than just your average rivalry. Almost all siblings compete with one another. For things to come to such a dramatic conclusion, there must have been a huge catalyst."

"Of course," the commissaire stated dryly. She seemed to want to say: a banal realization.

"Do they have families? Partners, children?"

"Neither have children. The parents are no longer alive. The older sister was married, I'm just driving over to see the husband now. The younger one is in a long-term relationship. I'll go to see her partner afterward. You will take the car you *borrowed*"—the commissaire seemed to want to continue her work alone now—"to the police school, just like you promised the owner. And then it's back to the classroom."

She didn't seem to mean to provoke him; at least, there was no hint of sarcasm.

"Regrettably I'll no longer be able to take part in the seminar," she continued, turning away from Dupin. "Very regrettably."

At the request he return to the "classroom," a violent protest had twitched on Dupin's tongue. But, as hard as it was to swallow, the investigation was the responsibility of the Saint-Malo commissaire—she was out of the seminar, and he was stuck with it.

At three fifteen, Dupin had reluctantly stepped back into seminar room B12 in the main building of the police school.

Without Commissaire Huppert and the host prefect from Rennes, there were now only five of them; the Morbihan commissaire had sent her apologies at the last minute due to a boating accident, and she was the person Dupin had been most curious about. She was the successor to Commissaire Sylvaine Rose, who had been promoted the previous year to prefect of the Département Loire-Atlantique, which, although historically part of Brittany, had been wrenched away by an administrative reform in the eighties.

No one had said a word about the incident when Dupin turned up, and group work had resumed almost immediately. Dupin had been partnered with the quite-likeable-seeming commissaire from Côtes d'Armor, and they were instructed to note on colorful little cards possible areas for improvement in the collaboration between the *départements*. As well as on the "optimization potential" in the collaboration between the commissaires and prefects. Dupin was torn between writing on dozens of the little cards, or none of them. His thoughts kept wandering to the terrible murder. To the two sisters.

Concealing his phone under his desk, he searched online

for the Trouin sisters and their restaurants. All incredibly impressive; the older sister, Blanche, in particular—the victim—seemed to be a veritable celebrity. Partly due to the Michelin star bestowed upon her two years before, she had been on her way to becoming one of the really *grand chefs,* as esteemed and popular in France as great artists or rock stars—and among whom there still weren't that many women. The number of features and interviews was astounding, in well-respected national and international newspapers and magazines. Articles about the younger sister were numerous too, and Lucille Trouin seemed only slightly behind the older sister. Both had clearly been inspired by their father, who had also been a chef, albeit in a simple yet highly beloved bistro. There were numerous quotes and comments—predominantly from Lucille—in which their sibling rivalry was an open topic of conversation. They seemed to make no secret of it. After the elder sister received the Michelin star, the younger one had boastfully announced that soon she would receive one too. In an interview, Lucille spoke about her older sister's "unfair advantage" in being able to refer to their father's recipe collection, which he had left to Blanche. Apparently, Blanche had discovered her passion for cooking as a teenager; Lucille, by contrast, not until her mid-twenties. Dupin hadn't found much about the father himself. Apart from the evident competition between the sisters, Dupin hadn't discovered anything that could explain such a brutal escalation. Naturally, he also looked for any update on the pursuit of Lucille Trouin, which was all over the news. The search still seemed to be ongoing.

With the "positive and motivational" words of the coach, the first seminar day had come to an end at a quarter after five.

"Come on, Dupin, tell us everything," his seminar partner,

Commissaire Gaston Nedellec, demanded once the coach left the room—everyone had stayed seated, clearly curious. Dupin willingly told his story once again, after which they all went their separate ways.

At six thirty, just a few minutes ago, the team—it seemed to be the buzzword, the "team"—was scheduled to meet at Porte Saint-Louis in the old town. The evening's activities were to kick off with a guided tour. Naturally, Dupin had contemplated skipping it, but decided it wouldn't be smart to be absent on the very first evening.

He arrived a few minutes late. With swift steps, he made his way toward the south gate, one of eight vast gates that led through the towering, house-high fortifications and into the old town.

Strong gusts of wind were coming in off the ocean, dense with salt and iodine; they were whipping up the Atlantic, driving massive waves. The sky was still a pristine blue. To the left, a large pier stretched in an elegant curve from the corner of the town walls far into the wide Rance estuary, toward Dinard.

High season hadn't yet begun, but there were already visitors from all over; Saint-Malo was a popular destination the whole year round, especially for short stays. On the pier, you could easily spot who was a Breton and who was just a tourist. The same game could be played all across Brittany. The uninitiated would venture out to the very tip of the pier in order to get spectacular views of the tempestuous ocean. Then it would happen: driven by the tide and the lashing wind gusts, some waves broke so forcefully against the walls that they shot up in wild fountains over the pier, with mighty clouds of spray. A spectacle of nature that, for those strolling on the pier, equated to a bath in the ocean. Regardless of what they were wearing, they were immediately drenched, all the way to their underwear and tights. Dupin watched one couple scream loudly and run away in panic.

He reached the city gate. The team had gathered in a passageway that was relatively protected from the wind. Locmariaquer, who looked somewhat over-the-top in his richly decorated uniform, couldn't resist a rebuke:

"And yet again we find ourselves waiting for you, Commissaire! This lovely monsieur here," he gestured toward a stocky, narrow-shouldered man with little remaining hair and round glasses, wearing an old tweed jacket, "is about to give us a tour of the city walls. The famous *tour des remparts*. And en route he'll tell us a little about Saint-Malo. Because—"

A wiry woman, who wasn't part of the team and who Dupin noticed only now, loudly cleared her throat: "The gentleman is Étienne Monnier, the nationally renowned Saint-Malo historian"—the man nodded in confirmation—"and we have the privilege of being guided through the eras of our illustrious city's history by him in person."

"She's one of Commissaire Huppert's assistants," Commissaire Nedellec whispered to Dupin. "She's here representing our hosts. There's nothing new on the Lucille Trouin pursuit, by the way, I just asked. I imagine this lady would know."

Dupin gave him a friendly nod.

"So, if we're all here now," the assistant continued, "we can start this evening's activities. The tour will be followed by a visit to the Maison du Beurre of Yves Bordier, the internationally renowned and multi-award-winning butter producer. We'll look around its exhibition on the cultural history of butter, and then dine in his Bistro Autour du Beurre."

Dupin suddenly felt incredibly hungry; the delicious home-made breakfast cake in Villa Saint Raphaël was the only thing he had eaten all day. He knew Bordier's butter, of course. The manufacturer was legendary. And in Brittany, butter—beyond its status as one of the most important food products—was something of an emblem.

"I want to assure you all," she made an assertive dramatic pause, "that we've put together a very fitting supporting agenda. Predominantly, and I want to emphasize this, thanks to our prefect. An agenda that will make you better acquainted with some of our extraordinary attractions and achievements, in particular the culinary ones. I'm referring to the culinary arts of some of the most prominent chefs of the region—well-known not only here, but all across Brittany, and even the entire nation. They will all open their gastronomic gates for us." The assistant broke off self-consciously. "Well, not all of them, of course. Blanche Trouin's restaurant will sadly now remain closed. And we've just made the decision to cancel the visit to La Noblesse, Lucille Trouin's restaurant." She looked uncomfortable. "But regardless, in addition to the restaurant visits, you'll get to know some other Saint-Malo specialties. Many are located in the Rue de l'Orme, where we're heading now. Including Bertrand Larcher's Japanese-Breton restaurant, where we'll eat tomorrow. This little street is kind of the culinary heart of the city."

Regardless of what could be said about the usefulness of the seminar, Dupin had to admit the accompanying program sounded impressive—the food part, at least.

"The motto of our internationally renowned cuisine is: *voyages et aventures*. Travel and adventure. These are the words of the chef of Saint Placide, where we'll dine on the last evening.

The city's history, too, has always revolved around travel, around dauntless adventure. Taking leaps of faith and living to tell the tale."

Dupin liked the motto, in spite of the overstated pathos. Travel and adventure: that's what life was about.

The commissaire's assistant began to move.

"Let's go. Along here. We'll make our way along the ramparts. It's time to start climbing!"

The steps were steep, and there were a lot of them. Dupin was the last to begin the ascent.

"Right, so." The historian who was leading the group along with Commissaire Huppert's assistant took over, in a deep voice and solemn academic tone. "One thing about the murder case that is currently on all our minds: I'm sure you're aware that human history is teeming with sibling drama, even as far back as ancient times."

He had stopped walking for a moment in order to make the random observation.

"And now to the subject at hand." He began to move again. "Unlike the inner city, the fortifications were mostly spared the terrible devastation of the Second World War. Some sections of the wall go back to the twelfth century. The classic shipowners' homes from the eighteenth century, which define the characteristic cityscape"—clearly well-versed, he pointed his right hand toward the church in the old city—"were all reconstructed after the war, true to their original style. Never, not once, has an enemy managed to conquer our walls in battle! Saint-Malo has always stood strong."

Commissaire Nedellec had fallen back alongside Dupin; the

two female prefects and Locmariaquer had caught up with the first small group.

"Chateaubriand, one of the city's many illustrious sons, and one of the most admirable authors in the French language, wrote that the Ville Close of Saint-Malo, which in surface area is no bigger than the Jardin des Tuileries in Paris, has given the world more famous personalities than many far larger cities."

It was remarkable how steady the historian's voice remained despite all the steps.

"As well as the corsairs, who ruled the oceans for almost three centuries, many world-famous explorers, physicists, doctors, and writers were born here. Jacques Cartier, for example, who discovered Canada, a country we enjoy a close relationship with to this day. Pierre Louis Moreau de Maupertuis explored the Arctic, René Duguay-Trouin conquered Rio de Janeiro. In Saint-Malo, you're connected to the whole world!"

"Trouin. Like the two sisters," mumbled Commissaire Nedellec.

They had now reached the top of the astonishingly wide wall. There was a steep descent on both sides, and a stone balustrade protecting them from the chasm. The wind was blowing twice as hard as down below. A clear, enlivening wind.

"But," the historian followed the wall northward, "let's start at the beginning. Everything began with a settlement in Saint-Servan, or more precisely: on the small peninsula of Alet, over there." He pointed in the corresponding direction. "That's where the Celts started a large gathering place in the first century BC. After the conquest of Gaul, it was developed into a small city by the Romans."

He had really meant it when he said "start at the beginning."

Dupin discreetly stepped a few paces to the side, enough to no longer hear anything with the wind, and to lose himself in the view for a moment. The enchanting light, the colors. He assumed, of course, that there was a good reason for the poetic name of the shoreline between Cap Fréhel and Cancale—"the Emerald Coast"—but he could never have imagined such a dramatic match. The sea genuinely was a sparkling emerald green, secretive and intense. Brighter in its tones toward the shore, with mysterious dark flecks on the horizon. It was turbulent, studded with bright white crowns of spray—sheep, or *moutons,* as the Bretons called them—which formed a rousing contrast. Beneath the powerful ramparts, a blindingly white beach stretched out, the waves crashing against it sweeping the sand repeatedly into a wild, watery chaos, creating a restless glinting and glistening; it looked as though myriads of tiny gemstones were swirling around. In front of the coast were numerous islets, whose brown and green shades of anthracite looked like Impressionist daubs of color. On a larger island, a defiant, buffeted fort towered up, a daring stronghold. Opposite he could see Dinard, some of its magnificent villas eminent. Past Dinard, his gaze was drawn westward to Cap Fréhel, which jutted wide and majestic into the ocean. The panorama, the beguiling colors, along with the strong wind gusts and the evening sun summoning all its strength, were enough to make one feel inebriated.

Dupin gave himself a jolt and followed the group.

At the top of a narrow, steep stairway they reached a higher plateau with angular expanses of grass and a bronze statue.

"This, by the way, is the statue of Jacques Cartier, the discoverer of Canada whom I just mentioned. But let's continue on in history: in the sixth century, the monk and missionary Maclou, one of the seven founding holy men of Brittany, came here from Wales and landed on the aforementioned peninsula Alet . . ."

It was so bizarre. Only a narrow street lay below, between the mighty walls they were walking on and the astonishingly tall high-rise buildings—and if you turned away from the ocean, you could see directly into people's apartments. Their living rooms, kitchens, and bedrooms.

A thought came to Dupin. The owner of the Villa Saint Raphaël, where he was staying, was from Saint-Malo and would certainly know about the two sisters. She knew her stuff about good food in Saint-Malo; just yesterday she had given Dupin a dozen culinary tips, one of which he had spontaneously followed, not ten minutes on foot, to the small bay of Saint-Servan.

Dupin paused and reached for his phone as the group walked on. He briefly caught the gaze of Commissaire Nedellec, and thought he saw a conspiratorial glint in his eyes. In the next moment, Nedellec too had distanced himself from the group.

"Villa Saint Raphaël, *bonsoir!*"

Dupin recognized the hotelier's warm voice. Emmanuelle Delanoë, roughly the same age as Dupin himself, was a very attractive woman, with an element of the mysterious to her, a special aura.

"This is Georges Dupin, the commissaire from . . ."

"Of course. How lovely. What can I do for you, Monsieur Dupin?"

Exceptionally friendly and clear.

"The two Trouin sisters, between whom this terrible tragedy

occurred today—do you know them?" Not having much time, he came straight to the point.

"I did. Both of them, personally. Not that we were friends, but we always had a chat when we ran into one another. And that was quite often. It's not that big a city, as you know. We don't have our own kitchen in the villa, so we often send our guests to their restaurants. And my husband and I really enjoyed eating there too."

Dupin had guessed right.

"And you, monsieur, do you have any thoughts on it all?"

He paused. He couldn't take any risks; she was sure to know the whole world and his wife. "I'm just curious, madame, that's all. I'm not involved in the investigation itself, it's in the very competent hands of Commissaire Huppert."

"Commissaire Huppert, oh yes," she said approvingly.

"Something quite serious must've happened between the sisters."

"I only know one thing. But Lucille would hardly have killed her sister over it."

Dupin came to an involuntary standstill.

"Tell me."

"I heard from my friend that Blanche was planning to nab Lucille's sous-chef. Colomb Clément. Some say he's the even greater genius. Only thirty-two years old, sensationally gifted, ambitious. In any case, he plays a key role at La Noblesse; it's been a while now since Lucille was there every night."

It sounded like a lead worth pursuing.

"Does Lucille know her sister was planning this?"

"I don't know."

"Does anyone else know about it?"

"I don't think so."

"It would be a heavy blow for Lucille Trouin, wouldn't it?"

"Certainly. But is it enough as a murder motive, Monsieur Dupin?"

"And how did your friend find out?"

"She's the sous-chef's sister. He told her. And swore her to secrecy."

"When was this? And did your friend tell you anything else?"

"The week before last, I think. He was visiting her. She only mentioned it, we didn't discuss it in detail."

"So Blanche made him a serious offer. Do you know when this was?"

"Quite recent, I presume."

"I see. Can you think of anything else worth mentioning?"

"I don't think so, no."

Out of the corner of his eye, Dupin had seen that the group were already some distance ahead. "Okay, then thank you for the chat."

"Gladly. Is there anything else I can help with?"

"No, thank you."

In fact, he had a few research tasks to delegate. But she wasn't Nolwenn—and this wasn't his case.

"Until later, Monsieur Dupin. *Bonne soirée!*"

She had hung up.

Dupin stood there for a moment longer. What was the significance of this unexpected snippet of information? Did it even have any? It seemed highly implausible as a motive, but perhaps it had been the last straw. It wouldn't be the first time. Sometimes things piled up, unexpectedly came to a head, and then suddenly . . .

Dupin swiftly made a few notes in his small red Clairefontaine notebook, then caught up with the group.

"Let's finally turn to the topic you've all been waiting for," the historian announced with visible relish. "The corsairs! Who, contrary to widespread misunderstanding, are not pirates, not in the slightest. Pirates unlawfully captured ships under the black skull-and-crossbones flag, in a high-handed and martial manner, for their own profit—the corsairs, on the other hand, were acting legally in service of the king and therefore all of France. We Malouins traveled with official letters of marque!"

"In practice it amounts to the same thing though, doesn't it?" The somewhat heavyset, constantly rather sullen-looking woman, the prefect of Département Côtes d'Armor, seemed to think the correction was necessary. "I read recently that some pirates followed a stricter moral code than the corsairs, who exercised their mission with extreme brutality and religious zeal. And the entire corsair empire lay in the hands of highly cunning Malouin tradesmen, who even founded stock corporations for their plundering trips. Many of the rich shipowners had the cellars of their houses extended to below sea level and connected to one another, creating extensive cave systems where they hid considerable portions of their bounty from the French king. Vast quantities of gold, silver, and jewels."

The historian raised his eyebrows. "I don't think we should pay any attention to biased interpretations. This proud chapter in the city's history . . ."

Dupin was only half listening. His mind was still processing the new information. And the question as to what he should do with it.

"As well as the supremely honorable task of capturing enemy

merchant ships, seizing their cargo, kidnapping the crew and releasing them again in exchange for ransom money, the corsairs fulfilled a second important function: acting as convoys for their own trade vessels. The enemy ships were mostly English, of course; they were particularly fearful of the Malouin corsairs' infamous flag, the white cross on a blue background. The oceans have never seen more daring seafarers."

The English element was sure to have provoked sympathy all across Brittany back then. And probably still did. Dupin made a mental note of it for Nolwenn.

"I think you should also tell us about the lucrative *commerce triangulaire*"—the prefect felt compelled to interject once again—"about the awful triangular slave trade between Africa, America, and Saint-Malo."

"A dark chapter, you're right," admitted the historian with surprising self-assurance. "With low-quality grain and cheap, colorful glitter, masses of slaves were acquired in Africa—the 'black gold'—then sold on, with enormous profit, to the huge sugarcane plantations in the New World.

"Yes, a terrible history—but it certainly doesn't represent the corsairs as a whole. The reality has many facets. Think of the many delicacies the corsairs brought to France and Europe. Rum, spices, and Arabian mocha—requisitioned by Malouin corsairs. You could smell the corsairs before you saw them!"

The part about "requisitioning" was, of course, a thorny affair, Dupin felt, who had pricked up his ears at the word "mocha," yet he would chalk it up as a point for the corsairs, given it was about coffee.

"In closing, I'd like to name a few of the most famous corsairs. For example, Pierre Porcon de la Barbinais. A curious story: after a failed ransom negotiation with the pirate sheikh of Algiers, he was bound to the front of a heavy cannon and blown to pieces by the ball."

An unusual understanding of the word "curious," thought Dupin.

"Or also . . ."

A particularly unpleasant, shrill ringtone interrupted the historian.

The assistant from the commissaire's office, who had remained astonishingly silent during the tour, reacted promptly.

"Yes?"

She stood still, her cell phone pressed to her ear.

"Oh! I see. Yes." She listened for a while. "Of course, yes, I'll do that. Yes. *Au revoir.*"

Everyone looked at her inquisitively.

"I . . ." She gave the group a bewildered look. "They've got her." Another pause. "They've got Lucille Trouin."

Dupin hadn't expected it to be so quick.

"She was arrested in Loudéac. At the train station. Someone recognized her car."

So Lucille had made it quite a bit farther.

"A judge has already ordered investigative detention," the assistant continued. "She'll now be briefly brought before the committing magistrate, but these are just formalities."

"And—has she confessed?" Commissaire Nedellec asked.

"She was arrested just half an hour ago and is being brought back to Saint-Malo as we speak."

"Commissaire Huppert hasn't spoken to her yet? Trouin hasn't said anything yet?" This time it was Dupin pressing for information.

"No."

"I'll be back in a moment." Without further explanation, Dupin walked ahead a little. He turned—they had reached the northwestern end of the ramparts—to the right around a corner and pulled his phone out of his trouser pocket.

"Hello?"

"Commissaire Huppert, this is Commi—Georges Dupin." He spoke quietly and, just to be sure, turned to look behind him. "I wanted to tell you something quickly."

"Go ahead."

"I just spoke with—" Dupin broke off. He racked his brain. He hadn't thought about how he could have obtained this information so suddenly and "coincidentally."

"I'm all ears," the commissaire prompted him.

"I was just speaking with the owner of a *maison d'hôtes* in Saint-Malo. I'm thinking of vacationing here for a few days at the end of the summer with my girlfriend . . ."

"And?"

"She told me she's friends with the sister of Lucille Trouin's sous-chef. From this friend she found out that Blanche Trouin was trying to lure him away from her sister. It seems she'd already made him an offer. Just recently."

Dupin waited.

"That was what you wanted to tell me?"

"I'm sure you're already aware of it, I just wanted to make sure."

"Thank you, Dupin. Talk soon."

"Wait, what's happened with Lucille Trouin, have you already . . ."

But she had hung up.

He wasn't any the wiser. Had she known or not? Did she think it was relevant?

He sighed, drew up his shoulders, and looked out to sea. Along the fortifications, the gaze was drawn to the craggy cliffs and a narrow strip of beach covered with foaming waves. A brazen seagull swooped down and settled on the moss-covered wall within an arm's length of Dupin. It stared at him challengingly.

Dupin turned, pushed his hands into his trouser pockets, and walked back the way he had come.

This time Dupin wasn't the only one who was late; this time they all were, the entire team. By more than half an hour. The historian had, despite stressing the importance of their pace in his lectures, taken significantly longer.

By the time they reached their destination—Rue de l'Orme—it was almost eight o'clock.

It really was the heaven on earth they'd been promised. The houses stood so close together that no cars could fit down the small street, which was paved with red-tinged cobblestones. One culinary sensation after the other: the Café Breizh, an extraordinary crêperie run by the renowned gastronome Bertrand Larcher, and next door was his Japanese-Breton restaurant, where they would be eating the following evening. Opposite, the Maison du Sarrasin, a small store that sold everything made from *blé noir*: potato chips, honey, mustard, cookies, caramel. The hearty crêpes called *galettes* here in the northeast were made from buckwheat. Lucille Trouin's restaurant La Noblesse was directly next to the Maison du Sarrasin. A handwritten sign hung on the door: *"Aujourd'hui exceptionnellement fermé—désolé"*—unexpectedly closed today. The restaurant was located in one of the beautiful old houses, no wider than ten meters, but with multiple floors. Next to the restaurant was a cheese shop specializing in Breton cheese, which, according to Commissaire Nedellec, also belonged to Lucille Trouin; this venture of the younger sister hadn't yet been mentioned. Both sisters had clearly expanded their business activities beyond their restaurants.

The Rue de l'Orme continued with a phenomenal-looking oyster bar with lots of flair, offering Cancale oysters. And the chef who had coined the motto *"voyages et aventures,"* whose restaurant they would eat in on the final evening, presented one of his specialties in his own store: *babas au rhum,* a ring-shaped cake made of sweet dough and doused heavily in rum. Next door was a country-style butchery. Then a fine *épicerie*; a shop selling only rum; and a very promising-looking fish restaurant with an emerald-green awning.

"The rum store belongs to Lucille Trouin's partner," Commissaire Nedellec whispered to Dupin. "He specializes in rum and opened stores here in Saint-Servan, as well as in Dinard and Cancale. He also sells online. And he's a partner in his girlfriend's cheese shop too."

All noteworthy pieces of information, not only because they demonstrated the gastronomic couple's industriousness, but because they revealed Dupin wasn't the only one interested in the case and who had suddenly come into the possession of revealing details.

"*Et voilà*, we're here," the woman from the commissaire's office said, smiling contentedly.

The Maison du Beurre—clad externally in sky-blue wooden paneling, with the name *Bordier* in white letters—wasn't particularly large either, so it was sure to be cozy. Inside was a cheese counter with an excellent selection, and opposite the entrance, its beating heart: the butter counter. A black marble surface held a tall mountain of butter, ready to be marveled at. *Demi-sal,* slightly salted, the Breton standard. Encircling the buttery summit was a display of small, pretty packets of all the different butter varieties. Including Roscoff onion, roasted seaweed, *piment d'espelette,* and Szechuan pepper.

Two staff members awaited them with friendly smiles.

"*Bonsoir*—and a warm welcome to the house of Yves Bordier. After a brief introduction to the history of butter and a glimpse into the production process"—the younger of the two women had taken on the introduction, and pointed toward the back room, which Dupin hadn't yet noticed due to the countless delicacies—"you'll have the opportunity to try some of our specialties in the bistro next door."

"If you could all join me over here, please?" The second woman, with blond curly hair and round glasses, had already positioned herself toward the rear of the store.

The group squeezed into the darkened museum area of the Maison du Beurre. Lightboxes had been affixed to the walls, documenting the individual manufacturing stages. In the middle of the room stood wooden appliances that had been used for the production of butter in days gone by.

The curly-haired woman went over to the lightbox entitled *The Genesis of Butter.* "Around six thousand AD, the nomadic hunter-gatherers in Asia and the Middle East discovered that a special cream forms when milk is shaken—and that's it, in a nutshell: the discovery of butter." This swift conclusion was encouraging. "Almost everywhere in the world, butter became the universal fat for preparing meals—with the exception of the Mediterranean basin, where olive oil played this role."

The infamous butter/olive oil border that divided Europe, and France itself, in two was one of the seemingly endless ways of defining the Breton identity.

From the looks on his colleagues' faces, Dupin could tell he wasn't the only one hoping dinner was imminent. He was queasy with hunger.

"In the course of a one-sided marketing campaign, olive oil was attributed with all the good qualities, and butter all the bad ones. In truth," she spoke with passionate emphasis now, "that's entirely untrue. Good butter is, as recent research has proven, incredibly healthy. And it became synonymous with fine dining. The general defamation of butter began with the Romans and Greeks"—her presentation seemed to be reaching further back now, after all—"who wrote it off as a 'barbarian fat'—completely in contrast to many other advanced civilizations: the Egyptians, Phoenicians, and Carthaginians, as well as all the cultures of Central and Northern Europe who devoted themselves to butter . . ."

A loud ringtone interrupted her. The woman from the commissaire's office pulled her phone out of her jacket pocket.

"Yes?"

She listened for a while. Then:

"Really? That was it? Nothing more? Not ever?"

A longer answer on the other end of the line.

"Okay. Yes, thanks. See you soon."

She ended the call and immediately turned to the group.

"Commissaire Huppert has interrogated Lucille Trouin in

the presence of her attorney. The investigative detention has been granted. It's . . ." She paused. "It's really strange, Lucille Trouin has declared she won't be testifying. Not a single word, under any circumstances."

Another pause; she seemed to be thinking.

"She told the police officers who brought her back to Saint-Malo. It doesn't make any sense, of course; it could be incredibly detrimental to her case."

"That's what she said?" The question slipped across Dupin's lips. "Not a single word, under any circumstances?"

"It seems so."

"How strange." Naturally, Locmariaquer felt the need to volunteer a comment too. "What does that mean? She doesn't want to say why she did it? Not even admit to doing it?"

The woman shrugged her shoulders in resignation. "Evidently."

"We'll see," protested the younger, red-haired prefect from Morbihan. "She'll soon come to her senses."

"Absolutely," agreed the stocky prefect from Côtes d'Armor, Nedellec's boss.

"I don't know, it doesn't sound too good to me." Locmariaquer didn't want to let them have the last word; his viewpoint sounded as vague as it did ominous.

A clueless silence spread through the group, which the guide swiftly seized to her advantage:

"In the Middle Ages"—it was a significant historical step forward, at least—"the consumption of butter was strictly forbidden by the Church during Lent. It was Anne de Bretagne, the last free reigning Duchess of Brittany, who won the right to eat butter all year round for her court and the whole of the region. That, of course, also contributed to the ascendance of Breton butter artistry—"

"Excuse me for a moment." Commissaire Nedellec interrupted the presentation and headed swiftly for the exit. "A private call."

"Of course it is," Dupin mumbled to himself. He walked along the row of lightboxes, his mind occupied by the latest news.

"I also need to make a quick call—a work one," Huppert's assistant added.

"I'd like to draw your attention to another interesting detail." The store guide seemed unflappable. "For a long time, well into the twentieth century, in fact, butter was also used as a miracle product in cosmetics."

Dupin ran his hand through his hair. It was all very peculiar. What usually came at the end of an investigation, here marked the beginning: the perpetrator was already known and in custody. Except she didn't plan to speak.

Through staying silent, Lucille Trouin really could compromise herself. In order to argue a crime of passion—and that would, after all, be the most favorable approach for her—she would have to make the passion element emotionally credible. Emotional, immediate, and personal. And this was the very thing she was refusing to do. Was she in shock? Her silence, of course, intensified the question that had been there from the beginning: Had it really been a crime of passion? And only that? Was it a crime of passion in the classical sense?

There was no doubt—Dupin's thoughts went back and forth—that emotion must have played a major role in the situation at the market. If the murder had been premeditated, Lucille

Trouin surely wouldn't have chosen a public place. And it didn't get more public than a busy market hall. She would, like all cold, calculating murderers, have attempted to commit a "perfect murder" in secret. In this sense, the crime *had to* indicate a moment of intense emotion. But perhaps there was more to it? A motive that extended beyond emotion? Something calculated? It could have been a combination of motive and passion, only: What had provoked each of them?

"Our manufacturing process," the woman was still refusing to admit defeat, "incorporates the entire savoir faire of butter production. One of the many secrets is the old technique of a special kneading process, both intensive and gentle, which eliminates more water than other methods, therefore reducing the butter to its essence. Finally, the butter is vigorously beaten with special wooden instruments, giving it that silky-soft consistency."

A single, high tone rang out. Dupin's phone, a text message. Nolwenn. It was just one sentence: *Stay out of it.*

She was really serious about this.

"The most important element, of course, is the choice of milk. Its exceptional quality and freshness. Which also means the butter looks and tastes different in winter than in autumn. According to the season, you'll rediscover the aromas of the meadows where our organic cows graze. In the bistro, you'll soon experience how butter from early summer tastes, with all the seasonal herbs."

"Wouldn't this," the sullen-looking prefect—whom Dupin found eminently likable either in spite of, or precisely because of her grumpiness—cleared her throat, "be the perfect moment for a visit to the restaurant?"

Dupin felt eternally grateful to her.

"That's exactly what I was about to suggest," said the store employee with a smile.

Less than three minutes later, the team was sitting in the bistro next door.

It was a phenomenal space; a rustic, spacious vault. The rough, lightly rendered stone walls lent atmosphere and warmth. Anthracite-toned steel beams stretched from the floor to the high ceiling, while spotlights on a decorative molding artfully staged the setting. Multiple black two-seater tables had been pushed together into one big dining table. They were the only people down here; in the upstairs rooms of the bistro, all the tables were occupied.

Dupin was sitting between Commissaire Nedellec, who had ended his "private" phone call, and the prefect from Côtes d'Armor. Only Commissaire Huppert's assistant was still absent.

Dupin was happy to see the bread and small granite platters with different varieties of butter already on the table.

"I'd like to extend a very warm welcome to you." A petite woman in her mid-thirties with long, light brown hair had stepped over to the group. "My name is Elen Delacourt, I'm the head chef. It's a great pleasure to cook for you this evening."

"Then you must be part of the region's inner epicurean circle, I imagine? You knew the Trouin sisters? What do you think happened between the two of them?" asked Commissaire Nedellec bluntly.

"Two phenomenal chefs." Her voice held heartfelt admiration. "It's an absolute tragedy. Incomprehensible. Of course, they were competitors, but no one would have expected it to go so far. It's beyond belief."

Dupin listened as he tried the butter with the Roscoff onions: a sensation. He turned his attention to the seaweed butter. No less delicious.

"Did you know the two of them well—were you friends?" Nedellec pressed.

"Not friends, no, but we held one another in great esteem."

Nedellec strove for a more casual tone: "Lucille Trouin is practically your neighbor. I'm sure you hear things from time to time, right?"

"What do you mean?"

"About conflicts, perhaps? Particularly explosive arguments?"

"I didn't hear anything, no."

Even the buckwheat butter was a poem. With little roasted kernels of buckwheat.

"Something particularly serious must've happened between the two of them," Locmariaquer joined in.

"The discovery of which," Dupin's neighbor resolutely intervened, "we can confidently leave to Commissaire Huppert. One thing's for sure, we won't be solving the case tonight here at this table."

"I completely agree," confirmed the red-haired prefect from Morbihan. She was small and wiry, and looked slightly lost in her magnificent uniform with golden epaulettes, but made up for it with her energetic assertiveness.

Dupin had arrived at the yuzu butter. Slightly bitter, a blend of lime and mandarin. He was gradually beginning to feel better.

"Here come the entrées." Two waiters and a waitress had appeared.

"We'll begin with *langoustines rôties* and white asparagus, and a carpaccio of pig's feet with a *mousse de lait fumée*," declared the chef, who seemed relieved to change the subject at last. "As the main course, we'll be serving a magnificent line-caught monkfish from the inshore fishery, with a consommé of spider crab with lychee, accompanied by *gargouillou des légumes d'été,* a blend of herbs, blossoms, and summer vegetables, and we'll conclude the menu with a sweet potato and carrot soufflé *à l'orange* as well as a cream cheese sorbet—and of course, with a cheese board. Which will include two Breton cheeses."

A question spontaneously escaped Dupin's lips:

"Do you—I mean, does the Maison du Beurre—also specialize in Breton cheese, like Lucille Trouin?"

"Not particularly. But we only include the best in our selection." The chef smiled: "Mesdames, messieurs. We wish you a *bon appétit.*"

With these words, she turned and made a discreet exit. The waiters too moved away.

In no time, everyone turned their attention to the starters, and didn't notice that the host prefect had entered the bistro.

"*Bonsoir,* my dear colleagues. I wanted to join you for a few minutes at least. I've just come from a meeting with Commissaire Huppert."

She sat down on one of the empty chairs. Dupin guessed that she was around sixty years old. With her gray hair and impressive uniform, she radiated self-assurance and experience.

"How wonderful that you could make the time. It's a real pleasure for us." Locmariaquer playacted the statesman. In contrast to the prefect's smooth appearance, his uniform with the golden epaulettes, golden buttons, and sleeve adornments made him look like a rooster puffing his chest out. But then, he always looked like that. He was very tall, perpetually somewhat flushed in his robust face, and had a noticeably oval, balding head. "And we're curious, as I'm sure you can imagine. How's the investigation going? We've just been discussing the case."

"The investigation is in full swing, but there aren't yet any clues on a really plausible motive or catalyst for a crime of passion. Even though Commissaire Huppert has already spoken with a number of people this afternoon. Including, as you know, finally with Lucille Trouin herself, but she's refusing to make a statement." She shook her head.

The waitress appeared with a plate for the prefect, who accepted it with a grateful smile.

"Please don't let me stop you from eating, everyone!" With these words, she reached for her fork. "The food here is really delicious!"

"Who has Commissaire Huppert spoken to?" Dupin had already eaten the last bite of langoustines.

The prefect slowly and deliberately picked up a second fork, taking her time to answer. "First with Kilian Morel, of course, Blanche Trouin's husband. He's completely in shock. Entirely understandable, and he doesn't seem to have a clue what could have happened. Nor does Lucille Trouin's long-term partner, whom Commissaire Huppert went to see afterward. Charles Braz."

"The guy has no idea what could've happened between the two sisters?" Nedellec was incredulous. "He has no idea what might have prompted his girlfriend to stab her own sister?"

"No. He seemed bewildered. Lucille Trouin called him

from the station earlier. Her one phone call. But she didn't say anything to Monsieur Braz about the murder either."

"Who else has the commissaire spoken with?" Dupin returned to his question.

"Flore Briard, Lucille Trouin's best friend," the prefect continued. "She's in the restaurant business too. In Dinard. She bought two faithful replicas of corsair ships, and opens them for fine dining in the evenings. She sometimes works with Lucille Trouin. But she's also clueless as to what might have happened between the sisters."

Dupin reached for his notebook, a reflex, but then stopped himself. It wouldn't be advisable to make notes in front of everyone. Much better to continue in a conversational tone.

"Blanche Trouin had two close friends," the prefect continued, "who theoretically might have known about any rising tensions: Walig Richard, an antiques dealer, and Joe Morel, her husband's brother, who seems to be a close confidant. Commissaire Huppert has already spoken with them too, albeit on the phone. But nothing came of it."

Huppert moved quickly. And the prefect was astonishingly open with sharing the updates, entirely in keeping with the desired team spirit.

"The commissaire also spoke with Colomb Clément, Lucille Trouin's sous-chef. Naturally, they see a lot of each other."

Dupin was all ears.

"It seems Blanche Trouin had made him a confidential offer to work for her instead. He was very open with the commissaire about it, and is relatively sure Lucille didn't know about it. Blanche had told her husband about the offer, according to the sous-chef's statement, which Huppert has already verified.

Whether she also told her friends Richard and Morel, we're not yet sure."

"When exactly did the commissaire speak with the sous-chef?"

For the first time, a look of surprise appeared on the prefect's face.

"I don't know, Commissaire."

"Perhaps the friends knew," Dupin blurted out, "and didn't keep it to themselves. I just mean," he added, trying not to seem overzealous, "it's entirely possible that Lucille Trouin could have found out about it."

"We don't know at this point," the prefect declared. "We haven't yet been able to locate other people in their close circle. The sisters didn't have much by way of private lives, they were real workaholics. Oh, and Commissaire Huppert already has the itemized records for Blanche's cell phone."

"What about family?" asked Nedellec, without letting a pause arise.

"The parents are deceased. Apart from a ninety-three-year-old aunt, the sister of their father, there's no one else left. She lives in Rothéneuf, in the east of Saint-Malo. She has advanced dementia, so is probably very confused. In any case, Commissaire Huppert said she didn't seem to understand what had happened. She wasn't able to help."

Dupin made a few notes after all, as discreetly as he could, balancing the red Clairefontaine on his thigh. As he did so, he noticed Nedellec tapping on his cell phone under the table.

"We're currently trying to find out whether anyone in the restaurant scene knew about a specific conflict between the sisters, beyond the usual competitiveness—but no results as of yet."

All around the table, the plates were empty and as clean as a whistle—the appetizers had clearly met with everyone's approval. As though summoned by some secret signal, the waiters appeared and cleared everything away.

"It all seems incredibly mysterious," mused Locmariaquer in a portentous tone.

"If only the two sisters knew what it was about, and one's dead, and the other won't say a word—then it's pretty complicated," Nedellec's boss summarized morosely.

"Did anyone who was there at the scene in the market"—it had been playing on Dupin's mind the whole time—"catch anything about the argument between the sisters? Has anyone come forward?"

"The witnesses we're aware of only heard something along the lines of 'You've gone too far.' An employee at Blanche Trouin's spice stand said she heard 'I hate you.' That's all there is, unfortunately; all very unspecific."

It was evidence, at least, of very strong emotion.

"It all happened very quickly, within just a few minutes, according to Commissaire Huppert's reconstruction. Blanche Trouin was standing in front of the spice stall when her younger sister turned up. They moved away to the side, by one of the columns, and that's when it happened. The other traders didn't know anything about a dispute coming to a head, Blanche had apparently seemed 'completely normal' that morning, in a good mood, in fact, which apparently she usually was."

The prefect broke off. All at once, she looked exhausted.

Nedellec frowned. "Did Blanche Trouin regularly work at her spice stall herself? I mean, she must've had better things to do. Or did she just happen to be there yesterday morning?"

"She loved the selling side"—the prefect was exceptionally well informed—"and was at the market every Monday. Everyone knew that, her restaurant was closed on Mondays."

"Is it possible"—Dupin wasn't sure how to formulate the question that had been on his mind since the afternoon—"that there could have been some kind of conflict in the area of cooking itself?"

"What do you mean by that?"

He didn't know how to phrase it more precisely. But cooking was the Trouin sisters' passion, their obsession. Their calling and profession.

"Their cooking styles and philosophies were vastly different," the prefect stated. "Blanche was known for her ingenious refinements of local aromas and products, at times she was even avant-gardist—her medlar concentrate comes to mind—but was incredibly strict in her regional constraints when selecting all her ingredients, likewise for *terroir* und *merroir*. That was her credo. Joined by imaginative, yet consistently calculated accents from her rich stock of spices. In essence, Blanche Trouin was an exceptional representative of the Nova Regio cuisine. She had her own garden, and harvested the majority of her vegetables from it."

The prefect paused and drank a sip of water.

"Lucille Trouin's governing principle, by contrast, is the development of the highest flavor finesse, differentiation and internal differentiation, often with diverse micro-elements. Regardless of the products' origin. They can be from all over the world—she deliberately doesn't focus on traditional Breton cuisine. She looks for completely innovative flavors and, in the process, masters the entire spectrum, from classic to purist to incredibly progressive."

Dupin had only understood the prefect's explanations in part, but they were interesting nonetheless. They presumably embodied something quite fundamental, because the opposing cooking styles would be linked with differences in their personalities.

"We'll now serve the main course." The waiters had returned. In the blink of an eye, a plate stood before Dupin.

"*Bonne continuation*."

The monkfish with consommé of spider crab and lychee was a wonderful idea, and the *gargouillou*, the vegetables with the blossoms, looked particularly beautiful, almost too good to eat. But only almost.

"Let's put this awful case aside for a while," decided the host prefect, "and turn our attention to enjoying the food."

At ten minutes after ten, the team had left the Bistro Autour du Beurre—the monkfish was the best thing Dupin had ever eaten. At around half past ten, Dupin had walked into the courtyard of the Villa Saint Raphaël. Only to leave it again a few moments later.

He had spontaneously decided to go for a nightcap in Bistro de Solidor, in Saint-Servan's pleasant harbor, which he'd visited the previous evening on the hotelier's recommendation. A splendid tip. And it was only a short stroll away.

Dupin sat by the window. With a view of the sea and the pier at the end of the harbor. The sun had only just set and the sky was a delicate pink, with a few blurred, more intensely colored streaks across the horizon.

Dupin liked Saint-Servan and its farthest coastal corner,

the—apparently famous—peninsula Alet, already a candidate for his list of favorite places. The narrow lanes, the harbor, the small shops, the wonderful old houses: former fishermen's homes as well as secluded villas. Gardens everywhere, small and large parks. Not to forget the market halls—in which, tomorrow, life would go on as normal—and the Café du Théâtre right by the market, where he'd had coffee that morning. Coffee that had been captured by the Malouins for the world and for him. Saint-Servan was already starting to feel like a familiar neighborhood.

The bistro's thoroughly attentive owner had talked Dupin into a special rum—"the city's signature drink, and a good while before it became fashionable everywhere else," he had clarified— "an old J.M.," neat, no ice. Created by a village priest in 1790 on Martinique, back in the corsair era. The bistro owner had told Dupin its whole history. Produced from nothing but freshly pressed sugarcane juice, "not cheap molasses." Golden brown in the glass, with a glint of copper and bronze.

"Aromas of cinnamon, baked apple, and coriander, perfectly balanced with vanilla and baked tropical fruits," enthused the bistro owner, "a silky-smooth bouquet, with hints of mocha, dried apricot, and flambéed banana. Long and harmonious in the finish, with a touch of mint."

Dupin took a long drink. And was impressed. The bistro owner saw it in his face.

"It's like nectar, am I right? From Elysian origins, it lets you forget all earthly suffering."

Surely no more beautiful a promise existed.

And it was fitting for Dupin's decision. There was no point in trying to secretly investigate this peculiar murder case. Unlike his case on the Pink Granite Coast, Dupin couldn't have a "chance" conversation with anyone, especially not the people the commissaire was already speaking with. He couldn't risk any collisions. What's more, it would be completely disrespectful to his colleagues here. And the commissaire seemed very competent.

Dupin let another sip of rum trickle down his throat. His gaze swept around the quaint bistro. He leaned his head back and closed his eyes.

The annoying thing was: not only was his *déformation professionnelle* nagging away at him, but he also felt personally called upon to investigate. Obligated, even. After all, the murder had occurred right before his nose. And he'd had to admit defeat in his pursuit of the perpetrator.

Dupin looked at the pink evening sky. He turned away. His gaze met the owner's, who was standing at the bar. Dupin nodded. A subtle gesture in the direction of his empty glass, and the owner immediately understood.

Rum hadn't previously been part of Dupin's repertoire; unjustly so, he decided on this evening.

He felt a contented tiredness slowly descend over him.

Before long, he lay in bed.

The Second Day

It didn't happen often, but last night it had: Dupin, undeterred by the events of the day, had slept wonderfully. Deeply and soundly, peacefully and without a single interruption. The rum had worked miracles.

The world was full of water this morning; it must have been raining heavily for hours. And it still was. The puddles in the garden had long become small lakes, watery landscapes with the occasional grass island dotted here and there. But even the weather couldn't mar Dupin's surprisingly good mood. Nor could the thought of the seminar and his decision to stay out of the investigation. The only sad thing was that he'd missed Claire's call, a drawback of the sound sleep. For differing reasons, this had already happened a few times since Claire had left the previous week for her fortnight of cardiological training in Boston. Now she was the one sleeping deeply and soundly—the window of time in which they could speak was small. Claire had left him a message, with loud music and animated voices in the background. She was with colleagues—Dupin had heard predominantly male names—in a bar. He had sent her a few text messages during the first few days, but she had only answered once. Claire didn't like text messages.

Dupin had got up at seven on the dot and drank a large café au lait in the cozy breakfast room. He had also eaten a generous piece of the homemade breakfast cake; today, it was a version with berries. Then, on the way to the police call, he'd made an impromptu stop at the Café du Théâtre—a parking spot had been free right before the door, a clear sign. He'd enjoyed a swift *petit café* at the bar, where the television was on, and naturally, like everywhere else, they were still reporting on the previous day's drama.

Only marginally late, Dupin had arrived in the École de Police.

The morning's task was to select, from the impressive plethora of "exciting points" they had discussed at length yesterday—like turf wars, personnel shortages, and fund distribution—the most important in each subject area. They would then focus on these intensively for the rest of the seminar.

"Let's get down to work!" Locmariaquer spurred on the small group after the coach had explained the program for the morning.

The seminar had been going for two hours already; it was shortly after ten. The rain was still pouring down. The room was hopelessly overheated, the air stuffy.

Dupin's good mood had expired. As one of the regularly interposed "learning interventions," the coach had just explained the systematic difference between efficiency and effectiveness. An avid discussion was underway.

"It's possible to be extremely efficient, yet also extremely ineffective. Just look at the world!" commented the prefect from Morbihan aptly. *Very true*, thought Dupin.

"I would say the opposite." Locmariaquer spoke up. "There's no effectiveness without efficiency."

"But look, my dear colleague," the prefect objected, now in quite a curt tone, "you—"

The door to the seminar room was flung open.

With a brusque "Good morning," the host prefect stormed in with a grim expression, Commissaire Louane Huppert a step behind her.

"How lovely to see you, mesdames," began Locmariaquer, "it's—"

"There's been another death," she said, cutting him off, "and it's clearly murder."

For a moment, there was complete silence. Everyone had paused mid-movement, as though they were frozen.

"That can't be!" Locmariaquer was the first to break the silence.

The prefect and commissaire made no move to sit down.

"I'm not surprised," murmured Commissaire Nedellec in a low voice. "This story isn't over yet, far from it."

"Well, I never." The brow of the stocky prefect from Côtes d'Armor gathered into deep folds. "This is really escalating."

"It's awful." The face of her red-haired colleague from Morbihan mirrored her shock.

"Who is it?" Dupin wanted to know.

"Kilian Morel, Blanche Trouin's husband," answered Commissaire Huppert.

"Where did it happen?" asked Commissaire Nedellec.

"Not far from the couple's house. At La Moinerie. Blanche Trouin's restaurant is in Dinard, not far from there. Morel looked after the staff and bookkeeping in his wife's restaurant. A rambler found him."

"His brother"—Dupin thought out loud, not sure himself how he came to the point—"is a friend and confidant of Blanche Trouin, isn't he?" It wasn't easy to remember who everyone was.

Commissaire Huppert's only response was: "Exactly."

"This means"—the host prefect's expression had darkened even further—"that there's a second perpetrator. Someone who murdered with intent." She took a deep breath in and out. "I'd like to speak with my fellow prefects for a few minutes. If the commissaires could be so kind as to excuse us for a moment."

Questioning glances rested on the prefect.

"We won't need long." A renewed request.

Nedellec and Dupin stood up and left the room together with Commissaire Huppert.

"What's going on?" Nedellec turned to the commissaire as soon as he had closed the door behind him. They stood in the long corridor: white walls, wooden floor; it smelled of wax.

"I have to make a call." Huppert's tone was friendly, but no less firm.

"Come on, tell us what this is about," persisted Nedellec.

"You'll find out soon enough."

With these words, the commissaire turned around and walked along the corridor to the stairs.

"Perhaps," said Dupin hopefully, "they're calling off the rest of the seminar."

It wasn't impossible; the case was clearly getting out of hand. Nedellec raised his eyebrows.

"Excuse me, Dupin, I have to make a quick call too." Before Dupin had time to respond, Nedellec had also darted off.

Dupin went to stand by the window. The downpour had relented. It must have happened in the last few minutes; suddenly there wasn't a cloud in the sky. The sun shone confidently, as though it had never done anything different. It shone down onto a thoroughly wet world—the glistening reflections in the soaked courtyard were blinding.

Now Blanche Trouin's husband was dead too. It was terrible, and utter madness. Yesterday, they had likely had breakfast together, everything still as normal, and now they were both dead.

This case was already a dramatic one, and before long it would be the talk of all of Brittany.

"We've finished our conversation." The host prefect was standing in the corridor, peering first in one direction, then the other. Commissaire Nedellec approached from one end; Dupin from the other. Nedellec was followed by Commissaire Huppert.

"We've conferred with one another," the prefect began again, once they'd all come back into the seminar room. Commissaire Huppert was staring at the ceiling, expressionless, and Locmariaquer had a kind of contented grin on his face; a disconcerting sight. "Commissaire Dupin, Commissaire Nedellec." Based on the tone, a clear instruction was about to follow. "From now on you'll be investigating this case together with Commissaire

Huppert. You three are now a team. You'll report to the four of us." A stern look. "What better way to strengthen cooperation between the *départements* than with a genuine collaborative investigation. Especially with a complicated case like this."

"What?" Dupin had been prepared for all manner of things—but not this.

"I'll be happy to." Nedellec was swift to express how pleased he was.

The counsel to the prefects nodded pathetically. Of course, Locmariaquer had to add his two cents: "An unprecedented occurrence! Historic!"

Dupin's feelings, carefully formulated, were incredibly conflicted. It was certainly better than the seminar. And it fit with how eager he was to investigate this himself. But the idea of a "team investigation" with three commissaires and four prefects went totally against the grain for him. It had taken Dupin a long time, as a dyed-in-the-wool loner by nature, to be capable of working with Nolwenn, Kadeg, and Riwal. How was he supposed to manage this off the cuff? With entirely new colleagues? And on command?

"There won't be an official lead among the three of you. In discussion with Commissaire Huppert, who, by the way, has given this her seal of approval"—all gazes moved from the prefect to the commissaire, whose expression betrayed nothing—"we've decided to leave it to you how to organize yourselves."

Well. That sounded better already. At least it implied more autonomy.

"You'll report back to us at dinner each night, so that we're kept in the loop," the prefect added. "The four of us have decided to continue with the seminar for now, with a slight shift in focus. We'll tend to a few of the main administrative pitfalls that hamper Brittany-wide police collaboration day-to-day. Formal things."

"I'm sure we'll produce historic results here too." Locmariaquer leaned back and beamed all over his eternally reddened face.

"You don't look too happy, Commissaire Dupin." The host prefect had addressed him directly. "Are you uncomfortable with our decision?"

Before Dupin could respond, Locmariaquer boomed in a threatening timbre: "I'm sure that even Finistère is delighted with our decision."

Dupin managed to force out a tormented "Absolutely."

"Okay, so that's decided. Now—solve the case! Show us your extraordinary Breton team spirit!"

Once again, Locmariaquer had to have the last word: "All of Brittany is watching you. Don't forget that. It's a blessing and a curse. And don't disappoint us."

He was a master of subtle motivation.

"Let's make a start." Commissaire Huppert sprang to her feet. "I'll bring you up to speed while we drive to the crime scene."

Before she reached the door, she clarified: "We'll take my car."

Nedellec and Dupin followed her.

It felt completely unreal. He'd just been sitting in a stuffy seminar room, and now Dupin was standing on a breathtaking beach, looking out to sea.

Blindingly white, fine sand in dunes that shielded the land

behind, covered with thick grass. The sky was a triumphant blue—apart from a single, self-assured white cloud above the sea, strangely triangular, like a puzzling sign. A gentle wind wafted the tufts of dune grass into yellow-green-brown smudges. Close to the shore: a wild and romantic-looking island, almost circular, with a steeply ascending, craggy rockface, and boulders coated in neon-yellow lichen here and there. On one of the rocks stood a solitary chapel of glistening granite, just a few meters in length and breadth but unusually tall, with a pointed roof, elaborately decorated. Between the island and the beach, protected from the sea's harshest raging, lay a dozen boats on colorful buoys. To the east, a stony headland jutted out into the sea, from which there was a wonderful view of the nearby Sables-d'Or-les-Pins.

It was enchanting. A landscape dreamed and painted by the deft summer light.

The journey here had been nerve-racking, and had taken them a good fifty minutes. They'd had to go across the Rance, as there was no other route, across the only bridge that led there and which strictly speaking wasn't a bridge at all, but rather the dam of the famous tidal power station. Extensive building work at the dam had led to a traffic jam—along with the laid-back convoy from the Dol-de-Bretagne classic car club: ancient Peugeots, Renaults, Citroëns. Likeable older people. Genuine pensioners, not rich snobs. Unmissable car stickers clarified the purpose of the gathering: *Journées Nationales des Véhicules d'Époque*. The national classic car convention. On the last car was a flag with the motto "Enjoying Life in the Slow Lane," and beneath it, "Speed Isn't Everything." Dupin felt his blood pressure rising. But the commissaires could only do one thing: be patient. During the journey, Commissaire Huppert filled Nedellec and Dupin in on the latest developments. Nedellec, and Dupin too—he couldn't help but laugh at himself, but there was no other way—had zealously made notes. Five pages he had by now, crammed full.

Dupin took a few deep breaths in and out. The beach, the ocean, the dunes, the sky, the colors—the landscape was overpowering. What's more, summer had arrived yesterday, and not even the nightly downpours could change that. Each year, you could clearly define the days when it arrived. Summer by the ocean gave Dupin an almost euphoric feeling, a sensation of great freedom.

Dupin pulled his attention back to the case.

The body lay about twenty meters away. A yellow tent with two open sides was stretched over it. Nedellec stood alongside—with the three gendarmes from Sables-d'Or-les-Pins, who had arrived just minutes after the rambler's call to the emergency services—and was making notes.

Commissaire Huppert had had the entire area of the shore sectioned off. The forensics team was already at work, and the astoundingly straightforward medical examiner had concluded his initial investigation, estimating the time of death at eight thirty that morning, give or take an hour.

Kilian Morel lay at the edge of the dunes, next to a small green dinghy with plastic pulleys at the stern. Both his arms were outstretched, and his right hand was buried in the sand. It looked as though he had been trying to crawl up the dune.

He had been stabbed, just like his wife the day before, except this time the weapon was missing. Four stab wounds, one of which, according to the medical examiner, had been straight to the heart. "Probably a pericardial tamponade." The blood had stained his beige shirt—which was tattered around the chest area—a deep red from the collar down to his dark blue linen shorts. A large quantity of blood had seeped into the sand. It was a brutal sight.

Blanche Trouin's husband was a few pounds overweight, but he wasn't fat; of average build, with longish, full, dark blond hair and a slightly plump face. Youthful, despite his forty-seven years.

He and his wife owned one of the sailboats, which were kept in the shelter of the small island during the summer. As the crow flies, it was less than two hundred meters to their house, the gendarmes had said. Presumably he had been heading out to his boat. Yesterday evening, his brother Joe had called and suggested he come by to keep him company. Huppert knew this from Joe Morel himself, whom she had spoken to during the drive, to deliver the terrible news. Kilian Morel had turned down his brother's offer and said he wanted to be alone, but that he'd be glad of his company over the next few days. Joe Morel—who according to Huppert had initially seemed devastated, but then relatively composed—had thought it likely his brother had wanted to do exactly that after the tragedy with his wife: sail out in the boat and look for solitude.

Some undefined footprints had been discovered in the sand near the body, misshapen troughs that could potentially be from the perpetrator. Or the victim. A beach rarely provided useful evidence. No cell phone had been found near the corpse.

"So?" Louane Huppert appeared behind Dupin as though out of nowhere. "What are you thinking?"

"Either," Dupin improvised, "the murderer knew Morel's boat was here. Or they followed the victim from the house. In any case, they knew where Kilian Morel and Blanche Trouin lived."

"That applies to everyone we have in our sights right now." Huppert positioned herself directly in front of Dupin. Her ponytail fell forward over her shoulder. "I meant more generally: Do you have any ideas about the case? You barely said a word during the drive."

"But he made no shortage of notes." Nedellec, who seemed not to want to miss anything, had joined them.

"No. No idea."

"Are you still thinking about the thing with the sous-chef?" asked Huppert in her typically prosaic tone. "Lucille Trouin would've had to know about it for that to come to a head. And even then, there wouldn't necessarily be anything more behind it."

That was exactly right.

"By the way, the sous-chef didn't volunteer the information when I spoke with him this afternoon. I called him back after your tip. But then he was really open and unfazed in talking about it."

"Well," muttered Dupin, "he should really have volunteered the information himself."

"Blanche Trouin first got in touch with Colomb Clément a month ago. Then she met with him in a bar late in the evening. Outside of Dinard. Clément asked for time to think it over. He called Blanche Trouin last Thursday to accept the offer. She quickly sent him a contract, and he had already signed it. Blanche Trouin wanted to tell her younger sister herself, Clément said, which was fine by him because he was nervous about having the conversation. Lucille Trouin, and I'm quoting here, could be 'very quick-tempered.' Whether Blanche had already done it by yesterday lunchtime, we don't know. Her sister is the only one who could tell us. I asked her outright. But in vain, as you know."

"Was there anything conspicuous in Blanche Trouin's cell phone records?" Nedellec changed the subject.

Dupin had wanted to ask the question in the car.

"It's hard to say at the moment. There were no phone calls to her sister, some with her friend Walig Richard, the antiques dealer, especially over the last two weeks—but according to what Monsieur Richard said yesterday, they weren't about anything special. Some with her husband, but none yesterday. One last week with Joe Morel"—Huppert seemed to have an extraordinary memory—"two calls with her aunt's housekeeper, about visiting, according to the housekeeper. Four calls with the sous-chef," she looked at Dupin, "which timewise fit in with when she was wooing him across, and Clément has confirmed them all. And, of course, dozens of other calls with suppliers, retailers, and so on; she was always very busy."

Dupin had noted it all down. At first glance, none of it seemed unusual.

"We've also filed a request to access her husband's phone records."

"We need the alibis of everyone on our list." Nedellec came to the next fundamental point. "Where they were this morning at the time in question."

"I've already assigned a colleague to each person."

That sounded good.

"And we'll also speak with each of them ourselves." Dupin's iron principle.

He realized that he was still unsure how investigating as a team would pan out. For him, the worst possible approach would be doing everything together. There were some essential questions to clarify on their modus operandi. The annoying thing was, if he asked explicitly, he would get an explicit answer, and lose the possible leeway that existed while everything remained vague.

"We should make sure people aren't having to speak with three commissaires at once."

He was relieved Huppert had formulated it herself.

"We'll have to figure out how to go about it."

It remained vague; Dupin was content.

Huppert started to make a move: "I think we should take a look at the couple's house. Two police officers from Sables-d'Or-les-Pins are waiting there for us."

She trudged through the heavy sand and the two commissaires followed.

"This recipe collection of the father's that you were talking about in the car," Nedellec asked, "do you reckon it's in Blanche Trouin's house?"

"I don't know. Maybe. Why?"

"Just wondering."

"It wasn't in Blanche Trouin's restaurant in Dinard, in any case. Forensics have already searched it. I asked her husband about the recipes yesterday, and he mentioned a notebook that Blanche kept in a pale blue box. But he didn't know where it might be."

Huppert hadn't mentioned these details during the drive.

"Did Kilian Morel say anything else about this?" Dupin asked, just to be sure.

"He merely confirmed that his wife often spoke about the recipes and saw them as a source of inspiration. He estimated that there were around eighty to a hundred."

"Do we know"—Nedellec was suddenly favoring the formal

"we"—"all the business activities of the two sisters and their partners? Beyond the restaurants, I mean?"

"I think so. We've had a list drawn up. You can get a copy anytime you want."

"I'd like to pay Blanche Trouin's two friends a visit." Clearly Nedellec already had a plan. "First Joe Morel. He could play a decisive role in this. As Blanche's confidant and the brother of the latest victim. And then this antiques dealer, Walig Richard. As close friends, they must know something about recent conflicts between the sisters."

They had left the beach now and were following a sandy path through the tall dunes. From a distance, it must look like a cheerful summer stroll. The officials from the forensics team followed a short distance behind them.

"Joe Morel and Richard claim they don't know anything. As I said, I spoke to both of them yesterday."

"You spoke with them on the phone." Nedellec summarized what the commissaire had told them. "The only ones you saw in person yesterday were Blanche Trouin's husband and Lucille Trouin's partner. And Lucille Trouin herself."

"It seems you've already solved this aspect of the case, my dear colleague," said Huppert, unruffled. "Whom I've spoken with on the phone and whom I've seen personally."

"And the aunt," Dupin suddenly remembered. "Did you speak with her on the phone or visit her?"

"I went to see her." Dupin's question didn't seem to bother the commissaire either. "Her niece was murdered, after all. It was a short visit. The aunt has dementia. I'm unsure whether she really understood what I told her."

Huppert came to an abrupt halt; Nedellec and Dupin did the same.

"That's it. The home of the two victims."

They were looking across at a modern bungalow made of pale granite, which, due to the natural shade of the stone and flat architecture, blended with astonishing harmony into the surroundings. Disheveled sea pines stood liberally distributed around the house, with stretches of grass in between. At the far end of the property, which was surrounded by bamboo fencing, lay a vegetable garden. There wasn't another house in sight far and wide, just trees and fallow fields.

The most noticeable thing about the building was its layout: it formed an elongated rectangle, with square structures to the left and right, each a little offset into the garden.

Two police officers stood in front of the light gray entrance door.

The path they were walking along, which fell away steeply within just a few meters, forked; one path ran parallel to the dunes, the other directly toward the house. From the west, a narrow, unsurfaced road led to the property. In front of the bamboo fence was a parking space, just large enough for one car, a dark gray Citroën DS 5.

"So," began Dupin, "I'll speak to Lucille's partner later—"

He was interrupted by his cell phone.

Nolwenn. A highly inconvenient time.

"Just a moment." Dupin turned on his heel and walked back along the dune path.

"Yes?"

"The almighty gods have spoken, and this is their wish. Then so it must be. It's clearly your fate: no sensational case without you." Her tone was combative; Nolwenn was obviously herself again. "The Commissariat de Police Concarneau is at your command, Monsieur le Commissaire! United, whenever you need us."

"Wonderful."

The forensics team were coming toward Dupin along the path.

"There's already a lot of talk online about the Breton 'Dream Team,' the 'Furious Three.' The 'Britt Team.'"

It sounded as though Locmariaquer had spoken to the press.

"They've forced us to work as a team."

"You'll survive. Think of Finistère! We represent Finistère!"

It was uncanny; for a moment, Nolwenn had sounded just like the prefect.

"And as I said: we're here when you need us, Monsieur le Commissaire."

"Thank you, Nolwenn." He spoke from the heart.

"Speak later."

She had already ended the call.

A smile darted across Dupin's face. Then he hurried back to join the other two commissaires. This *was* for Finistère. Their home *département*! The battle of the Breton tribes had begun.

The two police officers nodded in a friendly manner as the small group reached them.

"I'll take a look around outside," said Nedellec, marching off around the house. Without comment, Huppert headed for the front door. It was unlocked, which was quite normal in the

Breton countryside. The commissaire stepped in cautiously—and came to such an abrupt halt that Dupin almost walked into her.

"Well, would you look at that," said Huppert drily.

The house was in a terrible state. In the open-plan kitchen, cupboards had been flung open, drawers pulled out and emptied, their contents now in a chaotic mess on the parquet floor. The expansive living area that the kitchen led into looked no better. The cushions of the two elegant, pastel-blue sofas were scattered across the floor, along with everything else that must have previously been on the natural-wood dining table, now empty. One of the floor lamps lay on its side.

"Someone's really done a number in here." The commissaire strode toward the center of the room.

"Huppert! Dupin! Over here! Come and look!"

Nedellec's command echoed through the whole house. His voice was coming from inside the building, even though just a moment ago he had been outside.

To the right, a door stood ajar.

"You have to see this!" His voice was coming from there. "Someone was in the house! They were clearly searching for something."

Commissaire Huppert made no move to follow Nedellec's command. She went to the left, where, at the end of the kitchen unit, a further door led to the other square annex.

Dupin had moved toward the right-hand door, albeit somewhat reluctantly, and stepped in. The bedroom. From here, a sliding door led onto a small wooden terrace. Nedellec must have come into the house through here. From the bedroom, just like on the other side, you could also access the second annex.

"Look!" Nedellec pointed toward the opened closet. He was standing among mounds of clothing that had been yanked out. The chic wooden nightstands, too, were wide open. It was a complete and utter mess.

"It's the same in the living room," Dupin told him.

"Whoever it was, they seem to have searched randomly, with no idea of where to look."

Nedellec went toward the door to the annex, followed by Dupin. They would leave the bedroom to the forensics team.

"Not bad."

Nedellec had paused in the doorway. It was a separate, massive kitchen. A high-tech kitchen. Stainless steel, light gray stone floor. A colossal gas cooker, professional extractor hoods, an extra-large sink, two dishwashers, matte stainless steel cupboards, two open shelving units filled to the ceiling with dozens of small glass containers, various kitchen tools and utensils on stainless steel work surfaces. Above hung spatulas, spoons, scoops. Next to the door was a tall refrigerator.

The person who had searched the house had been here too, although the chaos seemed a little less pronounced. The cupboards were open, most of them full of foodstuffs, and the fridge too. But very little seemed to have been taken out.

"Anything, gentlemen?" Commissaire Huppert came in. "Ah, Blanche Trouin's kitchen lab." She looked around in awe. "So this is where the creativity happened. Her husband's office is in the other annex, by the way. Everything's been ransacked there too."

Nedellec peered into the fridge. "So the perpetrator was looking for something that could have been in either of their domains. We just don't know what."

Huppert stood in front of one of the cupboards. "I've asked forensics to keep an eye out for the recipe collection."

Dupin was by the shelves with the glass containers. They were spices. All kinds of spices, with the most beautiful poetic names. *Garam Masala, Dragonfire Curry, Harissa, Blanche's Provence, Curry Corsaire.* Spices from all over the world, and evidently Blanche's own creations too. "*Le monde des épices*" was written on the neat, visually appealing labels.

"If the recipes are even here in the house at all," murmured Nedellec.

"And of significance for our case," added Huppert. She frowned and went over to one of the other cupboards. "Doesn't it look a little *too* ransacked here? Maybe someone's trying to fool us? Send us off down the wrong path?"

"Or they didn't have much time, but still wanted to find what they were looking for no matter what," countered Nedellec.

Both were plausible.

"I'll take a look at Kilian Morel's office." Dupin made his way back through the bedroom and living area.

Morel's office seemed to also be a storage place of sorts. Along one entire wall, industrial shelving had been fitted right to the ceiling. Dupin saw all kinds of *blé noir* products—it reminded him of the store specializing in buckwheat in Rue de l'Orme. The shelf next to it was full of wine; the next, rum. Dupin glanced at the labels: *Opthimus, Diplomatico, Elements Eight.* Even the heavenly rum from the Bistro de Solidor was there: Rhum J.M.

"Yep, Saint-Malo and its rum."

Once again, Commissaire Huppert had appeared beside

him as though out of nowhere. Her expression was serious; her tone, matter-of-fact as ever.

"I've just spoken on the phone with an employee from Blanche Trouin's restaurant. Apparently, Kilian Morel was in the process of developing an online shop for rum and other Saint-Malo specialties, including Blanche's spice blends. The wines seemed to be for the restaurant."

"That would've put him in competition with Charles Braz, Lucille Trouin's partner."

"Rum is big business in these parts, a lot of people trade in it. He wouldn't have been targeting his brother-in-law in particular. But then again, who knows." Huppert paused. "Perhaps it does play a role. Maybe the rivalry between the sisters took hold of the two men too."

Nedellec came in. "We should discuss our plan of action. I'm going to—"

"Does Lucille Trouin know about her brother-in-law's murder?" It had only just occurred to Dupin; they hadn't yet discussed it, strangely, which was also the case for several other topics and routines—a result of the investigation's unstructured beginning.

"I drove straight to see her when I got the news. Her attorney was there the whole time. Once again, she didn't say a word. She's sticking by her silence. The investigative detainment, by the way, will be here at the station in Saint-Malo for the time being, not in Rennes, as it would usually be. Meaning that we can question Lucille Trouin at any time. Even if it's a little makeshift here."

It was an absurd idea that accompanied the investigation like an incessant dark bass in the background: Lucille Trouin was in police custody for having unequivocally murdered her sister. She knew why she had killed her sister. And possibly also knew why her brother-in-law had been murdered. Quite probably, even. And who had done it. The case could already be solved. But she was remaining stubbornly silent. Presumably one and the same motive lay behind both crimes—or, at least, there was some connection.

"So"—Nedellec was becoming impatient—"how do we want to proceed? I'm going to pay Morel's brother and then the antiques dealer a visit. I suggest we split up."

He had voiced Dupin's most fervent wish.

"In which case it's imperative"—Commissaire Huppert raised her voice—"that we confer with one another about everything. Each of us has to know whom the other is meeting and when, and what comes out of it."

Dupin very much doubted that this was possible.

"Let's say we'll inform one another as quickly as possible as soon as there's any news," he swiftly reinforced nonetheless.

"And we'll meet regularly," Huppert declared. "The entire Dream Team," she said without any trace of humor on her face, but Nedellec grinned. "Plus text messages and, if necessary, phone calls—we can do group ones between the three of us."

Dupin nodded. It was all going in the right direction, and he was slowly starting to have a clearer idea of the collaborative investigation approach.

"Everyone keeps to the rules, and if we take any, let's say 'unusual' actions, then we'll agree on it together beforehand." Dupin thought he saw Huppert glance in his direction. "And by that, I mean anything that goes beyond regular investigative inquiries. Dupin, whom do you plan to speak with first?"

He had already given this considerable thought. "Lucille Trouin's partner, Charles Braz."

"I'll call you both a car to take you to the station, so you can pick up your own vehicles."

Damn, Dupin had completely forgotten. He hadn't even come here with his car.

"I'll send a copy of the list of alibis for this morning to each of you, as soon as I have it. Then you can double-check them. My assistant will also send you the info on everyone who's relevant to the investigation so far. We'll talk later."

With these words, she turned and left them standing there.

"And whom are you going to speak to, Commissaire Huppert?" Nedellec called after her.

She glanced briefly over her shoulder.

"No one, for the time being."

She was already out of the door.

What was she planning? At least one thing was clear: the Département Ille-et-Vilaine had a massive home advantage.

A few minutes later, Dupin was walking along the narrow road in front of the house, his cell phone pressed to his ear. The list promised by Commissaire Huppert had already arrived in his inbox.

"Hello?" Charles Braz picked up straightaway.

"Monsieur Braz, this is Commissaire Dupin, I'm leading . . . I'm one of the commissaires leading the investigation"—he was still struggling a little—"and I'd like to speak to you. In three-quarters of an hour?"

"Certainly, monsieur. Is Commissaire Huppert no longer involved?" asked Braz in a friendly tone.

"No, no, she is. We've just—expanded the team."

"Okay. Where shall we meet? I'm at home."

Dupin saw a police car turn into the narrow street.

"I'll come to you. I have the address."

"Then I'll see you here."

"See you shortly."

Dupin pressed the Call End button, then immediately dialed the next number.

"Nolwenn?"

"Monsieur le Commissaire! We're just talking about the case. I'm here with the whole team: Le Menn, Nevou, and Kadeg."

Dupin almost felt emotional, thinking of them all sitting there together.

"I'm sending you a list of all the people involved so far. I'd be interested in anything you can find."

"We'll start right away."

"Just a moment." Dupin tapped around on his cell phone. "Here it is . . . and it's on its way to you. I'll be speaking with all of them personally. First Lucille Trouin's partner, his name is—"

"Charles Braz. I've already read about him online. I've already got a little tableau on my screen of the people, I'm just about to complete it. This Braz guy specialized in rum. He may also be involved in his girlfriend's cheese business and restaurant, but I've not been able to find out for sure yet."

Nolwenn's uncanny speed—like with Lucky Luke, whom Dupin had worshiped in his youth. Lucky Luke drew his gun faster than his own shadow.

"Try to find out about the business dealings of the murdered husband, Kilian Morel. He was building up an online shop of Breton specialties, including rum."

"I'm on it. Oh, your list just arrived. Whom are you seeing after that? Do you already have the order planned?"

Dupin looked at the list. "Flore Briard, Lucille Trouin's close friend. Then Clément, the sous-chef. There's something I need to clarify with him."

Dupin explained briefly.

"Okay. What about the ninety-three-year-old aunt who's noted down here? Perhaps it was about an inheritance?"

"At the moment, anything's possible."

Dupin realized that they hadn't yet discussed this in their team of three. And yet it seemed an obvious point.

"Okay. Then Team Finistère will get on with the research. Riwal's the only one who isn't here; he's battling the badger. Talk soon, Monsieur le Commissaire."

Nolwenn hung up.

The badger! Dupin had completely forgotten about it. And yet it had been the red-hot topic in their office over the last few weeks. More, even: a veritable reality show with daily episodes. Riwal's garden, his pride and joy, was under attack. In particular, his strawberries. And solely at night. Initially Riwal hadn't been sure who the attacker was; only a high-tech Wi-Fi camera and a night shift had brought clarity. He had immediately launched into defensive action, without wanting to harm the animal in any way, of course. As badgers, according to the experts he consulted, didn't like noise or light, Riwal had deployed exactly that in the "first phase": a radio placed in the strawberry beds, blaring away at full volume for several nights on end, and a floodlight steered by a motion sensor. Neither had bothered the badger. Consequently, protective measures of increasing intensity had been employed, albeit still ineffectively, including a borrowed cat, which was supposed to patrol the garden for a few days and nights—it was questionable whether she did it—and human hair, scattered over the garden, which Riwal had procured from his hairdresser. Badgers couldn't stand either, and both methods had been praised online as surefire fixes. As far as Dupin was concerned, it was all starting to get a bit strange.

Charles Braz's house was almost precisely in the middle of the Solidor quay, directly on Plage de Solidor. The bay, lined by the pretty quay, formed an almost complete semicircle. When the tide was out it lay completely dry, and dozens of boats, leaning lethargically on their sides, seemed to be resting before the next incoming tide. A promenade ran along the beach. One end of the picture-postcard bay was marked by an imposing church; the other by an old watchtower, the Tour Solidor.

There was a relaxed, serene atmosphere. The secluded bay, right on the edge of Saint-Servan, had the charm of a hidden gem. And of real life, following the same rhythm here day in, day out. *Les gens du coin*, the people from the local neighborhood, came here. It was a tranquil world. Dupin could happily sit in one of the cozy-looking cafés all day long, letting the sun shine on his face and watching the cheerful hustle and bustle.

The house with the number twelve was painted white, three stories high, with stucco decoration around the windows. Beneath was a shop selling rum. Pale, bleached wood, vibrant Caribbean tones: turquoise blue, deep bright blue, sunny yellow, fresh green.

Dupin was just about to press the doorbell when his cell phone rang.

Riwal. His first inspector. Who was actually supposed to be on a badger hunt right now.

"*Bonjour,* boss!"

"What's up?"

"I just got back to the office. I popped into the home improvement store to buy an electric fence. I got the tip off this special internet site, badger-in-garden-what-to-do.com."

"I see." That was all Dupin was prepared to say in response. "Was there anything else?"

"Well, this is a pretty great case, boss."

"Excuse me?"

"The crème de la crème." Riwal sounded really excited. "You're investigating in the most distinguished of gastronomic spheres. And think about the incredible restaurants you'll be visiting! My congratulations."

Dupin was too baffled to answer.

"Of course, it's a terrible tragedy." Riwal suddenly became serious. "Bitter rivalries between siblings can be hellish. The hurts pile up over the years. They go deeper and deeper, one leading to the next, like a terrible, inescapable cascade. And then—well, anything is possible."

They were bleak words. But sometimes, that was where you had to venture: into the darkest recesses of the human soul.

"Even murder?"

Dupin walked toward the watchtower.

"Put it this way: once things have gone so far, and the hate has burrowed its way deep down into the heart, sometimes all it takes is a catalyst that, to outsiders, might seem trivial."

Dupin knew what he meant.

"Having said that, it's looking completely different since the murder of Kilian Morel," Riwal said, preempting Dupin's interjection. "Is there anything else you'd like to know about rum before your visit to Charles Braz, boss? Nolwenn just brought me up to date."

Dupin hesitated. It would be a mistake to say yes. But apparently it would also be a mistake to say nothing.

"Saint-Malo has been the number one transit center for rum for centuries. Most of it comes from the Caribbean, which Saint-Malo has a close relationship with—just think of the French Antilles. It's no coincidence that the toughest sailing regatta in the world, the Route du Rhum, goes from Saint-Malo to Guadeloupe. In the discerning world of gastronomy, the main focus nowadays is on *rhum agricole,* rum from agricultural origins, which unlike industrial rum is extracted directly from freshly pressed sugarcane juice, not molasses, a preserved, nonperishable syrup. Definitely remember that detail. There's even an AOC quality seal, bestowed on rum from Martinique, Guadeloupe, and Haiti, among others."

"Thank you, Riwal, I think I'm now comprehensively informed."

"Do you know what the word 'rum' means? It's really funny— *tumult.* From the English word 'rumbullion.' Very fitting, don't you think?"

A shrill beeping tone rang out right by Dupin's ear. A text message.

"Riwal, I have to go."

"And we'll continue with the research."

Dupin had turned on his heel once again and was walking back to Charles Braz's house. He glanced at the message. It was from Nedellec.

News! Joe Morel was once romantically involved with Lucille Trouin. For a year. It ended nine years ago. She left him for Charles Braz.

Dupin came to an involuntary halt. That really was news!

The younger sister used to be involved with the brother of her older sister's husband. Was Joe Morel already a good friend and confidant of Blanche Trouin back then? And simultaneously the lover of her estranged sister? It was hard to imagine. But—life was like that, it often spun peculiar threads. And that was all a long time ago now, admittedly. It would surely only be an issue if the feelings between the two of them had sparked up again. If they had gotten back together. But even then: How would that have led to Blanche Trouin's death? And her husband's? Still. In the first phase of an investigation, it was important to pursue anything that seemed interesting, without exception and without overhasty judgment. You can only understand how a puzzle fits together once you have more of the pieces, which, if you're lucky, turn up suddenly and unexpectedly.

Charles Braz was a strikingly good-looking man. Lean, fine-boned but not lanky; instead, lithe and elegant. Tall, over six feet for sure, with tousled black hair, silvery gray at the temples. He was dressed in perfectly harmonizing colors; a polo shirt in petrol blue, dark blue linen pants. On Huppert's list, it said he was forty-five years old.

Braz had greeted the commissaire in a very friendly manner, at the apartment door on the first floor, and led him into a large room.

"I'm sure you find it hard to imagine that, as Lucille's long-term life partner, I have no explanation for the terrible drama that occurred yesterday. One would only assume I'd know what happened between the sisters." He had paused in front of one of the two large windows, which had a view of the bay and picturesque Rance estuary, and looked earnestly at Dupin.

"You're exactly right, Monsieur Braz. It does, of course, seem strange to the police."

Dupin held his gaze.

"I can understand that." Braz looked weighed down by grief.

The room was furnished in the same style as the store downstairs: bleached, pale wood, albeit with different colors, tasteful gray tones. A deep sofa, matching armchair, side table, a sideboard. Enlarged black-and-white photographs showing modern sailboats in an intense battle with the elements.

Braz had followed Dupin's sweeping gaze.

"I sail. The pictures are from a regatta."

"And you really have no idea what might've happened?" Dupin returned to the point.

"No. As hard as I try, I can't imagine what could have driven Lucille to do something so awful." Braz's expression, his voice, his posture, now emanated intense horror. "It's a nightmare."

"Do you remember any conflict between the sisters over the past days or weeks, a particularly bad argument, perhaps?"

"I really don't, no. I knew, of course, what everyone else did: they couldn't stand each other, and that's putting it mildly. They had entirely different ways of looking at things—people, the world, life in general. Even since their childhood. They—"

"They both devoted their lives to cooking, became famous chefs, stayed in the area they grew up in . . . Where exactly are the fundamental differences?"

"That's only on the surface. The differences lie in their fundamental attitudes, outlooks, and opinions. In their character. I know *only* differences. The fact they're both in the restaurant industry—and in the same region—only made things worse."

Braz spoke calmly now, analytically. Intelligently.

"Give me a few examples."

"Well, Lucille is incredibly ambitious. She wants to accomplish great things. And she's hungry for it. She's a workaholic. Blanche, on the other hand, hated ambition. She said she did things because she loved them, out of passion. She was blessed with incredible talents and simply wanted to enjoy discovering them. She didn't plan to become famous, or a Michelin-starred chef, it just happened along the way, and none of that interested her. That's what she said, in any case"—Braz recounted it without judgment—"and that's also how it seemed. Lucille, on the other hand . . ." He hesitated, then began again: "Look, it's incredibly difficult for me. I love Lucille, more than anything."

He moved away from the window and sat down on the armchair, but only perching on the edge, an awkward posture.

"The two of them have—had—their gridlocked way of seeing things. If I explain it to you like this," he looked concerned, "then, of course, I'm telling you how Lucille saw things. For the most part, at least. I'm giving you Lucille's perspective." He had gotten back to his feet and began to walk up and down in the room. "Naturally I have my own too. But I don't want to seem disloyal. Lucille has my support."

Dupin understood what he meant.

"In order to help us solve this, you should say everything that's on your mind, Monsieur Braz. In the end, it will help your partner too."

Whether this was true, of course, depended on Lucille Trouin's motivations, which so far remained obscure.

"I think Lucille sees everything relating to Blanche in an extreme way. She immediately interprets everything in a drastic way. Above all, in a very personal way. That applied to them both: whatever one of them said or did, the other would take it personally. Like when Blanche began to specialize in spices. Up until then, they'd both had the same supplier, a small company near Dinard. But then Blanche bought it, and Lucille immediately sought out a different supplier. She saw it as a personal aggression. She thought Blanche only did it for one reason: to hurt her. Which certainly wasn't the case, not in such an exaggerated way, I'm sure of it." A noble defense of his partner's fiercest opponent. "And I told Lucille that too. But her pattern of perception was too stubborn. And that's just one example."

It was a good one.

"It's really complicated. The difficult thing is that there are always multiple and often conflicting motivations for all human behavior." This was very similar to how Dupin saw it. "When Blanche bought the spice company, I'm sure her main aim wasn't to hurt Lucille. But she knew it might, and did it regardless. Who knows, maybe even with a little schadenfreude. People are rarely entirely without blame."

"Do you have other examples of the differences?"

"Lucille loves expensive, chic clothing, whereas Blanche always dressed very simply. Lucille always drives exquisite cars; Blanche drove a battered old Renault. She always seemed very humble, never made a big fuss, seemed at peace with herself, even-tempered, treated her employees like friends. Lucille is the opposite in all respects. She's, let's take the last point, very

authoritarian with her employees. Albeit fair and dependable."
He had returned to the armchair, and sat down once more,
again on the edge. "I could continue the list of differences as
long as you want."

So far, Dupin hadn't moved away from the window; he
couldn't stand it when other people walked up and down in a
room. That was *his* thing.

"And the jealousy, the deep envy, the distrust, this incredibly
bitter rivalry—do you think it was equally pronounced in both
of them?"

"Absolutely. They begrudged each other everything. Both
of them felt constantly disadvantaged, inadequate, ignored—
the other one always had more . . . more beautiful things, better things." Dupin felt he kept noticing in Charles Braz a kind
of distance to his life partner, either feigned or genuine. "There
are so many stories. Even going back to their childhood. Each
of them always thought their parents loved the other one more.
That their achievements got more praise, more attention. They
were constantly slighting the other." Now Braz sounded like an
experienced psychologist. "In any case, it began an endless chain
of hurt. A vicious circle."

"Would you say they hated each other? Did it go that far,
Monsieur Braz?"

"Hate" wasn't an easily definable word, but it meant something that no other word could capture, something that went
far beyond other negative, aggressive emotions. It marked something unbounded, blind, obsessive, violent.

"Yes," he confirmed in a subdued voice, "I think so."

Dupin glanced up at the sky. The wind seemed to have turned;
thick-bellied, pitch-black clouds were gathering from inland. For

now they were still isolated monstrosities, chased across the sky by gusts of wind, but it already looked threatening.

He turned away from the window. "Lucille called you yesterday evening from the police station after her arrest. Did you ask her why she did it?"

"Yes. But . . ." He paused; the question seemed to have hit a nerve. He seemed conflicted. "She wouldn't say a word. She said very little in general. Only that I should call her attorney. And come by to bring her a few things. She's allowed to receive visitors in investigative detainment."

"Did she call you while she was trying to escape the police?"

"No."

"When do you plan to visit her?"

"Straight after our conversation. I've already cleared it with Commissaire Huppert."

Huppert hadn't mentioned it.

"I'd like you to call me straight afterward, Monsieur Braz."

"Sure."

"Another thing." Dupin was now walking up and down the room. "Where were you this morning? Between seven thirty and nine thirty?"

"Here. At home. The whole morning. I just went out once to buy a baguette. I spoke to two friends on the phone, on my cell, and with Lucille's attorney. Twice, at around seven and then again around eleven."

"So we'll be able to see all these calls on the itemized telephone records."

"Yes. I maybe spoke with one friend at around ten thirty, with the attorney around eleven, and then with another friend."

Dupin sighed softly. With regards to Charles Braz's alibi,

that meant only one thing: it was vague, very vague. They'd be very lucky if—apart from the phone calls and the baker—they managed to verify what he said. He could have easily made it to La Moinerie and back. Precisely between seven thirty and nine thirty. It would have been enough time. For both the murder and the ransacking of the house.

"Do you have any thoughts on the murder of Kilian Morel, Monsieur Braz?"

"None at all. That only makes everything much more mysterious. You'd have to presume a connection with what happened yesterday—but what? It's all incomprehensible. As I said, I can't even imagine that Lucille . . ." His voice broke. Braz ran his hand through his hair.

Dupin paused in front of a picture that showed a small sailboat tilted at an alarming angle in a trough of waves.

"How was your relationship with Kilian Morel, with your—as it were—brother-in-law?"

Charles Braz raised his eyebrows. "Good. We didn't see each other often, due to the circumstances. Usually only at official events. And even then, we would just exchange a few friendly words."

"When did you last see him?"

"About three or four months ago."

"And did you talk about your shared passion for rum?"

"About all kinds of things, really. He was a laid-back guy, and always seemed very likable. Interested in all kinds of topics. Including rum."

"Weren't you taken aback when he set up in competition with you?"

"No, not at all. There are so many rum traders on the Emerald Coast."

He seemed generally relaxed about it.

"He mainly worked in the restaurant," commented Braz. "He looked after the business side, and the wine list too. He really knew his stuff."

"Where is your car, Monsieur Braz?"

Dupin had meant to ask sooner.

"My car? Almost directly in front of the house. A little to the right. Toward the watchtower. A Volvo XC60."

"And it was there all morning? You haven't yet driven it today?"

"No. It's been parked there since yesterday."

That would also be hard for them to verify.

"You just mentioned," Dupin changed the subject again, "that you spoke to two friends on the phone this morning. Who were they, exactly?"

"I spoke with—"

Dupin's cell phone interrupted Braz's response.

"I'm sorry." Dupin glanced at the display. Nolwenn. "Just a moment, please."

Before Braz had time to reply, Dupin left the room and went along the hallway to the stairs.

"Yes, Nolwenn?"

"So, a few bits of info from us, Monsieur le Commissaire." Nolwenn had clearly gotten straight to work; she didn't waste any time.

Dupin clamped the phone between his ear and shoulder and pulled out his notebook and pen.

"There's almost nothing on the internet about Kilian Morel, Blanche Trouin's husband—our new victim—except a few mentions in a report about his wife, that's it. He seems to have kept a low profile. His shop went online on January 7 and was registered in his name. It looks quite professional. Charles Braz, the boyfriend of—"

"I'm just at his place now."

"I know. We found a few interviews, about rum and sailing, irrelevant for us. In one of them he says he wasn't very involved with his life partner's 'business.' Apart from the rum company, I can't find any others in his name. On to the antiques dealer, Walig Richard, the victim's friend. He has two shops, one in Saint-Suliac and one in Saint-Malo. He is also a hobbyist vintner, evidently a real passion of his."

"There's wine cultivation here? In Brittany?"

"But of course, Monsieur le Commissaire." A peeved tone. "There's one single, but very large vineyard hill on the Rance, right by Saint-Suliac. Don't you remember the big lead story in the *Télégramme* last week—about all the specialties that are now being grown here?"

A rhetorical question. How could he have forgotten? Riwal had spent the entire lunch break enthusiastically discussing the scientific details in the article. Due to the influence of the Gulf Stream and climate change of recent years, practically everything now grew in Brittany. Pineapple, white tea, rice, aloe vera, bananas, Szechuan pepper, even saffron and ginger, pepper, lemongrass, vanilla. And there were sixty-four buffalo on a Breton meadow—for Breton buffalo mozzarella, *mozza breizh*.

"Should I put you through to Riwal, Monsieur le Commissaire? He'll explain the wine element very precisely."

"Maybe later."

"Then let's get back to the antiques dealer: in the few articles there are on him, there's unfortunately nothing noteworthy. They're about the antiques industry and wine growing, things like that. There's quite a lot on the sous-chef, Colomb Clément, though, including a few interviews. He sounds promising, a rising star in gastronomy. There isn't much on Lucille Trouin's friend, Flore Briard, the one with the culinary boat trips. Just one longer interview. She's from a wealthy background, parents are dead, very pretty, early forties, expensive taste. She owns one of the most magnificent villas on the entire coast. And that's saying something, there are masses of them up there."

"I'm meeting with her this afternoon."

Dupin had called Madame Briard on the drive here from La Moinerie. And had arranged to visit her at home at four o'clock.

"Last of all, the aunt: at some point there'll be a sizable inheritance, for whomever it's going to. The property, at least, because the woman also lives in an extraordinary villa. There's nothing online about the aunt herself."

"What about the victim's brother, Joe Morel? He was in a relationship with Lucille Trouin ten years ago."

"Aha, there's a story there . . . He owns a popular oyster bar in Cancale. Riwal knows it."

Cancale clearly wasn't subject to the same excommunication as Saint-Malo for Nolwenn and Riwal.

"Obviously we've checked all these people to see if they've ever been in conflict with the law. Nothing. Law-abiding citizens, according to what we've found so far."

None of it was particularly new, and certainly there was nothing eye-opening, but for Dupin it was still useful to find out more about the circle of people in the investigation.

"Thanks, Nolwenn."

"It's not easy when we're so far away. I mean, Saint-Malo is foreign to us."

Saint-Malo wasn't actually any farther away than the other places where Dupin—with Nolwenn's energetic assistance—had investigated over the years. It had never been an issue before.

"We'll continue the research, Monsieur le Commissaire."

One minute later, Dupin was back in Charles Braz's living room.

"We were just talking about the friends you spoke with this morning." Dupin picked up the thread. He had noted the questions he wanted to ask Braz in his Clairefontaine.

"You're right." Charles Braz was now leaning against the wall between the two windows. He looked tired.

"First I spoke with Eric for a long while, an old friend who lives in Cancale. We grew up in Dinan, a little below the Rance."

Dupin knew where Dinan was, and not to confuse it with Dinard. He made a note regardless.

"Then with Flore Briard, Lucille's best friend. She and I are also friends."

"The rich heiress. The two women also work together, is that right? The culinary boat trips along the Emerald Coast?"

"Yes, Lucille and her sous-chef create the menus for the trips. Well, he does predominantly. There's also a cook, an employee of Flore's, on the boat itself. But naturally Lucille is paid for providing the recipes, and Flore emphasizes that in her marketing."

In this respect, too, the loss of the sous-chef to the elder sister was sure to be a blow.

"Did Lucille know that Blanche was planning to steal away her sous-chef?" Huppert hadn't been able to ask Charles Braz about this yesterday; she had only received the information afterward.

"Really? Blanche was planning that?" He seemed genuinely amazed. "Lucille didn't say anything about it. But that would be really awful. It would cause Lucille major problems. Colomb isn't easy to replace." He moved away from the wall, walked over to the armchair, and sat down. "Is that really true? When?"

"She didn't mention it?"

"No."

He really seemed not to know.

"We've seen very little of each other recently, I have to admit. I've been away a lot, just recently in Paris. At a gastronomy fair. And Lucille doesn't talk that much about what's going on with her. Sometimes it takes weeks until she shares what's bothering her. She's the same with Flore, her best friend."

With this claim, Charles Braz was putting himself in a strategically comfortable situation. But perhaps it was simply the truth.

"By luring Clément away"—Braz seemed to feel personally impacted—"Blanche would have done considerable damage to Lucille's business. That really would have been a personal attack. How else should Lucille have seen it?"

This time he was clearly taking a side.

They were silent for a while.

Dupin changed the subject again: "Are you in any way involved in your partner's business affairs? Or is she in yours?"

Dupin's cell phone beeped.

A text message from Commissaire Huppert.

Telephone conference, urgent. 3 o'clock.

Dupin glanced at the clock: 2:25. At three he would be in

the car, on his way to see Flore Briard. So that was easy—and there'd be time for a *petit café* on the quay, too.

He gestured for Braz to continue.

"No, not at all. Lucille would never want that. And neither would I." In a quieter voice, he added: "Five years ago, she lent me some money. One hundred and fifty thousand euros. To expand my business. I paid it back to her in full at the end of last year. I was earning two hundred and fifty thousand myself, I used to be an interior designer—an architect, strictly speaking. It was going well. And"—for the first time, there was a hint of a smile—"it's going well now too. The rum business, I mean."

"And each of you has their own house?"

"Yes. This one belongs to me. Lucille lives around two hundred meters away in her own. We—we're both very independent people." This was clearly important to him. "I designed Lucille's cheese shop in Rue de l'Orme. And her restaurant after the renovations three years ago. She paid me, of course."

Braz seemed to value transparency.

"Madame Trouin's cheese business—how big is it intended to be? Does she want to expand?"

"She wants to gradually open shops all across Brittany, eight or nine. Including another around here, bigger than the one in Rue de l'Orme."

The plan was proof of Lucille Trouin's ambitious nature.

"How far along are the plans?"

He hesitated. "I think she wanted to start next year."

"We know there was a dispute over the father's recipes." Dupin needed to escalate the conversation a little.

"You can say that again." Braz took a deep breath in; it was clearly an emotional topic. "I don't think Lucille will ever get over it. She wrote Blanche a letter at the start of the year, demanding that she share the recipe collection with her at long last."

"How would you explain its enormous significance?"

"Purely emotional. Psychological. There's no miracle recipe in there. They're the father's legacy, his craft. The symbolic passing of the baton, in a way. Whichever of the two sisters has them, also holds his approval. The grotesque thing is: Lucille wouldn't even have been able to get them, because their father had already passed when she properly started cooking. I think"—he stood up from the armchair—"the recipes also played a significant role in the start-up phase of Blanche's restaurant, which was initially in Saint-Malo: they helped her swiftly establish herself with the locals, because her father and his cooking were so popular. I mean, it was a heartwarming story, for the press too."

"So the recipes were still a source of inspiration to Blanche Trouin?"

"I couldn't say. I think the significance of the recipes lies elsewhere."

Dupin walked up to Charles Braz and paused right in front of him. He locked his eyes on his. "It must have been strange for you that your partner and the brother of Blanche's husband were once together, given how complicated things were between the sisters?"

Braz showed no particular reaction. "That's all a long time ago now. They went to school together. I personally never had contact with Joe Morel." His tone made it clear that for him, there was nothing more to say.

"Were Blanche and Joe close even back then?"

"They were, yes."

"Then it must've been very difficult for Blanche."

Braz's gaze darkened. "Yes. I think it must've been quite intense for her back then. She can only have seen it as Lucille intentionally interfering in her life. A perfidious attempt to take something away from her. Blanche wanted her husband to exercise influence on his brother, which he tried to. But in vain."

Braz and Dupin were still standing opposite each other.

"Are your partner and Joe Morel still in contact?"

"No."

If that was the truth, the story really might be of no significance. But either way: Dupin needed to bring the conversation to a close, especially if he wanted to grab a quick coffee before the next appointment.

"I . . . I think, Monsieur le Commissaire, that . . ." Braz seemed uneasy all of a sudden, speaking hesitantly. "There's something else I should tell you." For a moment, even he himself seemed a little shocked. "Lucille wouldn't agree, I'm sure, but I think I'm obligated to share it with you."

He took a deep breath.

"I should have told your colleague yesterday, but I was so overwhelmed at the time. And I didn't see any connection—I still don't, for that matter, but . . ."

"Just tell me."

"Last week, Lucille told me over dinner that she might have a problem. A financial one."

"In what sense?"

"She didn't explain."

"She didn't tell you anything else? Just that?"

It was hard to believe.

"That's how it sometimes is with her. As I said, she doesn't find it easy to open up. She wants to solve her problems by herself, that's important to her. And I can understand that."

"She didn't say another word about it?"

"No."

"When was this?"

"Wednesday evening."

Five days before she murdered her sister.

Dupin turned away. He began to pace up and down the room again.

As interesting as this piece of information was, it wouldn't get them any further right now.

"What about their aunt?" The last point Dupin had noted down. "Do you know her?"

"Lucille took me with her on a visit once, the year before last. She was already very confused back then. And eccentric. If it weren't for her housekeeper, she would have been in a home long before now."

"The property in Rothéneuf must be worth several million. Will Lucille inherit it?"

"She won't inherit anything. Blanche wouldn't have either. It will all go to the aunt's younger sister, who lives in Canada with her three children and numerous grandchildren, in Québec. Until a few years ago, the aunt visited her there every summer. Lucille and Blanche have never met her. Commissaire Huppert already asked me about a possible inheritance yesterday."

Which, of course, explained why the commissaire hadn't even mentioned that point to them; the potential motive had evaporated.

"Okay, Monsieur Braz. That's it for now. Thank you. That was all incredibly useful information." Dupin had spoken with a strange emphasis, as though Braz had said more than he'd wanted to.

"Gladly, Monsieur le Commissaire. I really hope you"—Braz seemed unsure what words he should choose—"can solve the case soon."

Dupin left the room. Braz accompanied him.

They reached the apartment door.

"We'll be in touch again soon. And call if something else comes to mind. No matter what it is."

Dupin was en route south, toward the tidal power plant whose dam connected Saint-Malo and Dinard, and which he had already driven across twice today.

It was exactly 3:02 when he dialed in to the telephone conference from his car. He had drunk two *petit cafés* standing—they were bitterly necessary. Despite the absurd circumstances in which this investigation had come about, Dupin felt that special feverish mood taking hold of him, the one he always went into during a case.

"Finally." Huppert picked up at once. "Commissaire Nedellec has already dialed in. I'm in a hurry. Lucille Trouin is almost bankrupt."

"What?" Dupin blurted out.

"I've spoken with her bank, the mayor, the municipal property office, and a real estate agent. Lucille Trouin has bought a huge plot of land near Rothéneuf. From the city council. Around two hundred and fifty by two hundred meters. Right on the ocean, near Le Bénétin—a restaurant on the shore. She was planning to set up a kind of flagship store for Breton cheese there. As well as a restaurant. All strictly ecological, sustainable, powered solely by regenerative energy. A project only very few people knew about. She had the initial, confidential conversations in the middle of last year. The plot wasn't actually intended for construction purposes, but the mayor was still very interested, because the city's really keen on environmentally aware projects. And sustainable tourism. At the start of the year, she was given the green light during a discreet preliminary survey, that's when she bought the land." Huppert raced through her report. "One point one million euros. She put up five hundred thousand euros of capital herself, by borrowing against her house. And she took out two large loans totaling over six hundred thousand. For the construction, she took out another five hundred thousand euros. She already had a renowned architect in mind. Her restaurant is only rented, by the way."

Huppert paused briefly.

"But then, four weeks ago, a report by the environmental agency arrived at the municipal property office. Apparently, an extremely rare roseate tern is nesting on the land. That makes the entire project obsolete. She's got no chance. But the land is already hers. A piece of land in the most beautiful of locations, and she can't do a thing with it. It's essentially worthless. And it gets worse: the bank is now pushing for a swift repayment, because the conditions of the loan haven't been fulfilled. The city had expressly drawn Lucille Trouin's attention to the outstanding ecological report beforehand, but it seemed she ignored it."

"Interesting," Nedellec commented drily.

"The first breakthrough." Dupin meant it in earnest. This was more than interesting.

And the new information fit perfectly with what Charles Braz had just told him. Above all, it gave them—possibly—something very important: the urgent, acute element that had until now been missing. A potential reason for the sudden drama. In summary, it meant that Lucille's livelihood was under threat; for her, as things looked, everything was on the line. Which brought another possible motive into play—beyond only the competition between the sisters.

"I've just come from Charles Braz's place. Lucille told him about a financial problem last week, but left it vague. That's what he says, at least. It's likely she could have been talking about this."

"Is that really believable, Dupin?" Nedellec muttered. "His long-term life partner goes bankrupt and doesn't say a word? Did he know about the land and the project?"

"Apparently not. He only mentioned her idea of opening a second, large cheese shop in the area and several additional shops in other cities around Brittany. But he didn't seem to know the details."

"Seems to me like he's lying through his teeth," remarked Nedellec.

"Only Lucille could tell us for sure," Huppert said.

"I'll speak to him again." Both were conceivable: that Braz really didn't know anything—and that he had lied.

"How do you know the loss is bankrupting Lucille?" Nedellec pressed deeper. "Maybe she has savings?"

"As I said, I spoke with her bank. I know the manager there. The situation will most likely ruin her. A situation like this can push people to do almost anything."

"But how could murdering her own sister solve the problem?

How could that have given Lucille access to a large sum of money?" Dupin pondered out loud.

Huppert was still calm. "We'll see. I also have some intel on the financial circumstances of Blanche Trouin and her husband. Everything looks very stable there. Significant assets, amounting to over half a million. The house and restaurant are already paid off."

"Dupin's right," Nedellec agreed. "As her murderer, she wouldn't be able to get the inheritance anyway."

"She wouldn't have inherited from her sister in any case. That's crystal clear from the paperwork. Everything went to Blanche's husband," said Huppert. "And the aunt's leaving everything to her younger sister in Canada."

The latter piece of information corresponded with what Dupin had heard from Charles Braz.

"Then that finally brings us to my point." Nedellec had become impatient. "The former relationship between Joe Morel and Lucille Trouin."

Dupin had now driven up onto the road that crossed the dam.

"What kind of scenario could make something from so long ago an issue again?" asked Huppert coolly.

"Blanche Trouin must have seen it as an immense betrayal back then. As a provocation, an intentional attack. Just think about their dynamic of jealousy and rivalry."

"I can believe that," persisted Huppert, "but it would only be relevant today if they'd gotten back together again. I mean, it's clear Lucille didn't manage to destroy the friendship between Blanche and Morel, if that was even her intention. Dupin, you were just with Braz, what did he have to say on that?"

"It was dramatic, he said. But he doesn't see any significance for the here and now. According to him, Lucille and Joe Morel aren't even in touch anymore."

"See, Nedellec, there you have it."

"And since when do we believe a suspect's statement without questioning it?"

A good point. There was a brief combative pause.

"You're right," Huppert conceded. "It's good we know about it. I've got another call with the mayor now, so let's talk more later. I suggest we meet at six o'clock. Our report to the prefects is scheduled for seven-thirty, so that'll give us time to synchronize our thoughts."

"And where are we meeting?" Nedellec didn't seem reconciled yet.

"I have some things to do in Dinard after this. How about we meet in the Restaurant du Petit Port," Huppert suggested. "You'll find the address online."

"Sounds good." This fit perfectly with Dupin's plans.

"By the way," groused Nedellec, "I haven't been able to reach Blanche Trouin's friend, the antiques dealer."

His announcement didn't receive a response.

"In Petit Port then, at six o'clock," repeated Huppert. "Then we'll discuss all the other things too." She ended the call.

Dupin had almost reached the other side of the dam; to his right was the sea, the bay between the two cities, and to the left, an unhurried riverscape. Dupin estimated the width of the Rance here at one kilometer.

Just a few weeks ago he had read an article—in connection with the climate debate—about the pioneering tidal power plant and its revolutionary use of the Atlantic energetic forces. Built in 1966, it was the first of its kind in the world and capable of supplying up to 350,000 inhabitants with green energy. Thanks to the immense tidal differences, gigantic masses of water flowed through the dam's turbines twice daily, an awe-inspiring idea.

The black cloud behemoths in the sky had disappeared as swiftly as they'd appeared. There wasn't a single cloud in sight now, just brilliant blue—and it was an azure that seemed to intensify more and more. The erratic shifts in the weather seemed even more extreme up here than down in southern Finistère.

Dupin pulled out his phone and placed a call.

"Monsieur Braz?"

"Yes?"

Dupin could hear engine sounds, indicating that Charles Braz was also in his car.

"Commissaire Dupin here. I find it hard to believe"—he came straight to the point—"that you had no knowledge about the purchase of the land in Rothéneuf at the beginning of this year."

"The what?"

"I think you know what I'm talking about."

"No, absolutely not."

"I don't believe you, Monsieur Braz."

"But that's how it is, Monsieur le Commissaire." A despairing insistence.

"Your—"

Dupin braked sharply. A traffic jam had appeared on the last few meters of the dam. He couldn't believe it—it was the same stretch they had driven just this morning, and again he saw the convoy of classic cars in front of him. He came to a standstill just a few centimeters behind a Citroën Traction Avant Cabriolet.

The passengers in the back seat, two elderly ladies, turned and gave him a cheerful wave. A sticker on the protruding tailgate declared: "Ninety years of automobile history."

Dupin pulled himself together and returned to the matter at hand: "Your partner spent one point one million euros on a plot of land where she intended to set up a large cheese store and a second restaurant. A massive project—and she told you nothing about it?"

"I swear she didn't."

Braz sounded heavyhearted; Dupin could hear it. It was sad.

"And she also didn't tell you that she's learned it can't be built on and that she now owns practically worthless land, for which she had taken out two loans?"

For a while, only muffled engine and traffic noise could be heard.

"I told you that Lucille was planning to expand the cheese business. The—"

"Your partner is facing bankruptcy. That's what this is about, not the cheese business."

Dupin had turned right beyond the dam and was already in Dinard, recognizable by the quantity of villas and parks.

"We—Lucille and I . . ." Braz spoke in a deflated tone; it was difficult to even hear what he was saying. "We've had a few difficulties over the past year. In our relationship. And recently, we—took a break. Perhaps there are a lot of things I don't know. Even—important things."

"Was this break Madame Trouin's idea? Was she the one who wasn't . . . content with the relationship?" Dupin spoke more gently now.

"Yes." Again he sounded miserable. "But she couldn't tell me why. Or—she didn't want to."

"Had you properly separated?"

"No. We hadn't. But since then, we've seen each other only very occasionally. Everything is up in the air. She said she needs time."

Those fatal words.

Evidently a lot had been happening in Lucille Trouin's life recently. And it was vital to get a clear picture of it. It always was—for the sake of what a famous commissaire had once called the "atmosphere of the crime." Dupin was convinced that feeling this out was the most important work during an investigation. You had to develop a sense of the key figures in the drama.

"Okay, Monsieur Braz. We'll be in touch. Are you on your way to see Lucille?"

"I'm nearly there."

"Call me straight after the visit, okay?"

"Of course."

Dupin drove slowly; everything here was a thirty-kilometer-per-hour limit. He followed the GPS, according to which he should be there in three minutes. Just after he had turned off onto Avenue George V, the row of houses opened up, revealing a view of the sea. You could see the gorgeous bay between Saint-Malo and Dinard. Less than two kilometers divided the two cities; now it was Saint-Servan that lay directly across. Dupin spotted the quay, the tower, the harbor where he had just been, the imposing church on the right.

A little farther toward the open sea was the impressive Ville Close of Saint-Malo, defiantly enthroned on the island with her mighty ramparts. He saw the pier where the tourists had been caught out by the Atlantic breakers the day before. To the right of the large harbor, you could see the ferries that took people to Guernsey and Jersey—it was only around fifty kilometers to British territory. The most exquisite view of Saint-Malo was said to be from Dinard, more impressive than from anywhere else. Dupin now knew that this was true.

The perfectly sheltered, placid bay stretched out toward Saint-Malo, and its shore was the location of the most magnificent, well-known villas of Dinard. The wind had disappeared along with the clouds, and the sea was now nothing but a gentle ripple. The shallow depth and sandy seabed gave the water a bright, particularly beautiful emerald tone. There were easily a hundred boats moored in the bay. A sea of boats, wildly scattered dabs of white all the way across to Saint-Malo. Lots of green, copses and meadows directly bordering on the bay. Majestic sea pines. Dupin had rolled down the window: he could hear the lapping of the sea, boats shunting lethargically against jetties from time to time, the tinkling of the bells on the masts of the sailboats. A comforting tapestry of sounds, ideal for languorous days. Dinard possessed a legendary beauty and elegance.

Dupin turned off, the steeply ascending streets becoming increasingly narrow and winding, the ambience even more atmospheric and grand. He drove across a daringly small bridge. The Rue Coppinger led up to the Pointe du Moulinet, the last part of a rocky spit of land, which Dupin estimated as being a hundred meters above sea level—as though nature had thought to create a lookout point at this already perfect spot.

Flore Briard's villa had to be somewhere around here. La Garde. All the villas here were named. Dupin drove at a walking pace, and a small park with an unostentatious, half-height wooden gate appeared on the left. "*Privé.*"

Dupin came to a halt, turned off the engine, and got out.

On the other side of the road there was a dizzying drop, a phenomenal view of Dinard and the famous Plage de l'Écluse, a far-reaching city beach with a picture-postcard promenade. Opposite, at the other end of the bay, was another craggy spit, and again: magnificent villas on beautiful plots of land. Rich families from everywhere around—particularly from the capital—spent their summers here. Even in Dupin's bourgeois Parisian family there had once been a villa in Dinard, belonging to his mother's brother. But because the two siblings didn't particularly get on, the Dupins had, out of principle, spent their holidays not in Dinard, but in Normandy's Honfleur, another glamorous holiday destination for Parisians.

Dupin was just striding toward the gate when his cell phone rang.

A local number.

"Yes?"

"Good afternoon, Monsieur le Commissaire, I'm an employee of Flore Briard. I'm to tell you that unfortunately she won't be available until five o'clock. She sends her sincere apologies."

"Oh, okay."

There was little point in getting annoyed.

"Thank you. *Au revoir*, monsieur."

She had already hung up, evidently just as busy as her boss.

Dupin had paused in his tracks.

An idea had just occurred to him. An idea of what he could do with his sudden free time. He searched for something on his cell phone. Le Désir. Blanche Trouin's restaurant in Dinard. Dupin would take a look at it. Just to see how it looked. It had certainly been a key location in both the victims' lives.

There it was: Rue du Maréchal Leclerc. Perhaps ten minutes on foot; probably it was easier to leave the car here than look for a parking place by the restaurant. And the walk would do him good. As would another *café*. During an investigation—this was of vital importance—you had to make use of every opportunity that presented itself. On the way here, Dupin had seen a café that seemed just to his taste.

It was a good idea. And it would give him the opportunity to think. He set off, smiling.

The renewed ringing of his cell phone brought the smile to an abrupt end.

Riwal. He was clearly planning to be in touch regularly.

"Boss!"

"Yes, Riwal, what is it?"

Dupin made his way down a few incredibly steep steps. He wanted to take the path directly by the sea.

"Trouin—do you know where the name comes from?" A rhetorical question, for the inspector continued immediately. "From one of the most famous Malouin corsairs: René Duguay-Trouin. A naval officer, son of a wealthy shipowner. His heroic deeds played out in the late 1600s and early 1700s. He was most famous for conquering Rio de Janeiro, where he captured sixty trade ships, three liners, two frigates, over six hundred thousand cruzados, and other treasures."

Nedellec had commented on the name connection, too, but Dupin had immediately forgotten again. The historian had mentioned it during the city tour.

"Are you saying the two sisters are descendants of this pirate?"

"*Corsair*, boss! But yes: I read in an old article about the sisters that the lineage of their father, Georges Trouin, probably does go back to the legendary corsair. It's not all that long ago, really."

There it was again: the unusual Breton time reckoning. The past was always very close, regardless of how far back it lay. More precisely: the past was always present.

"And even if that's the case—how would it help us?"

"I just thought you should know, boss."

"Good. Okay." Dupin's thoughts were elsewhere.

"Where are you at the moment?"

"In Dinard."

"Oh, wonderful. The pearl of the Emerald Coast, the Nice of the North, the Queen of the Beaches . . . Dinard was the first genuine beach resort in Brittany, France—and the world. It all happened there first—Dinard was the epitome of chic vacationing as early as the mid-nineteenth century. Although one has to admit that the English played an important role there in the beginning . . . You can tell from the style of the villas, around five hundred of them, mostly neo-Gothic, with English verandas and sash windows. Rich and prominent people rendezvoused there, numerous artists. Victor Hugo, and Edmond Rostand, who wrote *Cyrano de Bergerac* there. Picasso painted his lovers on the beach. You must remember to walk across one of the most famous promenades in the world, the Promenade du Clair de Lune, the moonlight promenade. You feel like you're in a botanical garden full of exotic plants. It has the perfect Mediterranean atmosphere, boss. Palms, Atlas cedars, eucalyptus and weeping willows, flowerbeds in all their fantastic, vibrant glory. Agapanthus everywhere you look, with white, blue, and lilac blossoms."

If Dupin wasn't mistaken, he was walking along the promenade in question as they spoke. Right on the sea, four or five meters wide, lined by a strip of bountiful flora. He had to agree with Riwal: it was an exotic paradise. But this wasn't the moment for a lighthearted stroll.

"Riwal, I have to go."

"Get in touch if we can help, boss."

"Will do."

Dupin had no problems finding the café again. Le Mouillage.

Everything in it was just to his taste—simple and genuine. He could happily sit here every morning and every evening. Against the wall behind the entrance lay typical boating equipment, alongside piled-up bright green Heineken pallets, an entire phalanx. An old wooden surfboard, a panoramic sketch of the Côte d'Émeraude. A few standing tables with bar stools. Everything had a maritime feel.

There were tables on one side, and on the other, the bar with a counter, where two customers stood. A shelf with well-thumbed books, and affixed to the wall were miniature boats, old posters, large shells, an oar. Behind the bar, bottles in all colors, drinks from all over the world. The most extraordinary element, though, was the glass-roofed terrace at the far end of the space. And its phenomenal view of the bay.

Dupin had sat down in the corner and ordered a *café*, which was brought to him in next to no time. By the chef himself, to whom Dupin took an instant liking; three-day stubble, blue

T-shirt, blue cap. Dupin had pulled out his Clairefontaine and was making notes.

"Hey, you're the commissaire from Finistère—one of the 'furious three.'" Two women who were sitting next to him, one younger and one older, smiled at him warmly.

"Investigating in Dinard, you got lucky there! You must be here to meet with Flore Briard," said the older of the two.

Dupin was impressed that she'd guessed correctly on the first attempt.

The younger woman joined in.

"Blanche's death, and her husband's—it's a great loss for the city. They contributed so much to its allure. Gastronomy's very important here, along the entire coast. Even our chief of police used to be a chef."

Dupin noted a similarity in the women's features; presumably they were mother and daughter.

"Blanche moved her restaurant from Saint-Malo to Dinard fifteen years ago. After her younger sister opened hers in Saint-Malo." The message behind the feisty older woman's words was clear: Blanche Trouin had made the right decision—of course a person should go to Dinard if they could. "Blanche lived here in the beginning too. They moved out just four years ago."

It was an interesting acquaintance for Dupin to make; well-informed locals were always invaluable for an investigation.

The younger woman took over: "Saint-Malo and the east are more Lucille's territory—Dinard and the west, Blanche's."

"The rivalry between the two cities isn't anywhere near as bad as the sisters'," the older woman remarked. "But it does exist. It always has. The two places are very different."

"In what way?" Dupin drank his *café*.

"People from Dinard, like us, are warmhearted and cosmopolitan. Cheerful, easygoing, and high-spirited, perhaps even a bit lazy at times. *La joie de vivre*: that's us. Elegant, but never snobby or arrogant."

That matched the ambience of the city, Dupin felt: despite its noble old façade and grandeur, thanks to all its patina it never seemed pretentious or brash. He hadn't realized, though, the enormous role that rivalries and differences seemed to play in this small space, the Côte d'Émeraude was no more than forty kilometers long. But really, he should have known better: the closer together people were physically, the more significant their differences became.

"Blanche Trouin fit in well here," emphasized the older woman, "anyone can become a Dinardais if they share our values and ideas—but not a Malouin, you have to be born there. And your ancestors too."

"Maman, it's not like that anymore." Dupin had guessed right, she was her daughter.

"Did you also know Blanche Trouin's husband, Kilian Morel, personally?"

"Of course." The mother seemed almost indignant. "Almost everyone here knew Kilian Morel, there're only ten thousand inhabitants. An incredibly friendly, good-natured man. He wouldn't have hurt a fly. It's incomprehensible that he was the victim of a violent crime."

"He was a very dedicated man," continued the daughter. "Just like Bertrand Larcher, he was a real advocate for Breton buckwheat, which is massively under threat from industrial wheat. And Kilian was also hugely knowledgeable about wine."

"So you would find it unlikely that he was in conflict with someone?"

Perhaps they shouldn't entirely dismiss the scenario of two unrelated motives. But Dupin's instinct was telling him otherwise.

"He wasn't even capable of conflict. I'd say, that was his problem." The mother was resolute.

"Could someone stand to profit from Kilian Morel's death?"

"I can't even imagine—who would that be? No one here, certainly."

"Perhaps Charles Braz, Lucille's partner? By setting up his own rum business, Morel had become his competitor."

Dupin suddenly felt frustrated. Weren't they thinking too small with all these scenarios? The rum element, in any case. At the moment it wasn't much more than an unworthy prophecy.

"We can't help you there. Other than to say the murderer would have his hands full around here, there are so many rum traders."

"What about his brother? Joe Morel? Do you know anything about the relationship between the two of them?"

The daughter answered: "We don't know the brother. He moved from Saint-Malo to Cancale. That's—again—a completely different world. But I know he's very well-liked there. His oyster bar is popular with the locals."

"Objectively . . ." Dupin trailed off.

He had wanted to say: "Objectively, he stands to profit most from the two murders." He hadn't even spoken about this with Huppert and Nedellec yet; their conversation on Joe Morel had revolved almost entirely around the romance with Lucille. And yet this was far more relevant. Joe Morel was the one who was highly likely to inherit everything; the entire fortune of Blanche Trouin and Kilian Morel, his brother.

The older woman keenly spun an interesting end to the sibling story. "You mean, the sister kills the sister and then the brother's brother?"

Dupin glanced at the time.

"It was lovely talking to you, mesdames. Thank you for the information."

He got up and placed some change on the table.

"You've picked the right place, by the way. The fishermen come to this café to eat when they get in from the sea. That's Dinard too! It's not just villas. By the way, when you go to see Flore Briard, the incredible villa on the other side of the cape is up for sale. Sixteen million. You should factor in an additional ten million for the renovations, though." The mother laughed; it sounded like a direct invitation to buy. "La Garde, Flore Briard's villa, was built by Jean Hennessy, the Cognac King."

"One more thing." Dupin paused alongside their table. "Do you happen to know whether Flore Briard and Blanche Trouin were personally acquainted?"

"Definitely. They weren't friends, of course, but they were always polite with each other. There's not really any other way, we all get together quite regularly here. At openings, parties, gatherings. The two of them are engaged in lots of initiatives. I'm sure you're aware that Flore Briard is an important person here in Dinard. Even though she's—how should I put it—a little crazy, like her captivating late mother. Once Flore gets something in her head, it becomes an obsession. If you know what I mean."

"Is she married? In a relationship?" Dupin knew practically nothing about Madame Briard so far.

"Oh no. Her father left her mother just after Flore was born, for a younger woman, the classic tale. It had a lasting impact on her. There are lovers, of course, but not serious relationships."

Dupin began to make a move.

"Many thanks again."

"We hope you solve the case soon, Monsieur le Commissaire. None of this is particularly pleasant for Dinard."

"All the best, Monsieur le Commissaire," said the daughter.

Dupin stepped out on the street.

He generally had an excellent sense of direction, and would have no problems finding Blanche's restaurant.

Less than five minutes later, he had to admit that he'd taken a wrong turn. He had walked along the Rue Jacques Cartier, which was actually very simple, because it intersected with the Rue du Maréchal Leclerc. But he must have missed it. The smartest thing would be to check the map on his cell phone, which, as a rule, he strictly refrained from.

The town center, with its boutiques and shops, had a completely different atmosphere than that of the villa region. Here, little houses lined the streets—sweet, pretty houses, mostly with just one floor, occasionally with two, and predominantly made of wood, a style he hadn't seen before in Brittany. It reminded him a little of America's East Coast, of Maine, Vermont, Connecticut.

Surely he would find it soon. And he did.

Le Désir. Blanche Trouin's restaurant was also a beautiful old house, built around a corner; upstairs, a roof terrace with a brick balustrade. Next to the restaurant was a garden with an enchanting wooden veranda. Behind it, an annex that seemed to belong to the restaurant. The restaurant's wooden façade was painted dark blue. The windows were large. From inside, the customers could watch the hustle and bustle out on the street.

On the entrance door hung a somber-sounding handwritten note, fastened from the inside with sticky tape: "*Closed. Reopening unforeseeable. Thank you for your loyalty. Your Le Désir team.*" Above that, the restaurant's pride and joy, and its most effective advertising: the red Michelin star with the white border on a red background. In actual fact, it was shaped more like a small flower.

Dupin went up to the veranda. Here, as suspected, there was a second entrance to the restaurant. And one to the annex.

Dupin knocked loudly on both doors.

"Commissaire Dupin here. Is anyone there?"

No reaction.

He knocked again.

Nothing.

Dupin was just turning around when he heard movement inside.

"Coming!" called a voice.

The door to the restaurant opened. A young, decisively sad-looking man stood in front of him.

"How can I help you?"

"Commissaire Georges Dupin. And you are?"

"François Belfort. *Chef de service.* I just wanted to check on things. Take away any perishable food."

"I'd like to take a look in the restaurant."

"Of course." The man stepped to the side. "Come in, I'll show you the place."

They were standing in a small stairwell. To the right, wooden stairs led up to the first floor.

"What's upstairs?"

"A staff room and staff toilet, as well as a private space for the Trouins. The door's locked; the police took the key."

The forensic team had been here yesterday.

They crossed a large, impressive kitchen and reached the dining room. The blue of the wooden façade and shutters was echoed in the tablecloths. The walls were painted white, the chairs and tables natural wood. On the walls were white sideboards at hip height. Blue and white, the classic maritime color scheme. Potted plants stood on narrow wooden benches between the tables. The *chef de service* followed Dupin's gaze.

"Those are fresh herbs. Blanche's world. Local varieties, but lots of exotic ones too, from the most far-flung corners of the Earth. We alternate them according to the season and focus of the menu. The guests are free to help themselves."

The big, beautiful room looked sad, empty like this; restaurants needed life, people, lively conversation, a buoyant mayhem. Standing here, the brutality of what had occurred felt particularly stark: an entire world had been erased, the two people who had filled this place with life and love, who had given other people a moment of happiness. In times like these, you could feel the tragedy more intensely than in objectively more dramatic contexts like the crime scene itself. There, it was often abstract. Here one felt the unfathomable emptiness.

Dupin looked around for a while, then glanced at the clock.

It was 4:51. He had to go. He didn't have much time for his conversation with Flore Briard as it was. And he could come back here later, if he needed. But actually, he had already seen everything.

The gate opened as though by an invisible hand, soundlessly, smoothly. The commissaire was greeted by a large garden, a discreet gravel path, shrubbery, yellow flowers. Everything was well tended, but not fastidiously arranged.

At the end of the trees, the magnificent villa came into view: La Garde. Majestic, neo-gothic like most of the others here on the coast, but a lighter, friendlier variation. Pale gray granite at the corners of the building and around the generous windows, individual red-hued bricks giving lively accents here and there. Six pointed gables above the main entrance, and beneath it a dark wooden veranda.

Dupin was impressed. He'd seen dozens of villas in passing from the car, but this one put all the others in the shade. It looked more like an enchanted castle, with the promise of endless nooks and crannies.

He rang the bell.

A bright "Just a moment!" came out of the intercom system.

He waited awhile, then the immense door opened.

Flore Briard stood before him. Pretty. Very pretty. Blond, her hair loosely pinned up with a black stick, a few strands falling into her face. A loose, short dress in a reddish-violet shade. For Dupin's taste, she was a little too heavily made up.

"Here I am! How much time do you have, Commissaire?"

"It's just a few questions, Madame Briard."

"Good. Then we've got time for a short tour." She spoke at

roughly the same speed as Commissaire Huppert, albeit without her matter-of-factness; Briard's voice was full of melody and emotion, but not affected.

Dupin wasn't really in the mood for a house tour, but he was keen to find out what kind of person she was.

"*Et voilà*: my reception hall."

Dupin stepped in. He had never seen anything like it, not even in the houses of his upper-class Parisian mother's aristocratic friends. The space was reminiscent of a church. It was enormous. Around twenty meters long, certainly fifteen meters high, the open ceiling decorated with wooden beams and greenish-blue patterns. Parquet flooring. On the walls, a bright wallpaper with subtle silvery-white ornamentation. Wooden columns with golden light fixtures gleaming from them.

The building's former owner, Hennessy, as Dupin now knew, must have given the architect one sole instruction: maximum grandeur, maximum expense. And yet the space itself was almost empty: a few classical-modern leather armchairs, a matching side table, black like the leather. In a corner was a historic elevator with a half-height wrought-iron cage, inside which was a masterfully made wooden cabin, a priceless ornament.

"It's dreadful."

All at once, Flore Briard seemed deeply shaken and upset.

"It still hasn't sunk in. She's my best friend. And she stabbed her sister. Why isn't she talking? What's happened to Lucille, do you think? Have you discovered anything that could somehow explain it? I just can't believe it."

"But it did happen. As did the murder of Kilian Morel."

Flore Briard led Dupin through a small lobby, then along a hallway into a living room, which once again took his breath away. At least ninety square meters, Persian rugs on an old parquet floor, sparsely distributed antique furniture. Stucco ceiling, a stately chandelier. In the middle of the space was a gigantic wooden table, with a gray cat sitting on it, cleaning itself meticulously, surrounded by eight throne-like upholstered chairs.

Flore Briard paused in the middle of the room. "This is where I live during the warmer months. Here, on the terrace, and in the garden." She went over to the terrace door. Dupin followed her.

One entire side of the room consisted of panoramic windows. Seldom was the expression as fitting as here: it gave the feeling of living outdoors in the open air. Strangely, the room felt quite understated despite its splendor; it possessed a striking elegance, the opposite of gaudy.

"I knew Blanche's husband too, of course." Flore Briard picked back up on Dupin's statement. "Even though he belonged to the other camp. Yes, there was the Lucille camp and the Blanche camp. Naturally there were people who socialized with both, because they weren't close friends with them. I'm in Lucille's camp, of course. We're very close, and she means a lot to me. Even now, nothing will ever change that. Something very extreme must have been going on for her."

"And you don't have the slightest idea what that might be, madame?"

She stepped out onto the covered terrace. "*Et voilà!* The legendary bay between Dinard and Saint-Malo."

Simple furniture made of wood and cast iron stood on the gorgeous mosaic floor. Steps led down into the garden, which on this side consisted only of a few meters of grass, before, beyond a balustrade, it descended steeply toward the sea. The view was spectacular, even more captivating than the one from the moonlight promenade. And you didn't just see the bay, but far out onto the open sea. An endless, emerald expanse that seemed to push the horizon farther and farther away. A blue-and-white passenger ship was sailing through the bay, ferrying people between the two cities.

"No, I don't have the slightest idea." Flore Briard had stepped over to the railing, and came back to Dupin's question. "It's devastating. And completely unreal."

Dupin steered the conversation toward the most pressing subject. "What about your friend's financial ruin, the fatal land purchase—could it be related to that?"

"How would killing her sister in broad daylight solve her money problems?" asked Briard thoughtfully. "And why would someone kill Blanche's husband over that?"

A disarming counter-question, Dupin had to admit. But now it was clear: she knew about the financial debacle.

"Lucille was completely done in by the land thing, even though she tried not to let it show."

"And when I asked you just now if you knew what might be behind this—you didn't think to mention it?"

Dupin had come to stand next to her at the railing.

"Where do you see the possible connection?" she asked.

"When did she tell you about it?"

"On—"

Dupin's cell phone beeped, yet another text message.

"Sorry."

He pulled it out of his back pocket.

Nedellec. *More news! I'll report back later.*

Why didn't he just say what it was? Frowning, Dupin put his phone away again.

"She told me last Tuesday," Flore Briard continued. "We went for dinner in the evening. She'd found out about the nesting place on the property a good while before."

"She didn't tell her partner about it."

Flore smiled.

"He's no longer her partner. It's over. That whole story is done."

"Really?"

"Yes. Even if Lucille maybe hasn't formulated it conclusively to herself and to him. Things haven't been right between them for a long time."

"How long?"

"A year for sure."

Dupin made a note.

"What was wrong?"

"He's a weak person." Her tone sounded more regretful than disdainful. "And that constantly annoyed Lucille, it always had. It couldn't work long-term, even though he has lots of great qualities. She just didn't love him anymore. Then there's the fact that he wanted a family and she didn't. Do you need more reasons? I offered to lend Lucille money, by the way. To get her out of the whole mess."

A surprising piece of information.

Dupin could feel the blazing sun on his head. And up here, there was no breeze. It had gotten really hot. He wiped a few beads of sweat from his forehead.

"And?"

"She doesn't want money from me. Under any circumstances, she said. We'll see. This annoyance won't be her downfall. Anyway, she has other concerns right now."

Of course, the sums that were pushing her friend into financial ruin wouldn't even cause a rich heiress like Flore Briard to break a sweat. And you could see that just by looking at her.

"Come with me, Commissaire." Flore walked a little way into the garden behind the villa. "There, look."

There were two pretty, small stone houses attached to the main villa.

"I live in the front one during the winter. There's zero chance of getting the villa even moderately heated—impossible! Some of the staff used to live in these little houses. There used to be another villa over there, which blocked the view of the bay. Hennessy bought it back then just so he could have it torn down."

Dupin nodded vaguely. He was lost in thought.

"But he had a villa built closer to the street for his lover. Who later became his wife."

Slowly she made her way toward the stone steps that led back to the terrace. White, lush rhododendrons grew to the left and right.

"Where were you this morning, Madame Briard? Between seven thirty and nine thirty?"

Without intending to, Dupin had sounded brusque.

"I was on my boat, from seven. The *Épée du Roy*. She's moored here in Dinard. We had the celebratory sail to open the summer season last night. I presume you know about my enterprise."

"The trip happened despite the—events?"

"It was important." Her tone made it clear she had never even considered canceling. "It's my business, even though the menus are by Lucille's sous-chef."

"Was anyone else with you on the boat this morning?"

"I was alone until shortly after eleven. Then two of my employees joined me."

Which meant that Flore Briard, too, had no alibi for this morning.

"Speaking of the sous-chef, Madame Briard, what's your take on that? I mean, it affects you too."

Did she know about it?

She threw him a questioning glance, then went toward the living room.

"I have no idea what you mean," she responded curtly.

"Blanche Trouin had lured her sister's sous-chef away. Clément had already signed the contract."

"Excuse me?"

She seemed shocked. Or was acting it well.

"Yes, he would soon have been working for Blanche. And, as a result, no longer creating menus for you." That was what Dupin assumed, at least. Clément would have become part of the Blanche camp.

Briard seemed really wrought-up now. "When did Lucille find out about this?"

By now they had almost crossed the living room.

"We don't know for sure whether she had. Would she have told you, do you think?"

"Absolutely. Like you say: it involves me too. Look, Commissaire," she made no attempt to hide her outrage, "that's malicious. Really malicious. Of course, Clément is a sensational talent—but there are others out there. Blanche could have gotten anyone for her restaurant. And whom does she pick? Lucille's chef. It could only have been intended to hurt her."

They had turned in to the hallway.

"How long have you known Lucille Trouin, by the way?"

"Since primary school. We were always close friends, almost all our lives."

"So did you, Joe Morel, and Lucille Trouin all go to the same school?"

"Yes, and so did Kilian—albeit in different classes. Only Blanche was at a different school."

Gradually, the image of all their interconnections was becoming clearer.

"And here you have my winter refuge." Flore's mood had shifted within a fraction of a second, her anger seemingly forgotten. She had led Dupin into a bright, moderately sized room, in which there was a bed, and next to it an ornate iron fireplace.

"On the colder winter days, I rarely leave this room. Luckily, there aren't many of them."

Dupin realized that they must be in one of the annexes. She had probably had a wall knocked through to interlink the spaces. It was odd: Flore Briard's winter refuge amounted to a mere fraction of her "summer world." Old framed maps hung on the walls, along with paintings and a large frame containing historic postcards, aerial photographs of the cape and villa, its unbelievably privileged position easily recognizable. Several small cabinets stood against the walls, their surfaces holding quaint knickknacks. Plates and figurines made of old porcelain, little dolls, shells, candlesticks, jewelry. Rings, a long chain.

"If you've known each other so long, you would have been around when Lucille Trouin got together with Joe Morel."

Flore Briard led Dupin back out of her winter quarters.

"That was complicated, yes. Very, at times. Blanche was already married to Kilian and close friends with Joe. But it's a long time ago. An entire decade."

"Have Joe Morel and Lucille Trouin been in contact again recently?"

Flore blinked. She clearly knew what Dupin was getting at.

"Yes. To be honest, on several occasions I thought they might get back together. I teased Lucille about it. But no." She seemed resolute now. "There's nothing there."

"So they were meeting up again? Since when? How often?"

"They ran into each other at the start of the year. Then they met up maybe two or three times after that, but just for dinner."

This meant that either Charles Braz hadn't been telling the truth, or he simply hadn't known. Just like he apparently didn't know much about Lucille Trouin's life in general anymore.

"I would rule out an affair, Commissaire." An unmistakable clarification.

They had come back into the living room. The tour had come to an end.

"Shall we sit down?"

She pointed toward a sofa and two upholstered armchairs.

"Thank you, but I have to go in a moment." Dupin paused. "What are your thoughts on the father's recipe collection? It clearly held considerable symbolic importance for the sisters. It seems that only this year Lucille made another attempt to convince Blanche to share it with her."

"You're very well informed. For Lucille that's a wound that

simply won't heal. But I'm not sure how that would have come to a head now."

Dupin was getting the definite feeling that with some topics—thoroughly interesting ones—they just weren't making any progress.

"One last question: What was your relationship to Kilian Morel?"

Dupin had intentionally left it vague.

For the first time, Briard seemed lost for words. Dupin sensed she didn't really want to talk about it.

"We've always had pleasant conversations when we saw each other." She quickly got a grip of herself again. "He was a nice man. A little lethargic, but dependable, I think. Amiable."

"Did you see him a lot?"

"No. And only ever by chance, at the market, in a café. Or at events. The usual chitchat."

"When did you last see him?"

She thought for a moment. "I think at the closing evening for the comedy film festival at the end of April."

"Not since then?"

"No."

"Thank you again, Madame Briard. That was very interesting. I can see myself out."

"*Au revoir*, Monsieur le Commissaire."

Dupin crossed the living room, then the palatial reception hall. He paced swiftly out into the open air.

"Very well then." Commissaire Huppert sounded exasperated.

They had been sitting together for forty minutes now.

The initial report had been confined to the facts, in accordance with Huppert's suggestion that they "discuss things later." Each of them had set out the research they had done since midday, whom they'd spoken with and what they'd found out, all the new information. In the process, it became clear how the commissaire saw their teamwork going forward: Nedellec and Dupin giving central authority to Huppert, the frantic detective, the person who would bring everything together, analyze, and, what's more, carry out the especially important research beyond interviews with suspects. This didn't bother Dupin, because he had never seen his role as commissaire like Huppert did hers—though, strictly speaking, she was the living embodiment of a commissaire's job description. Dupin couldn't help it: he needed to be out and about, talking to people; this was the last thing he would delegate.

The facts had also included the alibis. The results of their inquiries were sobering. No one had a solid alibi. Joe Morel had stayed at the oyster bar unusually late yesterday evening, for a private function, and they hadn't managed to finish the cleaning up; according to his statement, this was why he'd been back in the bar by half past eight this morning. Alone. He didn't know whether anyone had seen him. One of Huppert's inspectors had spoken with the sous-chef: Clément—La Noblesse having reopened—had been at the market between seven and eight o'clock, which the inspector had been able to confirm with a few of the stall holders. Clément was last seen there at 7:50 A.M. After that he was in the restaurant kitchen alone, as usual, until around 9:50 A.M., when the other kitchen staff arrived. Although it would have been tight, he could technically have managed the "expedition." Nedellec still hadn't managed to reach Walig Richard, the antiques dealer.

By now they had Kilian Morel's itemized phone records, but nothing on them stood out. The only repeated calls were three conversations between him and Walig Richard on Monday afternoon and evening. But after Blanche Trouin's tragic death, that was easy to explain—after all, Richard was one of her best friends . . . Nedellec would ask the antiques dealer about it—when he finally got hold of him.

Dupin was the only one who had ordered something to eat—even though they were having dinner with the prefects afterward. His stomach was rumbling uncontrollably. Nedellec and Huppert just had coffee and water.

The Restaurant du Petit Port—the lettering of the sign on the façade was charmingly crooked—was fabulous. The location, the atmosphere. It was on one of the small streets that led down to the Promenade du Clair de Lune and the pleasure harbor and looked out over the palms on the promenade and bay. Now, toward evening, the colors were intensifying again, even the emerald green of the sea. If he were sitting here with Claire, it would be a perfect summer's evening.

"So, which of all this is really important?" Huppert pressed.

"The thing with the recipes, certainly," said Nedellec. "I really think it could be the key. The motive. And perhaps not only for Lucille's murder of Blanche."

Even if Nedellec was taking it quite far, Dupin felt he was on the trail of something potentially explosive. Nedellec had also discussed the recipes in his conversation with Joe Morel. Morel had told him that Blanche had been in contact with a well-known Parisian publisher, with whom she'd talked about the possibility of publishing a book. In the afternoon, Nedellec had called around to publishing houses until he'd eventually found the right one. A renowned cookbook publisher who had already commissioned a book with the father's recipes—edited by Blanche Trouin, including an afterword and some of her own additional recipes. The project was evidently quite advanced, a copy of the material was in Paris. Blanche and the publisher had reached agreement on the important details a good month ago via email, and she would have soon received the contract.

"I'm sure this would have made Lucille furious," Huppert acknowledged, "but it's like with the sous-chef: we have no idea whether she even knew about it. If not, it's irrelevant to us. And even if she did know, is it really enough reason to kill her own sister? Perhaps, at the most, as a catalyst for a crime of passion, if Lucille only found out about it yesterday. The drop that made the cup spill over. But how would that be connected to the murder of Kilian Morel? At the moment I can't see a link. It has to be about something else." She presented her objections in her usual matter-of-fact way, remaining completely calm. "But we should still definitely ask the publishing house to give us their correspondence with Blanche. The experts haven't been able to crack the two victims' passwords yet, neither for their cell phones nor their computers."

"I've already asked for the email exchange"—Nedellec waved her request aside—"it'll be with us today. But the publisher says there's nothing in there we don't already know. I think you're completely underestimating the emotional dynamics at play here."

"But the cookbook is irrelevant for Blanche's murder anyway," replied Huppert, unperturbed.

"Why? Kilian Morel might have let the book publication go ahead regardless."

"But why would someone kill him over it? Just so that Lucille could get the original recipes?"

It really did sound absurd.

A loud, deep honking sounded out. A ship's horn. Dupin spotted the blue-and-white ferry from earlier. It was back in Dinard.

"You mean Lucille incited someone to kill Kilian Morel?" Huppert seemed utterly unconvinced. "Who? Her partner? And she orchestrated the whole thing from police custody? How?"

"To win Lucille back—if he's desperately in love with her?"

Not a bad point, thought Dupin.

"Fine. The recipes, intensified by the book publication, stay on the list of possible motives," Huppert conceded.

"There's also the fact that Joe Morel is now a made man." Dupin couldn't stop ruminating on this. Commissaire Huppert had been informed that it was exactly as they'd thought: Joe Morel would inherit his brother's property and fortune; the will was unequivocal.

"That's on the list too."

This list, thought Dupin suddenly, was purely imaginary; nobody was writing it down.

Now it was Nedellec who wasn't in agreement: "You really think he'd brutally murder his brother for the money, even though they got on well, as far as I've heard? He'd have to be cold as ice."

Dupin had to admit, it did sound incredibly ruthless. He felt a fretful sense of unease—they had reached a critical point in the investigation.

"I'd like to have a word with Joe Morel too," Dupin suddenly declared. "Tomorrow morning." For Nedellec's sake, he added diplomatically: "It can't hurt."

"Nedellec, how did Joe Morel describe his relationship with his brother?" A neutral question from Huppert.

"He said they got on well, and always had. Not a particularly close relationship—but a good one. No conflicts or squabbles. They saw each other a few times a year. Kilian would mostly go to Cancale, to Joe's bar. Joe told me the bar is his life. I spoke with one of his friends as well, and he also portrayed the brothers as having a good relationship."

"Which doesn't mean much, but right now it's all we have." Commissaire Huppert's gaze swept across the sea. "And what's the significance of Joe Morel and Lucille Trouin meeting up again?"

Joe Morel had obviously spoken openly with Nedellec, outlining everything just as Dupin had heard it from Flore Briard. Which meant that Morel had headed off any speculation that they could be having a relationship or an affair.

"But it's also possible that neither of them is telling us the truth," mused Nedellec.

"It's on the list anyway," Huppert declared, this time refraining from adding her own thoughts. "And so is Lucille Trouin's impending bankruptcy, of course," she continued.

"*Et voilà*." A cheerful woman with long, dark hair put down a plate of delicious-looking red tuna in front of Dupin. Flash-roasted in the pan, still pink inside, with olive oil, lemon, and *fleur de sel*, the irresistible aroma of charcoal drifted up from the plate.

Dupin immediately began to eat, and thought he noticed an envious glance from Nedellec. He had just put the second forkful in his mouth when his phone rang. A highly inconvenient moment.

Dupin recognized the number. Charles Braz.

"Monsieur Braz?"

Dupin put the phone on speaker; Huppert and Nedellec had instantly shifted uncomfortably close to him.

"You asked me to call after I visited Lucille."

Braz was trying to stay calm, and not really succeeding.

"I've just come from the police station. I only saw her briefly. We hugged once. Under supervision." His voice was so strained it was almost unintelligible. "I asked her how she was doing, and all she said was 'Okay.' It was awful."

"Did she say anything else? About what happened?"

"No. I gave her the things I'd brought with me, mostly clothes. I forgot a few of them."

"Anything else?"

"She told me she'd barely slept. I mean, it wasn't the kind of situation you can talk properly in. Most of the time we were just silent."

Dupin knew what he meant.

"How did Madame Trouin seem to you? In general, I mean?"

"Calm. Composed is the right word."

"And that's it?"

"Yes."

"Okay. Then *bonsoir*, Monsieur Braz."

"*Bonsoir*, Monsieur le Commissaire."

Dupin pressed the red symbol to end the call.

"Nothing new then." Huppert leaned back in disappointment. "I'm a bit concerned that we can't track down the antiques dealer."

"Me too," muttered Nedellec.

Dupin turned his attention back to his tuna.

"No one's seen him today," Nedellec expanded. "He hasn't been in to either of his shops, nor telephoned in. But his employees say that happens sometimes. He's often on the road, in the countryside, attending estate sales and the like."

"Is there a partner or spouse?" asked Huppert.

"He's single."

"Perhaps we should put out a search for him. To make sure nothing's happened."

"Or"—Nedellec scratched his forehead; he seemed to be thinking out loud—"he murdered Kilian Morel, and he's now on the run. Even if we don't yet know what his motive was."

He drank a sip of water.

"I'll call the employee I spoke to in Saint-Suliac again. That's the main store. I'll ask him to think really hard about where Walig Richard might be. Perhaps he has a boat too."

"And don't forget the vineyard," Dupin remembered. Nolwenn had told him about it.

"Vineyard?" Huppert was surprised. "Is he one of the Mont Garrot vintners?"

"Could one of you enlighten me?" Nedellec seemed to feel excluded.

"Mont Garrot is a hill on the banks of the Rance, near Saint-Suliac. A whole seventy-three meters high. Fifteen years ago, a group of enthusiasts began cultivating wine there again. There used to be winemaking there as far back as the Middle Ages. Now there are around a thousand vines, producing roughly five hundred bottles a year. Everything's done by hand, no machines. Two grape varieties." Huppert seemed well informed. "Rondo for the red, Chenin for the white. The whites are similar to the

Anjou wines of the Loire Valley. Light, dry, but still fruity, with delicate citrus notes on the palate."

Sometimes, Huppert could be quite astounding.

Dupin had sped up; the last bite of tuna was gone.

"In any case"—Nedellec seemed a little thrown by Huppert's burst of enthusiasm—"we should . . ."

Dupin's cell rang again. An unknown number this time.

Without pausing to think, he accepted the call and put it on speaker: "Yes?"

"Monsieur le Commissaire?" A woman's voice, agitated and unsteady.

"Speaking."

"This is Francine Lezu. I'm the housekeeper to Madame Hélène Allanic-Trouin, the aunt of Lucille and Blanche Trouin. I mean, Blanche's when she was still alive. She's their father's sister and—"

"Yes, I know whom you're talking about, madame."

"Madame insisted I call the police. And repeat to you everything she told me. She's also insisting you come here at once. She's losing her mind, Monsieur le Commissaire, believe me. I need help with her. Madame has very bad attacks, even though she calms down again afterward. She's ninety-three. She . . ."

The housekeeper didn't seem any less agitated.

"Please take your time. What's this about?"

"Madame is completely beside herself. Since yesterday, since the terrible news. She keeps talking about her husband, who's been dead for fifteen years. She says she's a genuine Trouin and that her husband is sailing the oceans as a corsair, but will be back soon. That she's always taken good care of the gold and gemstones, and he'll bring even more home with him. She talks about Blanche too. About how Blanche has the precious spices and Lucille wants to take them away from her."

"I see." Dupin was baffled.

"And that someone has to transport her villa to Canada, on a large boat. That she's been robbed. They also took her sun hat, she says—she gets particularly worked up about that. Though I'm sure she's just misplaced it."

"Where is Madame Allanic right now?"

"I told her to lie down, and this time she didn't argue, but I had to swear I'd call you and tell you everything. And that I'd ask you to come by."

"Please tell her I'll come first thing tomorrow."

"Thank you, Monsieur le Commissaire." Deep relief echoed in her voice.

"You should call a doctor. Madame Allanic needs something to calm her nerves. Promise me that?"

"I . . . Okay, yes, I promise. I mean, I'll try. But she'll adamantly refuse."

"Perhaps she'll see it's necessary."

"You don't know her."

"Do your best. Right then, I'll see you tomorrow morning."

"And you'll definitely come?"

"Definitely."

Dupin hung up, at a loss. What was all this about?

"Good luck with that tomorrow morning." A light grin danced on Nedellec's face.

Huppert stood up abruptly. "We have to get going. The prefects are expecting us in Otonali at half past seven."

Nedellec followed, and Dupin too, still dazed from the confusing phone call.

The sun had sunk lower. The emerald green of the bay shimmered darker than before, but still gleamed.

"The concept of Bertrand Larcher's Otonali is about bringing together the two extraordinary food cultures of Japan and Brittany—which are actually quite similar in many respects—and in such a way that they cross-pollinate each other."

A promising concept, in Dupin's opinion. He loved both cuisines, and if they cross-pollinated, all the better.

The Japanese restaurateur formulated her sentences with great pride.

They were sitting around a very large table—the only table—in Otonali. A solid oak surface; tall chairs, varnished black, which were surprisingly comfortable. The entire team was there: the prefects, the commissaires, as well as Commissaire Huppert's assistant, who was responsible for the accompanying program.

Almost everything had been kept black and white; there was almost no color. The exposed pipes, ceiling lights, and simple frames around the large windows all conformed to the purist concept. And yet the space felt anything but cold and sterile; on the contrary, there was a warm, welcoming atmosphere.

"The sea and its delicacies are, of course, the focal point of both cuisines. Both cultures also prize high-quality meat and extraordinary vegetables. The principle is the same: it's about simplicity, the fundamentals, and the conviction that this is the very best. That you don't need a lot of ingredients, but a fantastic savoir faire. Brittany produces everything that Japanese cuisine celebrates, and our culinary skills elevate both to their very best."

"Bravo!" This came, of course, from the prefect who always had to make his voice heard. Dupin was relieved he was sitting at the other end of the table.

"If I may briefly add something," the commissaire's assistant interjected, "Bertrand Larcher is one of Brittany's international icons, just like Yves Bordier, or Olivier Roellinger, whose restaurant was the first in Brittany to be awarded three Michelin stars and who creates the most prestigious spice blends in the world."

The Breton pride was in no way inferior to the Japanese.

"Bertrand Larcher is also a passionate advocate for Breton buckwheat, which, in comparison to other varieties of wheat, possesses a multitude of unique taste possibilities and health benefits. With buckwheat," she elevated her emphasis once again, "he is defending our Breton identity."

That was the crux of it. In Brittany, ventures like these were also major societal and cultural missions; the chefs, impassioned visionaries. And always it came down to one great mission: the Bretonization of the world.

"He and his Japanese wife," the restaurateur continued, "also founded the Breizh Café, of which there are now nine in Japan." So Bretonization was well under way there too. "There are four in Paris, and of course, one in Cancale and here in Saint-Malo, where the couple also run an international crêpe-cooking school, the Atelier de la Crêpe. In Cancale you can also find Otonali's big-brother restaurant, which has been honored with a Michelin star."

The number of stars glittering across the Emerald Coast was truly impressive.

Dupin knew the Breizh Café from Paris, back when, for him, Brittany had still been far away. But he'd liked the crêpes in their heavenly creations even back then.

"Otonali means 'next door,' by the way—our restaurant is inspired by the Japanese spirit of *izakaya*, the simple neighborhood restaurants. Informal and uncomplicated. So. Now we'll prepare your dishes."

With a small bow, the restaurateur stepped discreetly to the side.

The host prefect stood up and responded with an equally respectful bow. "Thank you so much, that was very impressive. We greatly appreciate your hospitality and look forward to your creations."

The restaurateur nodded once more and retreated behind a counter that separated the open kitchen from the dining space. The small team of three had already set to work.

"Right then." The prefect turned back to the team, her tone now brisk. "We'll turn our attention to work for a short while too. What's the latest?"

"I'll summarize the current status of the investigation," began Commissaire Huppert, this role being unarguably hers. The three commissaires were sitting next to one another, Huppert in the middle.

After just ten minutes, she had finished her report.

Dupin felt she had delivered it masterfully. She had mentioned all the salient points in her consistently levelheaded manner, and had even given an indication of the direction the investigations would take next. Nedellec had nodded emphatically at crucial moments.

This was followed by the inevitable: a detailed, protracted

discussion, with Locmariaquer as the dominant voice. But Nedellec spoke up too. His sullen-looking boss didn't say a single word, and nor did Dupin. In essence, it was a rerun of the conversation the three commissaires had already had in Dinard.

And the inevitable really dragged out.

For a solid forty minutes. Nothing new—nothing at all—came out of it. And to top it all off, Locmariaquer insisted on a brief résumé of all the suggestions that had been put forward in the prefects' workgroup for improving collaboration. Dupin was so happy that he'd already eaten something.

"Right, we're all up to date now. If I were to give an overview, I'd say"—the host prefect's tone was serious—"that we're still missing a solid lead."

Her declaration held no judgment, she was merely stating a fact, and the three commissaires saw it no differently.

"I don't think I need to tell you that we're under immense pressure with this. There's never been such a prominent, publicly exposed investigation in Brittany. And with every hour that passes without us coming up with results, the pressure grows. Luckily, we've been able to describe it to the media so far as a 'familial incident.' The commotion is intense enough as it is. Otherwise the mayor would be on at me about a drop in tourism."

She reached for her wineglass and took a long drink.

"So. That's enough work."

She gave the signal to the restaurateur.

In the blink of an eye, the starters were on the table—the waiters seemed to have been waiting for the cue as urgently as Dupin.

"To start, maki sushi filled with Breton lobster, scallops,

and herring, and a platter of Breton gourmet fish, smoked Japanese-style and served with a sea urchin mayonnaise," the chef explained.

Dupin was already devouring everything with his gaze.

"For the main course, we'll serve veal carpaccio and tataki-style mussels, ravioli stuffed with Wagyu beef and duck's liver, and a tempura of freshly caught langoustines. To finish, a buckwheat ice cream sweetened with buckwheat honey. *Bon appétit!*"

For a while, a pleasurable silence reigned, with everyone enjoying what the generous platters on the table had to offer. Dupin was particularly taken with the maki sushi and the delicately smoked sea bream. Everything was sensational. That was the only word for it.

Locmariaquer engaged his three colleagues in conversation. Meanwhile, Commissaire Huppert turned to Nedellec and Dupin.

"A brief word about our plans for tomorrow." Before either of the two commissaires had a chance to respond, she made her suggestions: "Nedellec, the antiques dealer is still yours. On the drive here I gave orders for two colleagues to look for him. They're driving out to his house. As soon as there's any news, I'll be in touch. Dupin, you speak with the sous-chef—and, if you'd like, once more with Joe Morel."

Nedellec murmured something inaudible.

"Perhaps, Nedellec, you could also speak once more with Charles Braz? Maybe we can detect inconsistencies in their statements."

"I will." In his own way, Nedellec seemed content with that.

Dupin, too, was completely in agreement. It was just as he'd planned. He'd already sent the sous-chef a text message earlier.

Huppert turned back to Dupin: "And you're also," a brief pause, "going to see the Trouin sisters' aunt."

He hadn't forgotten.

"I'd also like to speak with Lucille Trouin myself."

It had been on his mind the whole day.

"Do you have reason to believe she might open up to you? Despite the fact she won't speak to anyone else?" Even now, Huppert's tone was completely objective.

Nedellec muttered something again.

"I think that given the special circumstances and the new information, we should try one more time, she—"

"I'll make arrangements tomorrow morning for you to visit her," Huppert interrupted. "Officially I'm the only one authorized, but we'll sort it out. The attorney also has to be present, as always. We'll have to think carefully beforehand about what we plan to tell her, and what we don't, regarding the status quo of the investigation."

Commissaire Huppert was right.

"I think all three of us should be there for the conversation." Nedellec spoke up.

The serving staff had begun to clear away the starter platters and plates.

"Of course," confirmed Huppert.

Dupin was silent. He actually wanted to see Lucille Trouin alone. To have all three of them sit across from her would be completely wrong; they had to take a different approach. But it would be wiser to discuss this tomorrow.

"And what inquiries are you pursuing tomorrow, Commissaire Huppert?"

Nedellec looked at her with interest.

"That depends on how things are going."

She was clearly playing her cards close to her chest.

Dupin felt a vague disquiet. There was nothing inherently wrong with their plans for tomorrow—but they were going into the day without a particular focus. Which was never a good sign.

"And now for the main course," announced the restaurateur.

Within seconds, new platters were carried over, and once again a blissful silence set in.

After less than an hour—the main course and dessert had been just as fantastic, and, of course, the case had been discussed in more detail too—the group dispersed. By then, everyone looked exhausted, and Commissaire Huppert wanted to drop by the station. And Dupin was planning his nightly ritual.

He had left the car at his hotel and made his way on foot through the balmy summer night to the harbor of Saint-Servan.

He walked through the large archway next to the church and, in the next moment, found himself by the sea. The atmospheric orange-yellow light of the streetlamps was reflected on the water, which was completely smooth. The tide seemed to have reached its peak. Only the occasional soft gurgle could be heard against the quay wall.

The sun had set half an hour before—it was ten to eleven now—but the last vestiges of the spherical pale blue light still lingered in the west. Dupin followed the promenade to the end, turned right onto the peninsula, and just two minutes later was sitting in the Bistro de Solidor. His spot was even free.

Nonetheless, Dupin was unhappy. With the whole situation, with the status of the investigation, and not least with himself. He was at odds with himself. He wasn't on form; he was lacking real inspiration. Which perhaps was due in part to the particular circumstances of this investigation; after all, he didn't have his usual free rein. Nolwenn and the Concarneau team hadn't been in touch again either, which could only mean one thing: they hadn't discovered anything new.

"*Bonsoir*, I hope you're well, Commissaire."

The owner of the Solidor sounded sympathetic.

"They just said on the radio that the investigations haven't uncovered anything."

Dupin merely nodded.

"A J.M.—like yesterday?"

"A double."

There was a lot of earthly suffering to forget. If Dupin was honest, he had already dreamed of this moment several times today. The rum—his new sleep aid. Tonight he would see whether it had been a coincidence, or whether the rum really did help.

The large windows in the bistro's covered porch were opened wide, drawing Dupin's gaze to the bay.

His thoughts returned to Lucille Trouin. It seemed that, due to the land fiasco, she was losing everything she had built up for herself. The accomplishments of years of hard work, to which, if he understood correctly, she had devoted her entire life. It was the field in which she'd wanted to defeat her sister, to finally be the victor in their terrible rivalry. A mighty coup had beckoned, and she'd bet everything—and lost. It must have pushed her to the extreme.

"Here you go, Commissaire."

The owner placed a bulbous glass on the table in front of Dupin. He had done himself proud; it was a generous double.

In one gulp, Dupin drank the glass almost empty. He pulled out his notebook and filled page after page. Tried out big and small hypotheses and theories, then discarded them again. Added exclamation points to already written notes, only to strike through them.

As hard as he tried, the vital flash of inspiration failed to come. Instead, a leaden tiredness set in.

It was midnight by the time he got up from his seat.

Twenty minutes later, Dupin lay in bed. And after one minute more, he was asleep. The rum worked its magic.

On the walk back to Villa Saint Raphaël, he had tried once again to reach Claire. Only to get her voicemail once again. Probably she was still in her seminar. Or already in a bar. This time he'd left her a longer message, updating her—the last she'd heard, he was still in his seminar—on the events and unexpected investigation.

The Third Day

Something was bothering him. Something annoying. Loud. Unpleasant.

Dupin tried to ignore it. Whatever it was, it had pulled him out of a deep sleep. He fought against it; every fiber of his being wanted to sleep on.

But it was no use.

It took him a while to gain a moderate level of consciousness and orient himself. Then all at once he was back in reality, and everything was completely banal: it was the penetrating ring of his cell phone, increasing in volume because he hadn't answered.

Dupin had to get out of bed in order to resolve the problem. His phone lay on a small table next to the sofa. Before he could reach it, it rang off.

He glanced at the time: 6:07.

Dupin jumped as the phone began to ring again in his hand.

A cantankerous "Yes?" was all he could muster.

"There's another victim, Dupin. Come right away. It's Walig Richard. At the foot of the vineyard."

"What . . . ?"

"We'll meet there."

"What's . . . ?"

The commissaire had already hung up.

It took Dupin a moment to grasp what she had said.

"Shit!" he exclaimed.

Another victim. Another murder.

The antiques dealer, Blanche Trouin's close friend and confidant.

Dupin got dressed hastily.

What was going on here? Now there were three victims.

Within minutes, he had left the room and was behind the wheel of his car.

A good ten minutes later, he was parking it again.

It had been eleven kilometers, an almost straight line southward on the map, along the Rance, no traffic. In the last few hundred meters, the road had ascended gently. Dupin had stopped the car right at the top, by a solitary, peculiar-looking round tower—with defense battlements, but only a few meters high—where two other police cars were already parked on the unsurfaced lot. He'd been expecting a few more, Commissaire Huppert's in particular. Everything seemed abandoned, there was no one to be seen. No vines, no signs, nothing.

Dupin walked along the narrow road that led away from the tower. Three or four stone houses stood on one side, a small wood with tall trees on the other. Other than that, nothing but fields and meadows. A few times he stopped and looked around.

The sun had only just risen, climbing a little above the horizon, an understated orange-yellow sphere; the rest of the sky was tinged white. To the west, the Rance flowed in sweeping arcs through the valley and formed a veritable lake before Mont Garrot. There was a silvery shimmer above the water, a milky-blue mist rising up.

Dupin came to a halt. It was utterly silent, not a sound to be heard. Still no voices, nothing. And strangely, no birds either.

This couldn't be, it was absurd. Where was the vineyard? The police officers? Where was the body?

His phone rang from deep inside his jeans pocket.

Huppert.

"What's keeping you?"

"I'm at the top of the hill, by the tower, where the other two police cars are parked, and . . ."

"The body's at the foot of the hill. Down where the vineyard begins. You needed to drive up the hill and down the other side, then turn to the right."

Precise information. But unfortunately, too late. Now he was stumbling around through the countryside.

"Okay. I'll go back to the car."

"If you're already at the top, just walk down the hill. Toward the river, you can't miss us."

"I'm . . ."

She had hung up.

"Damn it." Dupin veered left into the undergrowth and began to walk briskly downhill. Wild meadows of tall grass, brambles. Everything was wet, as though it had just rained, but it was only dew. Soon Dupin's shoes were just as wet, and full of mud. *Voyages et aventures,* he thought to himself. The freshness from the night was still tangible, a wonderfully clear air that smelled of dense earth and wet grass. And yet he could sense the day would be hot, especially here in the *campagne*.

Dupin made a wide arc around a particularly tall thicket, and suddenly there they were: the vines. Breton vines. And farther down, where they began, was a gathering of people. A large expanse of terrain had already been cordoned off.

Inside the cordon, toward the river, three men in hoods were moving carefully, two of them with cameras. The forensics team. Dupin hurried, and was soon with the group. Nedellec wasn't there yet. Dupin recognized the medical examiner, who was standing right next to the corpse with Commissaire Huppert, whose facial expression was as analytically matter-of-fact as ever.

"Stabbed—like Kilian Morel. And Blanche Trouin. The police recommenced the search at sunrise. His car was rather concealed, they found it at around five fifty-five A.M." Huppert frowned. "The most important detail, though, is that he's been dead for a while."

"What?"

The medical examiner—short, dark hair and angular gray glasses—joined the conversation: "The time of death is around twenty to twenty-six hours ago. I can tell you more precisely after the autopsy."

His phone rang.

"I have to take this." He moved away.

"Here I am!" Nedellec, breathing heavily, came to a halt next to the group. "I was up at the tower—"

"You're not the only one." Huppert cut him off, instantly returning to the time of the murder. "That would mean Walig

Richard was murdered yesterday morning between four and ten o'clock. The body's been here ever since."

"Which roughly ties in with the time Kilian Morel was murdered"—Nedellec voiced the thought that had shot into Dupin's mind—"meaning it could be one and the same murderer. Who," Nedellec paused, "went on a little tour yesterday morning."

"Mont Garrot would've only been a minor detour," Huppert added prosaically. "On the way to or back from La Moinerie, the perpetrator would have driven over the bridge near here instead of the dam by Dinard. Given their vague alibis, all of our suspects could have managed that timewise."

It certainly looked that way. Even if, of course, they couldn't entirely rule out the possibility that two murderers had been out and about at the same time. It was just incredibly unlikely.

"Maybe the examination of the wound can tell us whether it was the same weapon. The same knife." It was like Huppert had read Dupin's thoughts.

"What would Walig Richard have been doing here? So early? And alone?" Nedellec already seemed wide awake.

"There's not actually anything to do here in the wine region at the moment, the vines just need to be left to grow at this stage," Huppert informed them. "But the vintners still regularly check that all's well, make sure there aren't any diseases or fungi. I've already spoken with one of the other vintners, the mayor of Saint-Suliac. Walig Richard had apparently come out here regularly over recent weeks. Always at roughly this time of day."

"Someone's working systematically here," Nedellec declared emphatically. "It's brutal, but clear. They're eradicating the

Blanche camp. Only Joe Morel is still alive. Everyone else has been eliminated."

For a moment, everyone fell silent.

"I'll go pay him a visit now." Dupin had actually been planning to meet with the sous-chef first, but perhaps under these circumstances he would drive over to Morel's first.

"You're seeing Morel at twelve," Huppert countered. "In his bar. I spoke with him a short while ago. I just wanted to make sure he's okay, hear his voice. He's out in the oyster beds right now, he'll be busy there until midday."

The call had been important, Huppert was completely right.

"To be on the safe side, I've also spoken with Braz, Clément, and Briard. I mean, you never know. Flore Briard dropped off a few things for Lucille at the station yesterday evening, by the way."

Dupin gave the commissaire a questioning glance.

"Things that Braz forgot. He and Briard must have spoken on the phone after his visit to Lucille. She offered to take them in."

Dupin remembered that Braz had mentioned having forgotten a few things.

"The perpetrator," Nedellec thought out loud, "also knew where he could find Walig Richard, just like with Kilian Morel."

"That would probably apply to all four remaining suspects," responded Huppert drily.

Dupin had to run it through his mind first: there really were just four left now. He was being incredibly slow this morning, he could feel his brain resisting the work. It was pitiful.

He stepped closer to the corpse and crouched down.

Walig Richard lay between two rows of vines. He was of a

short, stocky build, and had a sloping forehead with thinning hair. A wide nose, his face deeply tanned—he had clearly spent a lot of time outdoors. He wore jeans and a wide, blue-gray T-shirt; both looked like work clothing, well worn, rips at the knee. The "technique" the murderer had used to stab him looked—at least at first glance—very similar to that with Kilian Morel: three wounds in the region of the heart. The blue-gray of the T-shirt had stained a reddish-black around the chest. The antiques dealer lay on his back, his legs outstretched, head turned to the side slightly, one hand on his wounded chest. There were no obvious signs of a struggle. Nor were there any tracks on the ground, which was hard and dry, with withered clumps of grass here and there. There may have been a brief tussle, but probably nothing more—if at all. Either the murderer had ambushed Walig Richard, or Richard had known the murderer.

"Can I have the corpse taken away?" The medical examiner had rejoined them.

"Fine by me." Huppert seemed deflated. "We're particularly keen to find out whether it was the same knife that was used on Kilian Morel."

"I'll look into that first. By the way, the forensics team haven't found anything of note yet. Not here, nor the parking lot or in the car. No clues regarding the perpetrator. And no cell phone either."

At that moment, Dupin's telephone beeped.

The message was from Clément, the sous-chef, answering Dupin's text from yesterday evening.

Eight-fifteen. In Café du Théâtre. I have to go to the market and be in the restaurant by nine.

That didn't give them much time.

Okay, Dupin responded, short and to the point. Then he turned to Huppert.

"We should take a look around Richard's shop and house. Saint-Suliac is only a few minutes away."

"Ah, are you back with us, Commissaire Dupin?" asked Huppert with a touch of sarcasm.

Nedellec spread his hands in a gesture of agitation. "Now it's gotten even more complicated." It sounded like a complaint. "Joe Morel wouldn't stand to gain anything from Richard's death. There's no inheritance there. The question is: Who would profit from the antiques dealer's death? And even trickier: from the deaths of Morel *and* Richard. And where's the connection to the sisters? If there even is one . . ."

"Is there a café in Saint-Suliac?" Dupin interrupted. Before he could start to ponder everything, he needed caffeine. He urgently needed to get his brain into gear.

"There is," Huppert replied tersely. "Why?"

"Who's going to focus on Walig Richard, speak to his co-workers, his friends, the other vintners—find out if he has any family?"

Nedellec's question was clearly rhetorical.

"Richard is your man, so it's your assignment." Huppert didn't dither in her response.

"We have to find out everything about him, that's the most important thing now," confirmed Nedellec.

"Let's meet in fifteen minutes at Richard's antiques store." Dupin turned away; he had to go up the hill to get to his car.

"It's not fifteen minutes away," Huppert corrected him. "It's not even ten."

Dupin didn't react. He set off uphill between the vines.

The Rance lay to his left, a docile, well-tempered riverscape. Its banks were lined by picturesque villages; dense, deep-green forests; far-reaching meadows and fields on harmoniously undulating hills. This world bore no resemblance to the wildness of the nearby Emerald Coast.

The sun had swiftly gained strength, and color too; it now bathed the early morning in a warm orange light.

"No, genuinely, Nolwenn. I can't think of anything right now."

It was a grave situation. One that had never occurred before. Nolwenn was far from happy about it. But what was he to do? Right now, he really didn't have any tasks to delegate.

Dupin had just sat down on the terrace of the Bistro de la Grève—right by Saint-Suliac's long pier—and ordered two *cafés* and two croissants, when Nolwenn called. She had already found out about the latest murder, and was on her way to the station. She had called a meeting for the entire team at eight o'clock. Admittedly, though, they had run out of ideas yesterday as to what else they could do from Concarneau. They had found all the information the internet had to offer, and inquiries with authorities or banks about the victims and suspects had been taken care of by Huppert's team. Which made sense, because the local and regional police officers knew the area and people best. In addition, all the police stations and *gendarmerie* in the region were on the case. While there was usually a lack of personnel for difficult cases, this time it was the reverse; there was an abundance. Due to the enormous public attention, which would expand to even crazier dimensions once they knew about the third murder, this was thoroughly justified.

"Okay then, Monsieur le Commissaire." Nolwenn gave up. "But it is and remains a dissatisfying situation. We can't do anything but jab holes in the wind."

"I know."

It was an old Breton expression for demoralizing, involuntary idleness.

"By the way, Riwal is still pursuing the biographical connections between the Trouin sisters and the legendary corsairs."

Dupin hadn't expected anything less.

The waiter arrived with the *cafés* and croissants.

"Thank you," whispered Dupin.

"Quite right, too"—Nolwenn suddenly seemed conciliatory—"have your breakfast first."

It was unbelievable. As always, she seemed to know precisely where he was and what he was doing. Dupin had long since accepted it as a supernatural, druidic gift, yet it still amazed him every time.

"You know, I'm sure that Saint-Suliac was declared one of the most beautiful villages in France by the national initiative *Les plus beaux villages de France*. And rightfully so."

A large national beauty competition, of which there were numerous similar initiatives, where the Breton villages consistently came out in first place.

"Call if there's any news!" A sharp command. "This case is really something."

"Speak later, Nolwenn."

Dupin leaned back in his chair. He hurriedly drank his first *café*, then, without pausing, the second.

Saint-Suliac lay in a paradisical, crescent-shaped bay. The

riverbank was strengthened with an ancient stone wall, behind which was a well-tended strip of grass and inviting benches at regular intervals. The main village street, which led to the *port de plaisance,* ran straight onto the jetty, which stretched out far into the sea and sloped away very gradually. The Bistro de la Grève was located just before the jetty, on the most beautiful spot, and Walig Richard's antiques store was just a few houses away— Quai des Lançonniers, directly on the narrow coastal road.

Everything here felt peaceful, sedate, tranquil. Idyllic was the right word. And quiet, absolutely quiet, at least at this early hour. A grandiose panorama, wide and free.

The water was rising, though it was still low tide. The milky-blue mist that hovered over the water was still unfurling its magic, and had now taken on an intense silvery shimmer.

The excellent coffee immediately took effect. Dupin could literally feel the caffeine, pure energy, reaching his brain; like electricity being switched on and instantly spreading out into all the connected networks. As his alertness grew, so did his awareness of the extraordinary brutality of this case. What on earth was going on here?

Dupin was just about to order a third coffee when he heard cars approaching. A few moments later they came into view: a convoy of vehicles, he counted seven, led by Huppert's dark blue Peugeot 508. Commissaire Nedellec was behind her in his dynamic silver Renault. All of them stopped on the coastal road in front of house number 6.

Dupin stood up, realizing his third coffee wouldn't happen, and swiftly made his way across to meet the others in front of the courtyard gate of the antiques store.

"It took a little longer than I thought," Huppert greeted him. "We had to get the key from an employee because we couldn't find them on Walig Richard's body, nor in his car."

"I had a few calls to make," responded Dupin. The commissaire didn't need to know about his extreme, almost medically indicated caffeine consumption.

Huppert strode past him into the courtyard.

"This shop is Walig Richard's property, by the way, as is the house where he lives. It's nearby, also right on the shoreline."

Nedellec and Dupin followed her.

It was a beautiful old house. Exposed granite stones in differing sizes, shapes, and colors—dark gray, brown, but also red-toned, and gray. In front of all the houses in this incredibly beautiful village were flower boxes, colorful flowerbeds, and blooming shrubs. Lavender, oleander, rhododendrons, rosemary, agapanthus. It was fascinating: the village, just like the entire surrounding landscape, exuded an entirely harmonious beauty. As though the inhabitants had wanted to make everything just as beautiful as nature itself had.

The wooden doors and window frames of Richard's house were painted a dark blue-green, the gutters light gray, tastefully coordinated. A luscious, pale pink climbing rose between the two entrance doors had grown to just beneath the windows on the first floor. Above the left-hand entrance, a discreet sign indicated the antiques shop. Pale gravel in the courtyard, and behind the low stone wall, blossoming artichokes.

"Some of the employees, as well as Monsieur Richard's friends and acquaintances, will be arriving soon," Nedellec informed them. "I arranged for them to come at intervals, one after the other."

Nedellec had been busy. Dupin was glad; they urgently needed some new leads. And some luck. Someone who knew something, something significant.

The rest of the team had now gathered in the courtyard.

"The employee responsible for this shop," Nedellec continued, "said he didn't notice anything conspicuous in here yesterday morning, it was all as he'd left it the previous evening. They opened at around eleven, like always. So if the perpetrator came into the shop after the murder, they must have done it discreetly. They clearly didn't ransack the place."

Huppert unlocked the door.

"I still want forensics to go through everything meticulously and document it. The whole house."

"Of course." The three men with hoods, whom Dupin had already seen back at the vineyard, instantly made their way to the front.

They plunged into the dull light typical of old stone houses with few and small windows.

Huppert turned on the light. An immense chandelier hung from the middle of the ceiling.

The entire room was artfully filled with old furniture and objects, but didn't feel cluttered; the bare white walls staged them as tasteful arrangements. A brief glance was enough to see that the items for sale here were very classy. Of superior quality. The typical scent of furniture polish, oil, dust, and multiple centuries hung in the air, mixed with notes of citrus and lavender.

The forensics team had already gotten to work.

Opposite the entrance, at the far end of the room, stood a long wooden desk on which there was an old-fashioned cash register and a large computer. An upholstered wooden stool and a black leather armchair behind; it looked cozy. Next to the table was a dark-wood vitrine filled with old jewelry: bracelets, necklaces, rings, some with expensive-looking stones, hairpins inset with pearls, cuff links adorned with mother-of-pearl.

"What do you think?" asked Huppert, who was standing next to Nedellec in front of the vitrine. "Is there anything valuable there?"

"No idea." Nedellec shrugged. "The employee didn't notice anything missing. And in our case it won't be about a jewelry theft."

Commissaire Huppert walked around the table and opened the drawer of a rolling file cabinet. She rummaged around, pulled out a black notebook, and laid it on the table. Then she opened it at a random page.

It seemed to be Richard's accounting book, as there were sales noted on the opened pages. The object and a number, presumably the inventory number, price, date, client name, and, written very small, the client's address along with an ongoing case number. The old-school method.

Huppert leafed through the book. There were similar entries on all the pages. She looked for the most recent sales.

"Two picture frames were sold yesterday. To a Georges Duras. A Parisian address."

"By which time Walig Richard," Nedellec added, "was already lying dead in the vineyard."

"A mirror was sold the day before, that's in a different handwriting, possibly Richard's."

"He was here in the shop the day before yesterday," Nedellec confirmed.

The men from the forensics team had now turned their attention to the jewelry display case.

"To a Pierre Comment from Saint-Brieuc," Huppert read on. "And a wardrobe to someone from Cancale, a Madame Swann Muity. And a gold bracelet. Quite pricey, one thousand fifty euros. To Marie Fesnata from Rennes."

Dupin had leaned forward a little in order to see. The handwriting was barely legible, almost as bad as his own.

"*Bonjour*, madame, *bonjour*, messieurs."

A stocky man had come in. Black beard, short black hair, in his mid-fifties, Dupin estimated, with a lackluster posture that matched his drawling voice.

"Your colleagues told me to come in. I'm Matthieu Boldin, I'm responsible for this shop. Even when Monsieur Richard is here himself," he hastened to add.

Huppert waved him over. "Then I'm sure you can tell us whether he made these entries? Here, in this book."

The employee leaned over the notebook. He looked a little nervous.

"That's his handwriting, yes."

"And this is where all the sales are recorded?"

"That's right."

Nedellec took over the questioning: "Did Monsieur Richard know the customers from the day before yesterday personally?"

"As far as I know, only Madame Muity from Cancale; they were vaguely acquainted."

"Had there been any conflict with her? Or with any other customer recently?"

The man looked confused.

"Absolutely not, no. Monsieur Richard ran his business in a highly dedicated, personal way. And so do his employees. I can assure you that our clients are always satisfied."

"And outside of work, can you think of any conflict in Monsieur Richard's private life?"

"He never argued with anyone. He just avoided people he didn't get on with—it was one of his vital principles. And Monsieur Richard seemed to have very good friends."

"One of them being Blanche Trouin."

"Oh yes, very much so, at least as far as I could tell."

"Do you happen to know when they last saw each other?"

"I don't. She didn't come here that often."

"Do you know whether they met up in recent weeks?"

"I think they met up last week. But I can't remember which day it was."

"And Kilian Morel—do you know whether Monsieur Richard had seen him recently? Or if they were even in contact at all?"

"Unfortunately I don't know that either."

"Did Monsieur Richard specialize in anything in his business?" Huppert joined in.

"No. For him, it was about the really special pieces. The ones with character. With history and soul, as he put it. He didn't focus on any particular era either."

"Did that apply to the jewelry too?" Huppert nodded toward the display cabinet.

"Yes, but he only moved into that in recent years. He quickly became an expert, though. He was an expert in all the areas he turned his attention to."

"Who was the last person to leave the shop the day before yesterday?"

"Monsieur Richard and I left together. At seven in the evening."

"Did he seem any different to how he usually was?"

"No, not at all."

Huppert looked at Nedellec. "You told my colleague on the phone that you didn't notice anything out of the ordinary here in the shop yesterday morning."

"Yes, that's right."

"Can you entirely rule out the possibility that something's missing? In the entire shop, in the display cabinet?"

"I think so."

"I'd like you to check again and make sure."

"Of course."

Huppert, who was more than a head taller than the employee, seemed to have made a strong impression on him.

"Were there any other valuable items here in the building besides the antiques?"

The man looked perplexed.

"I—no. Only the antiques. And there isn't much cash either. Almost everyone pays by card."

Huppert took a step toward him. "So you have no idea why someone would have wanted your boss dead? And who it might have been?"

"No." The employee gave the commissaire a despairing look. "It's all so terrible, I've no idea why someone would have done something so awful," he blurted out.

Nedellec looked at the time. "Monsieur Boldin, I've arranged to meet two of your colleagues as well as some of Monsieur Richard's friends and acquaintances here. Is there a quiet room in the building we can use?"

"Upstairs. On the first floor. It's predominantly a storeroom, but there's a table there too."

In the next moment, Nedellec turned to Huppert. "I think the conversations with Walig Richard's friends and acquaintances are the highest priority now. You'll have to manage without me for searching his house."

He headed decisively toward the narrow wooden stairs in the corner of the room.

"Take our colleagues from forensics up there with you," Huppert instructed him.

Dupin looked at the time. It was 7:50. He was due to meet the sous-chef in twenty-five minutes. In the meantime, he decided to take a look around the shop. And to leave the search of Richard's house to Huppert and the forensics team.

Colomb Clément, with thick, reddish-blond hair and dark, lively eyes, had a well-groomed one-week beard. He was a strong-looking young man—thirty-two, Dupin knew—a little rough-and-ready, perhaps, also in his facial features. The sensory subtlety he must surely possess as an up-and-coming *grand chef* wasn't obvious to look at him; Dupin had expected someone quite different.

Clément had been standing at the counter with unforced ease—dressed in jeans and a plain dark brown T-shirt—with an espresso cup in his hand, when Dupin came in through the door a few minutes late. The café was full to the rafters and bustling with activity, a constant coming and going.

Dupin had recognized him by his searching gaze. They had greeted one another with just a few words.

"Right then." Clément set down his cup. "Let's go shopping."

The sous-chef had admittedly said he needed to go to the market, but Dupin hadn't realized he'd be accompanying him.

"I'll be ready in just a moment." Dupin swiftly addressed the man behind the counter. "A *petit café*, please."

He couldn't let the opportunity slip by.

A brief nod, and the man immediately turned to the impressive-looking coffee machine. Clément seemed to take it stoically; in any case, he didn't show any reaction. He waited in silence until Dupin had drunk his coffee. Meanwhile, Dupin had stared in surprise at the front page of the *Ouest-France*, from which his own picture stared out at him. Beneath the headline "The Britt Team Takes Over" were photos of the three commissaires.

"We can go," signaled Dupin.

They left the café and turned left, arriving almost instantly at Place Bouvet, the center of Saint-Servan, where not only the impressive market halls were located, but the church too. Clément paused at the side entrance to the market, which by now had reopened for business.

Dupin realized he would have to get the conversation going.

"You've already spoken with Commissaire Huppert, Monsieur Clément." Dupin came straight to the point. "It's very significant for us to find out whether Lucille Trouin knew her sister had headhunted you. Has anything else on this come to mind?"

"No." He did, however, manage an afterthought: "Like I already told your colleague: Blanche wanted to tell Lucille herself."

"The question is whether she did that in the hours or days before the crime."

"That I don't know."

His taciturn nature didn't come across as unfriendly, but Dupin still found it onerous.

They stepped into the halls. Clément steered his way confidently through the aisles.

"Commissaire Huppert said you also didn't know whether Blanche Trouin had told anyone beside her husband about it?"

"Exactly."

"And why didn't you tell Commissaire Huppert about this matter of your own accord?"

"No idea."

"What's that supposed to mean?"

Clément had paused by a vegetable stand and was appraising *cœur-de-bœuf* tomatoes.

"I didn't think it was important, Lucille wouldn't have killed her sister over that."

His first proper sentence. One that made it clear how futile it was to discuss the topic any further. The whole thing with the headhunting, in any case, had taken a back seat since Walig Richard's murder.

"Why did Blanche's offer appeal to you?"

"She offered me a lot of creative freedom. And a significantly better salary."

He walked on—the tomatoes seemed to have been only of fleeting interest; he was on the hunt for something else.

"You didn't have this creative freedom with Lucille?"

"She's very authoritarian."

"Did you argue at times?"

"No."

"How much more money did Blanche offer you?"

"About fifteen hundred more a month."

A sizable leap. It was a strong argument.

Clément turned left and headed for the last stand in the aisle.

"*Marie-Annick, Maraîchère*" was written in green lettering on a white sign, along with an illustration of a vegetable cart.

"I also didn't want to do those culinary boat trips anymore. It bores me."

The first point that Clément himself had volunteered.

"Were there arguments over that?"

"No."

"*Salut*, Colomb," the stallholder greeted him, seeming to know him well.

"*Bonjour*, Marie-Annick."

The owner herself.

"What's it to be today?"

"*Petit pois.*"

The woman, who fulfilled every idea of a vegetable grower and stallholder in the loveliest of ways—a weather-beaten face, headscarf and dungarees—went over to the piled-up crates behind her, reached into the top one, came back with a single pea pod, and handed it to Clément. It was a practiced ritual: with seasoned dexterity, he retrieved the peas from their pod with just one hand. Then he rolled a pea softly between his index finger and thumb and tasted it.

For a while, there was only silence. Then, a laconic "Okay."

Judging by Marie-Annick's facial expression, she'd had no doubt regarding the quality of her peas, but a joyful smile danced on her lips nonetheless.

"They're fabulously sweet right now. Just how you like them."

"Give me ten kilos."

"Pierre will bring them over right away."

Clément nodded.

"Anything else?"

"*Cocos de Paimpol.*"

"You're in luck, I've got the first of the season."

The pea procedure was repeated with the white beans, except without tasting them. Although the stall owner must have noticed that Dupin was with Clément in some context, she paid no further attention to him.

Clément nodded once more. "Ten kilos again," came his verdict.

"That's everything?"

Neither of them seemed to require many words.

"Yep. See you later, Marie-Annick."

Clément had already turned away and was walking on.

"You heard about the latest murder, I presume. Walig Richard."

"They're talking of nothing else on the radio."

"Did you know him personally?"

"No."

"Do you know anything about him?"

"No."

"And Kilian Morel—did you have contact with him?"

"Again, no."

"You would have run into him from time to time, I presume?"

"Very rarely. Sometimes at parties, public events."

They had arrived at a butcher's stand. Inside a large glass display case was everything the heart could desire: gigantic *côtes de bœuf*, sumptuous entrecôtes, filet steaks, legs of lamb, Ibérico pork cutlets, venison sausage, entire rabbits, and a variety of offal.

"What about Joe Morel, the brother of Blanche's husband?"

"I know who he is, but I don't have any contact with him."

"Have you . . ."

Dupin's cell phone. The peace had lasted an unusually long time.

Commissaire Huppert.

"Excuse me for a moment. I'll be back in a second." Dupin went off into a quieter corner.

"Yes?"

"Flore Briard. Her finances don't exactly look rosy either." As always, Huppert wasted no time on small talk. "From the one point seven million euros she inherited ten years ago, only twenty thousand remain, in a money market account. That's everything. It looks like she's living off of her business with the culinary boat trips. She owns her villa, admittedly, but that costs her a fortune in upkeep. And it seems she recently contemplated renting part of it out. Last year she sold a very expensive Rolex at auction, an heirloom."

"Interesting."

It really was. Not spectacular, but interesting.

"How did you find this out?"

"I have my contacts. Just like you."

Information like this wasn't usually obtained through entirely law-abiding methods. After all, in strictly legal terms, Briard wasn't a key suspect. Huppert clearly had her terrain in the palm of her hand.

"So it's unclear how she would've been able to lend Lucille money. Unless she's planning to sell her villa. But I haven't heard anything about that."

"I'll call Madame Briard. Is there anything else?"

"I haven't been able to reach Nedellec, I think he's carrying out his interviews. I'll try again later. I'm still at Richard's house."

"And?"

"We haven't found anything relevant yet. By the way, I've arranged for you to visit Lucille Trouin. You can go from early afternoon onward—she has a clinical-psychological examination before that, which she initially refused. But we'll need to talk things over beforehand."

"Absolutely. Talk soon."

Dupin hung up and, within moments, was back with Clément.

The sous-chef was holding a piece of meat, pressing his thumb into it and studying it closely.

"Okay."

For him, this seemed to be an expression of the highest possible satisfaction.

"Twenty of those."

"Your *souris d'agneau* with white beans, *petit pois,* and *la ratte* potatoes?"

Clément mumbled an affirmation.

Unlike the owner of the vegetable stand, the butcher definitely took notice of Dupin:

"You absolutely have to order this dish of Colomb's, monsieur, it's one of his masterpieces. Mind-blowing. The lamb hock is marinated in cinnamon, blossom honey, and a little premium caraway, then gently braised for hours."

Just the mention alone of *souris d'agneau* was enough to make Dupin's mouth water. He also loved white beans and fresh green peas. And the marinade sounded equally heavenly.

"Absolutely."

"It's a really simple dish." Clément played it down.

It was always the way: when an exceptional cook says "really simple"—and in their mind, it really is—for laypeople that means: no matter how hard you try, you'll never be able to make it taste the same.

"Need anything else, Colomb?"

"That's everything."

"We'll bring it over."

The sous-chef had already left the stall.

"Had Lucille Trouin seemed any different to you lately, Monsieur Clément?"

"No."

"Perhaps a little preoccupied?"

He shook his head.

"Did you know about the difficulties she was having?"

"No."

Clément steered toward a stall with strawberries from Plougastel. "*Les meilleures fraises du monde*" proclaimed the sign. It was entirely true. Introduced in the eighteenth century from Chile and further refined in Plougastel, they were nothing like the standard European strawberries. Dupin couldn't get enough of them.

"You also work for Flore Briard in a sense, if I understand correctly."

"No. Not directly." The distinction seemed important to him. "I create the dishes and menus, and another chef then prepares them on the boat. But La Noblesse sells the recipes; Lucille Trouin's restaurant, not me. I get a salary bonus. Not much of one, though."

He pushed his hands into his trouser pockets and joined the small queue in front of the strawberry stand.

"Still, Madame Briard would struggle if you left."

"She'll find a solution."

"You must sometimes have cause to meet with Flore Briard, I presume? To discuss the menus, for example."

"From time to time. Usually at the start of the season. She was in the restaurant last week. Friday. She came into the kitchen after service and said she wanted a quiet word with me soon."

"About what?"

"No idea. She said she'd be in touch. But she hasn't yet."

A topic for Dupin's next conversation with Flore Briard.

"Whom did she usually come to La Noblesse with?"

"Mostly with girlfriends, as far as I'm aware. I'm always in the kitchen. On Friday she was there with a man."

"Who?"

"Blanche Trouin's brother-in-law."

"What? Joe Morel?" Dupin's eyebrows shot up.

"As I said, I don't know him personally, I just know who he is."

"Are you sure it was him?"

"Yes. One of the customers wanted to speak to me, so I was in the dining room briefly."

Flore Briard and Joe Morel. That was noteworthy.

"Did they seem—intimate with each other?"

"I don't know."

"Was Lucille there that evening?"

"No."

The man at the strawberry stand greeted Clément warmly.

"How's things, Colomb? I have some wonderful Gariguettes, Séraphines, and Surprises, which would you like?"

Three of the Plougastel strawberry varieties.

"Gariguette today, please."

The man handed Clément a single strawberry, and the sous-chef took his time.

Dupin thought he could make out a smile on Clément's lips as he let the strawberry slowly dissolve in his mouth.

"Five kilos."

"You got it."

Clément lifted his hand by way of good-bye and left the stand.

"I have to get back to the restaurant," he said, turning to Dupin.

"Then thank you for your time, Monsieur Clément."

The sous-chef had paused for at least a moment.

"*Au revoir.*"

Clément made a beeline for the exit through which Lucille Trouin had fled on Monday, after the murder.

Dupin got into the car, shut the door, and entered Madame Trouin-Allanic's address into the GPS.

The route would take him along one of the bigger roads beneath Saint-Malo's old town directly to Rothéneuf, past the large industrial port.

He dialed Flore Briard's number.

It took a little while before she picked up.

"Hello?"

"Commissaire Dupin here. I have a few more questions for you, madame."

"That doesn't surprise me," she answered confidently.

There was noise in the background; she seemed to be on her way somewhere too, on foot, probably out in the street, Dupin presumed.

"It's about a few things you didn't mention when we spoke yesterday."

"Then there'll be quite a lot."

"You said you wanted to give your friend Lucille Trouin a loan, and I'm assuming a considerable one. But we've discovered you're not in a financial position to do so."

Flore Briard answered without hesitation: "I don't know what you've heard and from whom, Commissaire, but I know my financial circumstances. Don't you worry."

"Our information is unequivocal, madame."

"Ridiculous. My inheritance was manifold."

Dupin remained firm. "This means you're more dependent on the culinary boat trip business than we thought."

"You're wrong, Monsieur le Commissaire." She didn't seem at all irritated. "But I love my little business. It's very important to me."

How reliable was Huppert's source? Did Flore Briard perhaps have an account or funds abroad that no one knew about? Dupin wouldn't be able to push any further than he already had. What's more, there didn't seem to be any obvious link between her financial situation and the murders.

It was futile.

"One more thing, Madame Briard, what's your—" Dupin slammed on the brakes; the tires screeched. A slow-moving convoy of cars crossed the arterial highway. The classics club. It looked like a procession. Today the banner on the last car read: "We Love the Classics." Once again, a few people from the vehicles waved at him.

Dupin picked up the thread of his conversation again: "What's your relationship to Joe Morel, Madame Briard? On Friday evening you ate out at Lucille Trouin's restaurant with him. You didn't mention that yesterday."

She was the one who had spoken of the two "camps" yesterday—and Joe Morel belonged to the other camp. The Blanche camp.

"Joe and I have known each other a really long time. We've always gotten on. From time to time, we catch up over dinner. Not often, though."

"What did you talk about on this occasion?"

Dupin had reached Saint-Malo's industrial port. On the dock, countless blue plastic crates were stacked into towering piles, presumably waiting to be loaded onto boats.

"Everything, really. My work. His bar. How things are going. Nothing in particular."

It was clear Dupin wouldn't get anything out of her.

"Was it an impromptu get-together?"

"No. I went out to dinner in Cancale a few weeks ago. With a girlfriend. We stopped off at Joe's bar for an aperitif beforehand. Joe and I chatted and made a plan to catch up. And this was it."

"Have you had any contact with him since the day before yesterday, since the incident at the market?"

"Of course. We've spoken on the phone twice. And messaged. In moments like this, you have to be there for people."

"How did he seem on the phone? In particular, after his brother's murder?"

"He's not the type to express his emotions. But they're there. Of course it's a terrible shock for him. Perhaps you should speak with Joe yourself."

"I will. You asked Colomb on Friday evening if you could meet with him soon. What did you want to talk about?"

Dupin had passed the sign for Rothéneuf. So this was the location of the plot of land that was bankrupting Lucille Trouin.

"I think you knew about Blanche headhunting him," Dupin continued. "And that Lucille did too."

In all honesty, he wasn't sure what to think.

"I didn't know anything about it, Commissaire." Her voice took on an element of sharpness. "I meet up with Colomb two or three times a year. To find out what ideas he has for the coming season. With Lucille, I only discuss the business side, after all. The menus play an integral role in the boat trips. And I need variety. So that people always have a reason to book again, even though they're already familiar with the views."

"It was a bit late for a conversation about the summer season, wasn't it?"

"I've decided to invest in a large grill for both boats. Barbecue cuisine is all the rage right now. That was the main reason I wanted to speak with him. The trips continue until late October or early November, that's still another five months."

Dupin couldn't think of a substantive response. It was disillusioning. But then something else occurred to him.

"What were the items you dropped off at the police station for Lucille yesterday evening?"

He had meant to ask Huppert as soon as she mentioned it.

"Just a few things that Charles forgot. Flip-flops, contact lens solution, moisturizer. And a few things I knew she'd be glad to have."

"Such as?"

"Her favorite cooking magazine. A book I knew she'd been wanting to read. A bar of chocolate with nuts."

"Okay, Madame Briard. I'm sure you'll be hearing from me again soon."

"I look forward to it, Commissaire."

Dupin hung up.

He was nearly there. One more right turn, then he would reach the Allée Notre-Dame des Flots.

While Madame Allanic-Trouin's villa didn't possess quite the dimensions of La Garde, it certainly had no reason to be bashful. It too had an impressive neo-gothic splendor; Dupin particularly liked the light shade of stone.

The setting was just as magnificent as the villa itself. A small, semi-private road, lined by wild meadows, led out of Rothéneuf toward the sea and ended there. More precisely: at the villa, which towered, grand and solitary, over the Atlantic on the very last sweeping cliffs. Just a stone's throw away was a steep descent into a wide bay, which was framed by high rocks and connected only narrowly to the open sea; almost encircled by the land, it itself formed a little sea. An inland sea, which at high tide—as it almost was right now—became a part of the wild Atlantic; at low tide, by contrast, a gigantic, blinding sand basin. This was a phenomenon that could be marveled at in countless spots on the Breton coast. Small groves of windswept sea pines lined the shore, with the bright blue watercolor sky above—it was breathtaking. The inland sea was a glistening turquoise, primed with white sand. A pleasant breeze carried salt and iodine from the ocean. Dupin loved it; it was so restorative.

He had parked at the side of the road, some distance from the gate to the villa. For a while, he stood motionless next to the car, ruminating over how the meeting might play out.

Presumably the aunt wouldn't know a great deal about the two sisters, and even less, or nothing at all, about the other people involved. By all accounts, her memory was fading.

Dupin let out a sigh and set off.

Behind the gate, which looked like a show-jumping obstacle, began a dark gravel path that led to the villa.

An elderly lady came out of the entrance door and hurried toward him.

"Pardon, Monsieur le Commissaire, I'm Francine Lezu, Madame Allanic's housekeeper. I only just spotted you, otherwise of course I would have come to open the gate." She looked over at his car with a frown. "You could have parked inside. I'm so sorry"—she spoke without pausing for breath—"I'm so glad you've come, I'm at my wits' end. Madame is saying crazier and crazier things, the doctor has prescribed her a sedative but she's refusing to take it and doesn't want any injections either. But she's getting worse and worse. I'm hoping your visit will help, which I'm sure it will." She took a deep breath at last. "The visit from Commissaire Huppert yesterday—how shall I put it?—didn't go so well."

The housekeeper and Dupin were standing directly opposite each other. He estimated that she was in her mid-to-late seventies, with a wiry, almost bony frame, thinning hair, and her clothes seemed from another era: a long black skirt, a ruffled white blouse, and a pleated gray apron.

"It's a pleasure to meet you. And I look forward to meeting Madame Allanic too."

She turned on her heel. "Along here—if you'll follow me. Madame is waiting for you on the veranda, her favorite spot. She's just had another angry outburst, and I was afraid she was going to completely break down. Sometimes she wants me to look in the house and find out where her husband might be hiding."

"What was her husband's profession?"

"He was a shareholder in one of the big shipping companies here in Saint-Malo. The biggest."

This detail seemed important to Madame Lezu.

"How long have you been working for Madame Allanic?"

"Oh, nine years and three months."

"Has Madame ever spoken with you about what will happen to her fortune after her death?"

She looked indignant. "Of course not, what are you thinking? I'm the housekeeper. An employee. Madame would never do that, it would be completely inappropriate. And of course, I wouldn't want her to either."

"When were the Trouin sisters last here?" It probably made more sense to ask the housekeeper.

Madame Lezu didn't need to think long. "Lucille three weeks ago, Blanche just last week. She always took very good care of Madame; she brought delicious ingredients and cooked for her."

Dupin pulled out his notebook. They had reached a wide, semicircular set of stone steps, which led up to the villa's entrance.

"How often did they each come, as a rule?"

"Blanche every few weeks. Lucille less often. Sometimes they came when I wasn't here. I work the whole weekend, but have Mondays off. But Madame would tell me about their visits." Madame Lezu paused. "I got the feeling they preferred coming when I wasn't here."

"Why?"

Her face reddened a little: "Perhaps, how shall I put it—they felt less observed."

They had paused in front of the large entrance door.

"Were the two sisters' partners with them, the last time they came?"

"No. Neither of them."

"After her nieces' recent visits—was everything like normal? Or did you notice anything different about Madame afterward?"

"Not at all, no. By the way, I should tell you that she can't hear very well anymore."

"I'll keep that in mind, Madame Lezu."

"It's a long time since Madame has left the house; her life only takes place here now."

The housekeeper opened the door and made her way through the magnificent entrance hall to another door opposite.

Within moments they stepped into a huge space that seemed to be the living room. Dark, heavy, and intricately adorned wooden furniture, unlike anything Dupin had seen before. Peculiar artwork, incomparable with any of the styles he knew.

A dark wooden floor with wooden mosaics, large paintings in bulky frames on the wall, nineteenth century, landscapes. A generously sized double door led directly out onto the terrace.

"Have you ever overheard any of the conversations between Madame Allanic and her nieces?"

The housekeeper glanced around nervously, clearly feeling uncomfortable.

"Of course not," she whispered. "I just made the coffee or tea. Served the cake."

"And you yourself don't live here in the house?"

"Madame wouldn't like that. There's a small house for the employees farther down the road, in the village."

"Are there other service staff, then?"

"There used to be. But for a long time now it's just been me."

"Thank you, Madame Lezu."

Immense relief emanated from the housekeeper's face as Dupin headed for the doors to the terrace.

It was like something in a film. The entire setting. The terrace—which had to be at least fifty square meters—was a kingdom in itself, surrounded by a curving balustrade at hip height in elegant white. A breathtaking sight: to the right, the small inland sea, and everywhere else, the endless Atlantic. The legendary emerald green shone in deep contrast to the white and blue of the sky. Then the noble green of the occasional sea pine and the gray tones of the rocks and cliffs.

Near to the wall of the house, sheltered from the wind but in the sunlight, stood a large wicker armchair, with a rectangular cast-iron table and three chairs alongside it. In the armchair: Madame Allanic. She was wearing a straw hat with a broad, sweeping brim and a deep-pink band. A small tray stood on the table, bearing a silver teapot, a blue-and-white porcelain cup, and a matching milk jug.

Madame Allanic sat there utterly motionless, as though she were frozen to the spot. Her gaze rested vaguely on the ocean. She didn't seem to notice Dupin and the housekeeper. Her combed-back, short, dark blond hair shimmered white at the temples, and her striking forehead was bare, her skin astonishingly smooth for her ninety-three years. She had a narrow nose, and subtly made-up lips.

"Good morning, Madame Allanic." Dupin spoke more loudly than usual.

She turned abruptly toward him, in stark contrast to the unmoving, withdrawn state she had been in. Out of the corner of his eye, Dupin noticed the housekeeper retreat discreetly.

"My husband will be back shortly." Madame Allanic seemed agitated. "And then he'll sort everything out here. He always straightens everything out, you'll see. I don't care when I die. He'll bring new treasures with him! Lots of new treasures, even more valuable than the old ones! They stole them, that's right, stole! They can't force me to speak, I won't say a word." All of a sudden, she stopped speaking and seemed to fall back into her paralyzed state, except that, this time, her gaze rested uncertainly on Dupin and not the ocean.

"I'm Commissaire Dupin, Madame Allanic, from the Police Nationale. You asked to speak with me."

Something akin to deep astonishment appeared in Madame Allanic's expression. Together with confusion. She was wearing a mixed-wool jacket, a Bordeaux-colored blouse beneath with white piping on the collar, and a golden brooch set with a single jewel. Pleated black pants. As elegant as her appearance was, her vulnerability was plain to see. And her old age. Particularly on her hands.

"You're too late." Now she sounded resigned all of a sudden, sad. "It already happened. They murdered her."

"You mean Blanche? Your niece?"

Once again, she looked surprised, as though she were wondering how he knew.

"She was my favorite. And she's coming to see me again soon." She paused again, motionless. Then she was gripped by a new impulse: "They came and took everything from us! Those evil thieves. They scaled our town's mighty walls. I'm going to Canada, you know. Canada belongs to us. To my sister in Canada."

"The one you're planning to leave your estate to, if I understand correctly."

Dupin watched her attentively.

"To Canada!"

She fell silent.

Dupin noted how deeply this whole situation and the old woman's condition was affecting him. She seemed imprisoned in her own darkly gleaming night. He didn't even know how to calm her down. A normal conversation was out of the question.

She began to speak again: "Blanche has them. Blanche! She has them all. The spices. The aromas of the world. From the most exotic of lands. No one knows them but her, only my husband. Blanche took the recipe book. It was her. From her father. She has the gift."

"Did Lucille kill Blanche because of it, do you think?"

Yet again, she gave him a look of intense bafflement. Then it seemed as though she were gathering new strength.

"The corsairs were proud men. We conquered the whole world. I'm a corsair woman. And I won't tell them, nor will Blanche."

"You won't tell them what, madame? What exactly?"

She looked down at the ground.

"Persian cumin, Afghan saffron, the most valuable spices in the world. Bourbon vanilla from the Comoros, Tasmanian pepper, cardamom from southern India, Arabic mace. Real treasures! But I didn't tell them."

The meaning of her words remained a mystery.

"I see you've found your sun hat. It's lucky it wasn't stolen." Dupin remembered the housekeeper mentioning it on the phone the previous day.

"They stole everything." She looked horror-struck. "Everything."

A beeping tone sounded out. A text message.

Dupin glanced quickly at the display on his phone. A message from Huppert: *Conversation with L. Trouin: 2:00.* So she'd sorted it, good. Dupin put his cell phone away.

He decided to have one more attempt with reality: "Madame Allanic, you know that Blanche's husband was murdered yesterday. Kilian Morel."

Dupin thought he saw the hint of a nod. It was something, at least.

"Do you have any thoughts on this, madame?"

"My husband went to Rio. With his magnificent ship. He sailed around the whole world." She gave Dupin an oddly penetrating stare.

"And this morning, madame, there was another murder. The

victim was Walig Richard, the antiques dealer in Saint-Suliac.
A friend of Blanche's."

She fell silent again.

Perhaps she simply didn't have any strength left. Dupin felt
sympathy for her. The conversation was clearly tormenting her.
Dupin was tormenting her. He decided to bring it to a close.
He liked this eccentric old lady, in whose head everything had
slipped out of place, where things that didn't belong together
linked up, reassembling themselves haphazardly. For her it was a
closed world—her world. Dupin wouldn't mind getting similarly
lost in his own world when his final days came.

"How's the investigation coming along? Kilian was a good
man. Where's Lucille?"

Dupin wasn't sure he'd heard correctly. These were clear
sentences in a clear voice, concrete, realistic questions, sentences
from this world. And they were obviously directed at Dupin.

"Lucille's with the police. In investigative detainment. But
she's refusing to talk."

Madame Allanic's reaction this time was a distinct nod.

"Do you know why Lucille did it? Why she stabbed Blanche?"

Madame Allanic was silent. But it was a different silence to
before, Dupin felt. Or was he just imagining it?

"We're trying to find the motive, madame. For Lucille's act
and also the other murders. The story that could be the key to all
of it. Do you have any idea what it might be?"

Madame Allanic seemed to be agonizing over something.

"Gone."

One loudly echoing word.

"What's gone?"

"But my husband will be back. He's already on his way."

"Did you mean your husband's gone?"

It hadn't sounded like that was what she meant.

"He'll put everything straight." She seemed to be slipping away again. "I don't know which ship she's on. Blanche was so fond of the vanilla. Like my husband. Lucille, she can be very wicked."

"What do you mean by that, madame?"

She looked at him with empty eyes.

The fleeting clarity seemed to have gone—if it had ever existed.

"I won't say a word."

Dupin waited. For a long while. But the old lady remained silent.

"Thank you, Madame Allanic." Dupin decided to leave it at that. "And I can assure you we'll do everything in our power," he paused for a moment, "to put things straight again."

For a brief moment, she looked alertly at Dupin, only for her gaze to then drift off again across the Atlantic.

"*Au revoir*, madame."

She had fallen back into her rigid state. Dupin thought he saw her shiver gently, even though the temperature had risen further in the last half hour.

He turned to go.

Dupin stood alongside his car feeling slightly disoriented; the last three-quarters of an hour had been surreal. For a while, his gaze wandered around aimlessly, then he jolted himself back into action and got into his car.

It was only just past ten, so he had plenty of time. He was meeting Joe Morel at midday. Then Lucille Trouin at two.

He turned the engine on, looked at the map on the GPS, expanded a section of it. He found what he was looking for.

Three minutes later, he was there.

He had taken a lane full of deep potholes, which branched off sharply from the paved road. Before him lay the plot of land that was now useless to Lucille Trouin, and that would likely push her to financial ruin. It was a meadow, surrendered to nature, full of hedgerows and bushes that stretched all the way to the cliffs. A fantastic piece of land, almost in the same position as the aunt's—which was just a few hundred meters away as the crow flies.

Dupin walked along a narrow path toward the sea. On the right, some distance away, was a modern, elongated building with a high, tent-like roof. It must be the famous restaurant Huppert had mentioned.

He wasn't pursuing any specific plan. It was pure coincidence that the property was so close to Madame Allanic's. But it was fitting of this peculiar case that prompted him to rack his brains, to the point of feeling dizzy, over details that quite clearly weren't connected.

The plot of land was located on a plateau a good thirty meters above sea level. A solitary, solemn cross stood on an overhang that was shaped like a sharp wedge.

Dupin walked down the treacherously steep path and came to a halt by the cross. And then, accompanied by three gulls that were circling and screeching above him, he ventured an even more treacherous descent down to the sea. He wanted to find a sunny spot to sit in for a moment. Which wasn't easy; the dark rocks were craggy and sharp-edged, and he also had to watch out for the waves.

After a short while he reached an abrupt dead end—a yawning crevice separated the cliffs, cutting off his path. He had to turn around.

Between two breaking waves, Dupin heard the penetrating ringtone of his cell.

Huppert.

Dupin picked up.

"Yes?"

"Dupin, Nedellec's on the line too. The medical examiner called me regarding the time of Walig Richard's death. He's specified the window as eight to ten yesterday morning. And, even more importantly, after closely inspecting the wounds, he found clear indications that both men were killed with the same blade. Probably a large pocketknife. A nine- or ten-centimeter-long blade, which creates a small, characteristic injury."

"Then," Nedellec immediately picked up the thread, "I was right with my hypothesis. The perpetrator killed them one after the other. We just don't know who was first."

"The examiner suspects that Kilian Morel was killed a little earlier."

Dupin was distracted. It was really odd. Probably just a strange figment of his imagination. On the other side of the crevice, in one of the rocks, Dupin could see a face. At first just vaguely, but then with increasing clarity. He briefly closed his eyes. When he opened them again, he suddenly saw human features in a second stone too. And in the one alongside it. It was eerie; the entire rock overhang opposite was coming to life: faces, heads, grimaces appeared everywhere. Dupin shook himself and tried to keep a clear head.

"This means," Huppert deduced, "we're another step further with the reconstruction of yesterday morning."

Dupin wrenched his gaze away from the cliffs. Was his imagination really so overheated that he was seeing apparitions?

"The key events of our case," emphasized Huppert, "took place between Monday at one fifty in the afternoon, and Tuesday morning, seven thirty to ten. Which also means that nothing has happened in roughly the last twenty-four hours."

Dupin clambered back without even glancing over his shoulder.

"There could be another incident at any time. This could still be ongoing. And claim more victims."

Nedellec's wording sounded unnecessarily dramatic, but of course he was right.

"We'll soon find out. Nedellec, how are the conversations going with Richard's employees, friends, and acquaintances?"

Perhaps the most important question of all right now.

"I'm making good progress."

"Meaning?" Huppert pushed.

"I've spoken to all his employees, but without finding out anything significant. And I talked to Richard's best friend here in Saint-Suliac. A musician—a pianist. He's also a vintner at the same vineyard. They liked going for walks together, or sitting in the bistro on the quay. He says he has no idea what his friend could have gotten mixed up in. He saw him on Monday evening, they had a few glasses of wine together, after Blanche Trouin's death. Richard must have been devastated, understandably. His friend said that alongside the grief, pain, and bewilderment, he also noticed another emotion. An uneasiness. Very clearly, at times. And he asked him about it. But Richard was evasive."

"Could it have been fear?" Dupin had—panting a little— reached the cross on the overhang.

"He just referred to it as an unease. The pianist was with him until eleven at night, then Richard wanted to be alone. By the way, he told his friend he was planning to go to the vineyard the next morning. Which he didn't consider unusual, as Richard loved the place, the hills, the vines, the solitude there. And he liked going there early in the morning. His friend presumed he wanted to take his mind off things. It was clearly a meditative place for him."

"Good. Whom else are you meeting with, Nedellec?"

"The mayor next, whom Richard knew really well. Then his neighbors. I'll call with an update later."

"Okay. And Dupin, how was your visit with the aunt?"

"There's not a great deal to tell."

Dupin struggled to give a proper account of it.

"I suggest we talk in detail after the interrogation with Lucille Trouin. Agreed, everyone?" A rhetorical question.

She had already hung up.

Dupin was back in the meadow. On Lucille Trouin's land. He glanced at the time: 10:35. Still a little early, but he would set off for Cancale regardless.

Dupin left the D201 just north of Cancale. He drove directly down to the harbor, straight toward the Atlantic. The street was lined by little white houses, which had presumably been built by oyster fishermen. He soon reached the shore, or more specifically:

the wide promenade, fortified by an imposing quay wall, which stretched along the whole neighborhood.

Dupin took an instant liking to the atmosphere here. The mecca of the oyster world—together with Belon, of course—an iconic shrine for oyster lovers, of which Dupin was definitely one. There they lay, in front of the quay wall, Cancale's famed, extensive oyster banks. The sea floor of the infamous Baie de Cancale, through which the Breton-Normandy border ran, consisted of nothing but white sand.

Dupin got lucky, immediately finding a free parking space next to the promenade. Joe Morel's oyster bar had to be somewhere around here. He got out, walked over to the edge of the quay, and stopped.

Now, at high tide, the Atlantic was streaming over the oyster banks. The oysters fed on plankton, for hours on end, the smallest of particles. Then they lay exposed to the air for hours, which today meant the hot sun. The banks were visible as dark shadows on the sea floor. In the Cancale bay, the tides showed off with all their might; depending on the coefficient, they reached Breton record status here, and not only that: with a tidal range of over twelve meters, the bay ranked in second place on the global tidal rating.

The view was captivating, the air lucid. You could see how far the bay stretched out, its impressive breadth. The gaze was drawn to the coast opposite; the shimmering beaches there belonged to Normandy. The silhouette of the legendary Mont Saint-Michel could be clearly seen. The ocean was as smooth as a mirror, like oil. No trace of the emerald green; a pure aquamarine dominated, with increasing patches of blue toward the horizon.

The landscape had a completely different feel to what Dupin knew from the rest of Brittany; it didn't seem at all Breton-like. This is where Brittany came to an end; that was the melancholic feeling. Perhaps it was the English Channel, that typical Channel atmosphere, becoming tangible here. Or, and this was also possible, you only felt the end of Brittany because you knew it ended here.

The proximity to Normandy made Dupin think of Claire. "His" Normandin.

He decided to try and catch her. Admittedly it was five in the morning where she was, but that at least made it likely she wasn't out and about.

He dialed the number. Waited. Once again, her voicemail kicked in.

Was she really so fast asleep? She usually heard the phone; an occupational hazard of being a cardiologist. But not on this occasion.

"Claire, it's me." He hadn't actually wanted to leave another message. "It's lovely to hear your voice—at least on here." What a stupid thing to say. "I hope you're doing well." An empty phrase. "I'll try you again later. Kisses."

He hung up. It was depressing.

Tucking his cell phone away, Dupin made his way toward the pier, which stretched far out into the sea. Only at the very tip of it did he come to a halt. A few of the oyster fishing boats were tied to the pier.

He ran through the day so far in his mind: Walig Richard's murder—he'd been "uneasy," his friend had said; had Richard seen it coming?—and the inspection of the antiques shop; the telephone call with Flore Briard; and, of course, the disquieting visit to the old lady.

Dupin watched three large red tractors driving along the coastal road. He headed back toward the quay. A dozen stands were set up at the start of the pier, selling fresh oysters. The canvas tents kept strictly to the Atlantic color scheme, predominantly blue and white. Large wooden crates contained oysters of differing sizes and varieties, and signs over the stands indicated the names of the respective oyster fishers. There was a wonderful atmosphere. The air carried the scent of the seaweed and algae on which the oysters were presented in the crates.

Dupin ran his hand across his forehead; he was sweating. Before long the walk would no longer feel pleasant; it was getting even hotter. He looked out for a café.

At 11:47, after two *petit cafés* and further intense ruminations, he was standing in front of Joe Morel's oyster bar. La Cabane des Huîtres.

The building's façade consisted of white-painted wood, everything simple and unfussy. Chairs and stools at a long bar. A small terrace with three tables; any more wouldn't have fit. There were still only a few guests, but it would soon pick up with the lunchtime service.

Dupin stepped in, then came to an abrupt halt.

A familiar face was heading toward him.

Flore Briard.

"What a funny coincidence, Monsieur le Commissaire. Given we were only just speaking on the phone." She paused right in front of him, in a pale yellow dress, large Creole earrings, and high espadrilles. She was wearing her blond hair down today, and a lighthearted smile. The situation didn't seem to be making her uncomfortable in the slightest.

"What are you doing here?" he blurted out.

"I was in the area for a meeting with my oyster supplier. Life must go on, after all. So I popped in to see Joe. It was lovely to see him. He's back there in the courtyard." She gestured toward a narrow corridor at the far end of the room. "I'm sure he'll be out in a moment."

Numerous questions danced on Dupin's tongue. But was it worth probing further? It could, of course, be just as Flore Briard had described it. Still, it was a little suspicious.

"Who's your oyster supplier?"

Not even his curt follow-up question seemed to rattle her.

"Marcel Duché. He also has a stand out there on the quay."

"And you get the oysters for your boat trips from him?"

"Exactly."

"Not through Lucille's restaurant?"

"No, directly. But he's the same trader. We both know him well."

"What were you talking to Joe Morel about?"

"About how terrible all of this is"—she spoke in a hushed tone now—"terrible and mysterious. By the way, just so you don't find out afterward and agonize over it: I'm just about to go and meet Charles Braz. In Lucille's restaurant. We felt the need to talk."

This meant that three of the four suspects would soon be in the same locale. Colomb Clément, the sous-chef, was in the kitchen. And Flore Briard had just visited the fourth here. Curious occurrences. There could be something behind them—or nothing at all.

"I see."

Dupin had endeavored to sound as masterful as possible.

"Okay—then, see you soon, Commissaire—you'd best go find Joe in the courtyard. It's just through the kitchen."

Dupin nodded and made his way toward the corridor.

He stepped through a swing door into a large room. On one side, there was a professional kitchen unit, on the other, an old wooden table with four chairs and a somewhat tired-looking black leather sofa. A young man and a young woman, who were working at the long counter, blinked at him with surprise.

"The toilets are to the left along the corridor."

The woman had a shucking knife in her hand, and was in the process of opening a Creuse oyster. In front of her was a wooden crate containing an impressive quantity of them.

"I'm here to see Joe Morel."

With a minimal head movement, she nodded toward the open door that led outside.

A moment later, Dupin was in the courtyard.

Joe Morel was sitting at a small blue table. He was leaning back, a cigarette in his hand, his legs outstretched.

Dupin stepped toward him.

"*Bonjour*, Monsieur Morel."

"Commissaire Georges Dupin. We have a meeting, I know. Your colleague was here yesterday." His voice sounded raspy.

Their gazes met. Morel wore old, worn-out jeans with a rip in one knee, and a black T-shirt. Athletic build, slim, certainly one-eighty in height. He looked younger than his forty-two years. Thick, tousled hair, as though he had only just got out of bed, defined cheekbones. And yet there was something uniquely gentle in his features. To top it off, he had sparkling bright blue eyes, which for sure dozens of women had fallen in love with.

"My sincere condolences on the loss of your brother, Monsieur Morel. And your sister-in-law."

He really had been hit hard by this.

Morel pulled a packet of cigarettes out of his trouser pocket and lit a new one. An empty espresso cup rested next to an ashtray.

"Thanks."

His sitting posture had remained unchanged. Dupin was now standing directly in front of him. It was a small garden, tucked away behind the building, with stubbly grass, high stone walls to the right and left, and two long palms that seemed slightly out of place.

"You're working? Despite everything?"

"What else am I supposed to do?" Morel answered. "It's my store."

Dupin decided to sit down on the chair opposite him.

"Are you back together with Lucille Trouin, Monsieur Morel?"

Morel looked at Dupin.

"No. But we get on well." He took a drag of the cigarette and inhaled deeply.

"Are you friends?"

Morel breathed the smoke out slowly.

"Friends is a bit of an exaggeration. We've seen each other two or three times over the last six months."

"And Blanche and your brother knew that you sometimes met up?"

"I didn't tell them."

"Not even Blanche?"

"Not even Blanche."

He took another long drag of his cigarette. His hands were remarkably steady.

"Your sister-in-law Blanche was also one of your close friends."

"Yes." His gaze drifted past Dupin. "We saw each other almost every week, mostly in some bar or another, or had dinner together. Sometimes we went out on my boat."

"Did she confide in you?"

"Presumably not about everything, but a lot."

"And from what she'd told you recently, is there anything that could be connected with what's been happening?"

Dupin knew this was quite an abstract question. But Nedellec had already discussed everything concrete—the recipes, the matter of the sous-chef—with Joe Morel yesterday.

"I wouldn't know what."

"Did Blanche seem different to you recently at all?"

"No. Not at all. I saw her last Monday."

"And you didn't feel guilty"—Dupin came back to the previous point—"about meeting with Lucille again and not telling your sister-in-law about it?"

"It would have made things unnecessarily complicated again. And it's also completely uninteresting. Sometimes the two of them just went a bit nuts."

"Because of all the competition between them?"

A nod. "Like kids—but deadly serious. Blanche knew that's how I saw it. She was okay with that."

"Is it possible that Blanche heard about your contact with Lucille from someone else?"

"I wouldn't have thought so. But obviously I can't rule it out. In any case, Blanche never challenged me on it."

"And she would have?"

Morel cocked his head to the side. "Definitely. Or maybe not, I don't know."

"When exactly did you last see Lucille?"

"Two or three weeks ago. She dropped in spontaneously because she was in the area. It was a short visit."

Evidently lots of people dropped in when they were "in the area."

"And nothing of what she said now echoes strangely, after all the terrible events?"

"No."

"Did Lucille tell you anything about having bought a plot of land in Rothéneuf?"

"No."

Joe Morel stubbed out the cigarette. And sat just a little bit more upright.

"Would you say your relationship with your brother was a close one, Monsieur Morel?"

He took his time with the answer, closing his eyes.

"I liked him. Very much. We got on well, always had really. But I wouldn't say we were very close."

That could mean everything and nothing.

"How often did you see each other?"

He seemed to be thinking it over. "Maybe once every two months. Mostly he came by here. Whenever I was in Dinard, I went to see him—at his place, I mean."

"When did you last see him?"

"About a month ago. We had some oysters here together."

Morel really didn't seem the type to show his emotions. And yet Dupin could feel his grief regardless.

"He didn't tell you about anything unusual? Any worries, financial difficulties, conflicts?"

"No."

Dupin had been sitting down for long enough. Abruptly, he stood up. "Now you'll inherit everything from your brother. Who in turn inherited everything from his wife. That'll be quite some sum."

Morel shrugged. "Could be. Yes."

"You don't have a proper alibi for yesterday morning."

"I've made a statement about where I was and when, and what I was doing." He slumped back down into his relaxed posture and took another cigarette. "You can believe me or not. There's nothing else I can tell you."

"You're aware that the quite considerable inheritance makes you a key suspect?"

Another shrug of the shoulders. Nothing more.

"What will you do with the restaurant? The spice business? The online shop?"

"Sell them, I think." He already sounded decided.

"Right away?"

"I think so. I don't want to have to spend time on them. My bar's enough for me."

There was always something brutal to it: a person had put their heart and soul into building something up, over the years, over the decades, dedicated their entire life to it—and a sudden death made it all null and void.

"Don't you want to expand your business? You'd have the money for it now."

"Definitely not."

"You live here in Cancale, right?" Dupin was walking up and down in the courtyard; Morel followed him with his gaze.

"Yes, just over there." He pointed vaguely toward the street at the back. "The house is mine."

"How well did you know Walig Richard?"

"He wasn't really my cup of tea. And Blanche knew that. It was okay. To be honest, I rarely saw him. But he meant a lot to Blanche."

"Are you in a relationship at the moment, Monsieur Morel?"

"No."

During the conversation, a frustration had been rising in Dupin. He felt they were still only scratching the surface.

"Flore Briard—is she just a friend?"

"Yes."

"She was just here. Had you planned to meet?"

They wouldn't have had time to agree on a story, and Dupin knew that.

"No. She just popped in. Very briefly."

"What was she doing here in Cancale?"

"Her oyster supplier's based here."

"And what did you talk about?"

"We didn't talk much. Flore's very upset."

"And you're not?"

"Of course I am."

Dupin's mood had become even more dejected. Everything was so incredibly arduous.

"That's all for the time being, Monsieur Morel. We'll be in touch."

"Fine." Morel, who seemed unfazed by the conversation's abrupt end, stood up. "It's just straight through there."

"I'll find my way."

Dupin left the bar and reached for his cell phone. He dialed Huppert's number.

"What is it, Dupin?"

"Can you send someone to La Noblesse to discreetly watch a couple of people there?"

Dupin was fed up; they had to change their approach. Be more aggressive.

"Who and why?" A calm follow-up question.

"Charles Braz and Flore Briard, they're meeting there for lunch. Colomb Clément will be in the kitchen."

In all likelihood, this would be futile too. If Braz and Briard were involved in the murders—or even Clément too—and wanted to discuss something delicate, then they would choose a different location. Not in public, not Lucille's restaurant. On the other hand: sometimes the most conspicuous thing attracted the least suspicion.

"Okay. I'll send someone."

"Right away?"

"Right away."

"I'll call again later."

Dupin hung up.

Without thinking about it, he headed to the left.

Dupin reached the colorful oyster stalls on the shore. Ever since he'd got out of the car in Cancale, his mouth had been watering again and again. The oysters were omnipresent; in the ocean, in the bars and restaurants, on the stalls, the advertising signs . . .

Perhaps it was sensible, even, to give in to temptation. Their meeting with Lucille was at two, and he should definitely eat something before then. He needed to have all his wits about him. What's more: nothing in the world nourished the tiny gray cells more efficiently than oysters. They were the best brain food.

He made his way decisively toward one of the stalls, where there was already significantly more hustle and bustle. The midday trade had begun. "Huîtres Simon" looked very promising. The taut fabric on the stall shone a dark blue with yellow stripes—and, together with the turquoise blue of the bay, created an atmospheric play of color.

"Six Plates and six Creuses, please."

With this one sentence, his mood improved immeasurably.

The man countered the order with the obligatory question: "A bottle of Muscadet with that? Or just a glass?"

Dupin turned both down with a heavy heart. He had to be fully focused for the interrogation.

He took a place at one of the standing tables, and was swiftly served the large plate of oysters, a basket with some baguette, a small jug of water, and the vinaigrette for the oysters. And—a glass of Muscadet. Dupin was just about to protest—but things were so busy here he would only create confusion; it wasn't worth it.

He drank a sip. Heavenly. Everything was just as it should be: the wine was perfectly chilled and tasted a little citrusy, the best preparation for his taste buds ahead of the first—famous!— oyster.

Dupin let his gaze wander across the wide bay, half Brittany, half Normandy. But soon, on his second oyster, his mind was once again occupied with the complexities of the case.

The Commissariat de Police Saint-Malo was in Rue du Calvaire, at the intersection with Boulevard Théodore Botrel—it was a modern, tall building constructed at an unusually sharp angle around the corner. The entrance was made entirely of glass, with the Tricolore resplendent above—*bleu, blanc, rouge*. The premises were part of the same complex as the police school. It felt to Dupin as though many weeks had passed since he'd sat in the seminar room; it seemed so incredibly long ago.

His short break at the oyster stall had played out differently than expected. He hadn't managed to get into any intense contemplation, as two calls had come in, one after the other. The first from Nedellec, with Huppert also on the line. The commissaire had succinctly reported back on his conversations with the friends and acquaintances of the antiques dealer, where nothing of note had arisen. Then, Huppert had informed them about the analysis of Walig Richard's cell phone records: apart from the phone calls with Blanche Trouin and her husband, Kilian Morel, which they already knew about, there were no other calls of interest. And still no sign of the cell phone itself.

After that, Nolwenn had called to remind Dupin, with great emphasis, about his home team's ongoing willingness to lend a hand.

Dupin was just a few meters away from the entrance to the police station when the glass sliding door swept open and Commissaire Huppert came hurrying toward him:

"You're cutting it a bit fine."

It was 1:57; he was perfectly on time.

"Follow me. I'll take you there. I think we should confront Lucille with everything we know so far," began Huppert, as they made their way to the elevator.

"That would be my approach too."

They needed strong ammunition for this conversation. And

the strongest they had was their knowledge about the plot of land and Trouin's financial situation.

They got out on the third floor.

"I'm in the room next door. Trouin's attorney, Monsieur Giscard, is already there."

In truth Dupin couldn't stand it when he had to do observed interrogations, but that wasn't important now. At least he would be speaking to Lucille Trouin alone.

They turned down a corridor, and at the end of it Commissaire Huppert came to a sudden halt.

"Room 318—here. They're already inside. With two police officers for the moment. As I said, I'm next door if you need me."

Dupin nodded and reached for the door handle. He was relieved; he had been expecting a more exhaustive pre-discussion.

He stepped in.

A long, narrow table, with three chairs on each side. Just one window, looking out over Rue du Calvaire. Dupin would sit with his back to the large mirror, through which the others were watching him; Lucille Trouin and her attorney were already sitting opposite.

The attorney, in an elegant suit with designer stubble, had gotten up as soon as Dupin entered and now came toward him.

"René Giscard. You know my client doesn't want to give a statement on the incident. So we see no reason for a renewed interrogation."

The two police officers who had been standing by the table left the room.

"We know that, monsieur. We know that."

Without any sign of haste, Dupin sat down and shifted his chair until he was directly opposite Lucille Trouin. She was an incredibly attractive woman, whom he would have estimated as being in her mid-thirties, not forty-two. Jet-black, shoulder-length hair, with a slight auburn sheen, if you looked closely. Big, dark brown eyes that were very close to black, eyebrows skillfully emphasized with pencil. A simple but elegant black pullover, a plain silver chain with a single, impressive stone, black jeans. She stared out of the window, her expression empty.

"My name is Georges Dupin, I'm one of the investigating commissaires. *Bonjour,* Madame Trouin."

She turned toward him, at least. It was impossible to read even the slightest hint of emotion in her face; Dupin had rarely seen such a neutral expression. Her immaculately made-up lips didn't move.

"Madame Trouin," the attorney took over, "has already been questioned by Commissaire Huppert, and as I said, doesn't wish to—"

"We know," Dupin interrupted in a calm tone, "about your financial ruin, the fiasco with the plot of land. We know you urgently need money in order not to lose everything. Everything you've built up is at stake." Dupin had fixed his gaze solely on Lucille, as though her attorney didn't even exist. "What's more, your bankruptcy would have meant, and this would perhaps have been the worst element, losing the lifelong, bitter feud with your sister. Your drastic financial situation must surely have played a decisive role in what you did." Dupin had to escalate things like this, there was no other way. "We doubt that your act was a crime of passion after all, and are investigating correspondingly. We also see the murders of Kilian Morel and Walig Richard as connected. It's just a matter of time until we get to the bottom of it all."

It was a shot in the dark. But that didn't matter: Dupin's aim was to trigger something within Lucille Trouin. If possible, to break down her reserve. She was a murderer. And she was keeping her silence. They had to break it.

Dupin waited.

Madame Trouin hadn't even blinked as he spoke.

He waited. Until the point where his words began to fade away, to lose force. In that very moment, he continued:

"We also know that your sister stole your sous-chef from you. Clément had signed the contract and would soon have been working for Blanche. And, in addition, we know that you ended your relationship with your partner and have been meeting with Joe Morel."

Once again, his aim was for the most intense provocation, to trigger the greatest discomfort. And anger. Dupin needed to make as much noise as possible.

"And finally," this—if she didn't already know—was sure to hit her hard, "we've found out about the imminent publication of your father's recipes, which your sister had been working on with a well-known publishing house. She was planning to show the whole world that she was the better chef."

A leaden silence. Lucille still seemed fully composed. It was unsettling.

"I don't understand what you're driving at, Commissaire." The attorney eventually interrupted the silence. "Why are you telling . . ."

Dupin stood up abruptly. The chair almost tipped over, clattering loudly back down.

"That's all from our side." He continued to ignore the attorney, looking Lucille Trouin directly in the eyes. "Madame, thank you."

Dupin went toward the door, and a moment later had left the room.

It had been a conscious, albeit spontaneous decision not to ask Lucille any questions, which she could once again have refused to answer. She had been playing that game for too long already—because, of course, it was a game that she was playing with them. All that remained was to wait and see whether he had aggravated her enough to make her speak.

He walked back down the corridor, in urgent need of fresh air. A door was flung open behind him, and Huppert quickly caught up with him. Dupin wasn't in the mood for a post-mission critique.

"That was a clever move, Dupin."

She looked at him from the side.

"But a dangerous one too. You really pushed her to the limit. Let's see what comes of it."

The critical postscript almost entirely qualified the praise she'd given.

They had reached the elevator.

"I'm in the process of examining Walig Richard's finances." Huppert changed the subject. "I've agreed with Nedellec that we'll meet at four in my office. By the way, I heard from my colleague who was watching Flore Briard and Charles Braz in La Noblesse. Unfortunately he was unable to get a seat where he could've heard their conversation—he said they were sitting at a table for two in a tucked-away niche."

Exactly as people do when they don't want to be overheard.

"And the sous-chef didn't come out even once."

"How did they seem with each other?"

Huppert obviously knew what Dupin meant: "Close, certainly, but my colleague couldn't make out any indications of a romantic relationship."

It had been worth a try.

"I'll bring Nedellec up to speed now."

"Speak later . . ." Dupin was just about to turn away when something occurred to him. "One more thing, Huppert."

He lowered his voice. He couldn't get it out of his mind; the experience had been too peculiar.

"Between Lucille Trouin's plot of land and the aunt's house, on the cliffs right by the ocean, I saw something . . ." He pondered how to best formulate the question.

Huppert spared him the ruminations:

"You weren't hallucinating, Dupin, don't worry. Toward the end of the nineteenth century, a monk chiseled three hundred stone sculptures into the rocks. If anything, he was the one who was delirious."

"I—thank you."

Dupin was relieved, even though the monk sounded a little sinister.

He said good-bye to Huppert, took a step forward, and the door of the police station glided soundlessly open.

Dupin had turned right, toward the kilometer-long beach that stretched all the way to Rothéneuf. It didn't take him long to reach it; the Ville Close lay to his left and, slightly in front, the powerful Fort National. He would use the next hour to go for a walk; for Dupin, this was the best way of thinking.

An unmissable sign greeted him as he stepped onto the beach: "*Grand Plage du Sillon—La plus belle plage de la France.*" Even the beach had won an award; a great accolade.

As Dupin replayed the interrogation in his mind, he began to feel more and more dissatisfied. Perhaps he should have given it a little more time at the end, to allow something to develop. By breaking it off abruptly like he had, perhaps he'd ruined everything. On the other hand: maybe it had triggered something in Lucille Trouin, and his approach might still pay off.

The overall course of the investigation was making him increasingly unhappy. Of course, there were moments of despondency in every investigation, but this time their progress seemed more hopeless than Dupin had ever experienced. The police statistics made it abundantly clear: with every hour that passed after a crime without the police shedding light on it, the chances that it would ever be solved sank drastically. Dupin felt resignation, but also an uprising against it, a fierce, desperate agitation.

The sand was unusually fine, and Dupin sank deeply into it. The Plage du Sillon was worthy of its honors; it was wonderfully long and wide, a true city beach. To the right were magnificent houses and villas. In front of the quay, which protected it from the raging tides, dense rows of tree trunks had been driven into the sand as an extra defense.

The beach had filled with the first holidaymakers, the weather prompting a summerlike cheerfulness. People were sunbathing, strolling, reading, children were playing, a few particularly brave individuals were even venturing into the water, which was divided into two colors today. A band of glittering turquoise near the shore, and a band of emerald green farther out. The sky was an intense blue, an even tone without shadows or nuances, resembling a painted backdrop.

Dupin was just reaching a flat rock ledge that overhung the water—he had been walking for a good twenty minutes now—when his phone rang.

It was Commissaire Huppert.

"What's up?"

"She wants to talk, Dupin. Right now. I'm just going to 318. Lucille Trouin requested a private word with her attorney right after you left."

"I'm on my way."

Dupin had already turned around and was hurrying back.

"It's best we don't wait." Huppert was out of breath. She seemed to be running. "I'll go in immediately. And I'll call you soon."

Before Dupin had a chance to reply, she was already gone.

Finally, something was happening.

A quarter of an hour later, as he turned in to the street where the police station was located, his phone rang again.

Huppert. He picked up at once.

"She's made a statement."

"And?" Dupin's nerves were stretched to the limit.

"She says it was a crime of passion. A sudden, irrational act. That she wasn't aware of what she was doing. Like she was in a trance. All she felt was rage and contempt. In the moment, all the indignities, slights, and hurt that had built up over the years and decades just erupted."

The way Huppert emphasized the words betrayed what she thought of the statement: namely, not much.

"She says that in the weeks beforehand she was so worn

down by her financial problems that she'd become mentally un-stable, and that she couldn't sleep for nights on end. She cited practically everything you can find in the judicial forensic sci-ence textbooks on 'victim situations' and 'explosive reactions,' every key term you can imagine."

"And what was the alleged trigger for this 'explosion'? What provoked the crime of passion?"

Dupin could already see the police station.

"Yes, well—here it comes. Brace yourself." Huppert's voice had taken on a peculiar tone. "She says she found out about the publication of the recipes last Sunday."

"Incredible. I don't believe a word of it."

"Wait, it gets even better. She was beside herself then al-ready, which is why she went to the market stall on Monday, where Blanche not only 'shamelessly confirmed' it all, but also told her about stealing Clément away. That, apparently, was the final straw. She completely lost it, and that's how the 'terrible drama' came about."

Dupin had come to a halt just a few meters away from the station. He was lost for words.

"After her confession, the tears flowed. She swore that she feels awful and wishes she could take back what she did. It's laughable. Anyway, Trouin now wants to speak with the psy-chologist she previously refused to say a word to. She was in a 'state of shock,' she says—and that was the only reason she hasn't spoken before now. She was simply incapable of saying anything. She claims that your 'vigorous outburst' earlier helped her to re-gain her senses. And to make the confession."

It was monstrous. And it exceeded all the brazenness Du-pin had ever experienced with perpetrators. Without hesitating,

Trouin had turned the tables and used—or rather, abused—his information to create a plausible reconstruction of a pure crime of passion. It didn't get more perfidious than that. Could he have predicted this? Either way, without intending to, he had helped her out of the tight spot. It became clear to him only now: after the crime, she couldn't simply have invented a "trigger" without taking the risk of being caught in a lie. That's why she'd *had* to remain silent. In order not to risk anything.

"She didn't know about either!" Dupin was furious. No one had ever made him look like this. Like a complete idiot. She was making fun of him. And she was approaching it very intelligently. Because how would they ever be able to prove the opposite of what she'd said? It was humiliating.

"Of course not. She didn't know about any of it." Huppert's confirmation unfortunately held no trace of consolation. "But it's come at just the right time for her."

Dupin was still standing there as though he'd been hit by lightning.

"And who allegedly told her about the recipes?"

"She didn't want to say, apparently in order to protect the person, who had nothing to do with the whole thing."

"That's complete and utter nonsense."

Dupin had started walking again. Not to the entrance of the police station, but back toward the beach.

"Shrewd, though."

It certainly was.

"Did she say anything about the other two murders?"

"Just that it's all very tragic and she doesn't have the slightest idea what's going on. That's when she ended the conversation. It's clear what position she's planning to take," Huppert summarized drily. "Crime of passion equals diminished culpability equals a significantly reduced sentence—and she has nothing to do with the other two murders. You've handed her on a silver platter what she was so far lacking: the plausible catalyst for the crime of passion. We'll see each other later, Dupin. Four o'clock."

She had hung up. Clearly, she was no longer expecting him at the station.

Just a short while later, Dupin walked onto the most beautiful beach in France for the second time. Compared with the state he was in now, his downbeat mood during the first beach stroll had been a joke, a fleeting gray shadow. This time, a colossal, pitch-black monster of a cloud hung over his mind.

He pulled out his phone and dialed Nolwenn's number.

"Monsieur le Commissaire, how are things going?"

Dupin hesitated. Where to begin?

"What's happened?"

He pulled himself together and recounted the interrogation debacle. And then everything else that had happened since their last phone conversation.

Nolwenn was silent throughout; no questions, no analysis, no comments. Then she said, "Well. That's Saint-Malo for you. Even the criminals there operate only in the superlative. All five of us are here, by the way. I've put my phone on speaker. We've got your back."

Dupin almost felt sentimental.

"Always remember: *Pa v ear fallán an amzer—E vezer an tostan d'an amzer gaer*, Monsieur le Commissaire. Right when the storm can't get any worse, that's when you're closest to the sunshine. It's true!"

A Breton saying. At least some things were the same as ever. And it was a particularly wise one, at that. It helped a little.

"Okay, so . . ."

"Riwal wants to speak to you."

She had already passed the phone along.

"*Salut*, boss," the inspector greeted him in a forcibly cheery tone. "You'll figure things out!" A well-meaning attempt. "Kadeg just forwarded me a newspaper article from last week. On the underwater sandbank, not far from the two frigates *Dauphone* and *Aimable Grenot*, which were discovered back in 1995, they've found another boat from the corsair era. Less than twenty kilometers from Saint-Malo! It probably sank around the same time. At the beginning of the eighteenth century. I have no idea how I could have missed the report."

"And?"

"It seems there's a mountain of treasure in the boat. They've already salvaged some gold and silver, and jewelry too. Diamonds, emeralds, rubies. There's even supposed to be some connection to the Duguay-Trouin corsair clan. But that's probably pure speculation, one—"

"Was there anything else, Riwal?"

"The electric fence at ankle height was a complete non-starter, boss."

"What electric fence . . ." Dupin broke off as he remembered. The badger! Of course.

"He was back again last night."

"Don't lose heart, Riwal."

For a moment, Dupin really had felt distracted from his own disaster.

"Don't worry, boss. Tonight will be a very special evening

for you. You'll be cooked for by Hugo Roellinger in Le Coquillage."

It had completely slipped his mind. It felt fundamentally absurd to go out for a fancy dinner after a day like today.

"Hugo Roellinger grew up among the legends of the corsairs, apparently in the same house in Cancale where the immortal privateer Robert Surcouf played as a child. Roellinger worked at sea for years before he followed in the footsteps of his father Olivier, an almost unearthly three-Michelin-star chef, by becoming a chef himself. With two stars of his own by now."

Dupin remembered the remarks of Huppert's assistant; she had mentioned the Roellingers.

"He says his main inspiration is the horizon. Make sure you get the lobster with cacao and chili three ways with sherry sauce. You've never had anything like it. An homage to the great seafarer Daniel de la Touche, who set sail from Cancale and came back with boats full of cacao, vanilla, and chili." Riwal seemed to be making the most of the fact that Dupin was letting him ramble on. "And bring back some of the heavenly spice mixes made by his father! You won't find better anywhere in the world—"

"Thank you, Riwal." Now it really was time to interject. "I have to go."

"Okay, boss." The inspector took it on the chin. "Good luck!"

"Speak later."

Dupin was still riled up. And in urgent need of a *café*.

In no time at all, Dupin had found a nice bar on the promenade, drunk two *petits cafés,* calmed down a little, and sunk back into feverish ruminations.

At 3:40 he finally set off, and at 3:59, entered the police

station for the second time. This time without being greeted; he'd needed to ask the way.

The meeting took place in Huppert's office, on the second floor, directly above the entrance. It was a generously sized room with windows overlooking both streets, furnished with emphatically modern office furniture.

The commissaire was sitting at her desk. Nedellec and Dupin took their places opposite.

They had proceeded just like the day before: first, recounting everything in order, reduced down to the facts.

Huppert had managed—once again in the gray zone of police work, Dupin presumed—to get at least a vague overview of Walig Richard's finances, as well as those of Colomb Clément, Charles Braz, and Joe Morel. So far, without discovering anything conspicuous. She had also told them about the final report from the forensics team. Nothing unusual had been found in either the vineyard, Richard's two antiques stores, or his home, and there was no indication that the perpetrator had searched them.

Finally, she had talked about the interrogation disaster.

"Well, that certainly backfired." Nedellec couldn't hold back a comment, albeit while giving Dupin a sympathetic glance. "So what do we do now?"

"We can't sit around waiting to see whether something else happens—and for the murderer to finally make a mistake."

Commissaire Huppert had said precisely what was on Dupin's mind.

It was grotesque: a brutal murderer out there somewhere, and in here sat three competent, experienced commissaires who were on the brink of giving up hope.

"We have to go through everything again. Starting from the beginning." Nedellec now sounded admirably constructive. "Speak with everyone again."

It was an act of pure desperation. But what else could they do? As they didn't have any new leads, they'd have to pore over everything again in minute detail. Maybe they'd overlooked something? Perhaps they had already found the key to this infuriating case?

"Okay," Huppert agreed listlessly. "We'll analyze everything again, try it from a different angle. We're meeting the prefects at seven o'clock. In Saint-Méloir-des-Ondes, right by Cancale. In Le Coquillage. We've got time before then."

"You mean, we're going through everything again together?" Dupin's gaze fell on the large flip chart next to Huppert's desk—his idea of a nightmare.

"I'll fetch coffee, and then . . ."

Huppert was interrupted by the shrill ringtone of her cell.

"Yes?"

She listened. Her expression froze.

"At Pointe du Grouin?"

The person at the other end of the phone seemed to be answering in detail.

"I understand." Huppert's tone had changed. Something wasn't right.

"Okay, yes, we're on our way."

She jumped up and made her way toward the door.

"Charles Braz! He was found a few minutes ago. He's dead!"

Her hand was already on the door handle. The two other commissaires reacted instantaneously and were right behind her.

They hurried along the corridor. "He fell from the cliffs. At Pointe du Grouin, between Rothéneuf and Cancale. They're the highest in the region."

They had reached the stairwell.

"Who found him?" Dupin was utterly focused.

"A couple from Alsace. They were hiking the coastal path. It's quite an isolated area. And today most of the holidaymakers are at the beach." Huppert was taking two steps at once. "It must've only just happened, or at least that's how it looks. Two officers from Cancale are at the scene."

It couldn't have been much longer than that. Braz had been in the restaurant with Flore Briard until half past two.

Dupin was running alongside Huppert. "Did the police find his car there?"

"It's up at the side of the road, properly parked."

"I'll call Flore Briard. She was with him earlier."

They had arrived downstairs.

"Are there any signs of a struggle? Any indications that he was pushed?"

It was a notorious quirk of Dupin's, asking for details when no one was able to answer them yet.

"The police officers only just got there," Huppert replied calmly. She turned and dashed over to her car. "See you both there."

She was already gone.

Fifteen minutes later, Dupin was the first of the three commissaires to park at the side of the coastal road that crossed the high plateau between Cancale and Saint-Malo. He left his car directly behind the police cars and ambulance.

Charles Braz's Volvo was a little distance away. The gendarmes had cordoned off the entire section of road. The forensics team would search scrupulously for evidence of a second car having been there. If it had been murder—and this was surely the most convincing hypothesis at present, even if the murderer hadn't used a knife this time—there were two possible scenarios: either the perpetrator had come here with Braz, or in their own car. The question of whether the previous two murders had been the last had been gruesomely answered: this was still ongoing. Someone was unwaveringly following a merciless plan, seemingly without much fear of being caught.

Flore Briard's phone had been constantly engaged; Dupin had tried again and again.

He got out of the car. A brisk wind immediately gripped him. He saw a vast coastal cliff—steeply descending, seventy meters high for sure—infinitely more rugged than the other stretches of coast he had seen over the past few days; a surprising landscape, especially in contrast to the shallow, gentle bay of Cancale just a few kilometers away.

He needed to find a safe descent down to the coastal path, and from there, farther down to the water.

Two cars came to a halt just behind him. Nedellec and Huppert.

"What are you waiting for?" The commissaire jumped out of her car. "Along here."

She ran ahead.

"On the drive here I gave orders for Briard, Clément, and Morel to be brought to the station for further questioning. They're the only three left. Even though we don't yet know the connection: they're prime suspects, and there's a flight risk. If they make a fuss, I'll have them temporarily detained." Huppert spoke calmly, as though she had all the time in the world. "We'll question them together later, including about their alibis for this afternoon."

It was serious, and Huppert had made the right decision. The circle of suspects had shrunk further still. Even more critical was the fact that, this afternoon, all three of them had been relatively close to the latest crime scene—even if their precise alibis weren't yet known.

The three commissaires had reached the coastal path, which was also cordoned off, and were now headed in the direction of Saint-Malo.

Behind a towering cliff overhang, they were awaited by two police officers.

"He must have fallen from over there," said the older, corpulent officer, pointing toward a spot around twenty meters away that was marked with a neon yellow sign. "In any case, he was lying directly underneath it."

"Forensics are nearly here." His younger, equally corpulent colleague spoke up. "There are lots of incredibly sharp rocks down there. He had no chance. There was a suicide in almost exactly this spot around seven years ago, by the way."

"A suicide, right here?" Dupin blurted out.

"It's the ideal place for it." The policeman paused briefly. "If you see what I mean. Of course, it would also be perfect for murder."

"Is the medical examiner here yet?" Huppert wanted to know.

"Should be arriving soon."

Nedellec had already walked a little farther along the coastal path, taking immense care to stay on the left-hand side, away from the cliff edge, so as not to disturb any potential evidence.

Dupin followed.

"I'm going down to the rocks." Huppert walked back along the path the way they had come. There must be a path there somewhere; she seemed to know the area like the back of her hand.

Dupin reached the marker, a folded neon yellow vest.

This was the spot.

He crouched down next to Nedellec. The path here was seventy centimeters wide at most, and consisted of well-trodden earth and stones, some short, scrubby grass at the sides. From the edge of the path, it was less than thirty centimeters to the cliff edge.

At first glance, there didn't seem to be any obvious clues. On one spot where the path transitioned into grass, there was a small scuff of earth, perhaps a centimeter high. It could have been caused by the tip of a shoe, a heavy tread. It was too small to judge clearly.

Someone really could commit the perfect murder here. The perfect murder—something humanity had puzzled over for centuries. It crossed Dupin's mind every time he found himself at a particularly dangerous stretch on Brittany's coastal paths. There would be no need for a struggle, not even a heavy shove. Just a nudge would be enough, while someone was looking at the breathtaking landscape, and they would lose their balance.

Nedellec pointed toward the potential shoe scuff:

"We should leave that to the experts."

"You're right. Let's go back down. I just want to try Flore Briard again quickly."

Nedellec nodded and walked ahead, Dupin a little behind, his phone to his ear.

This time the call went straight through.

"Yes?"

"Madame Briard, this is Commissaire Dupin."

"How can I help you, Commissaire?"

She sounded as though she didn't know. Or she was pretending not to. Dupin wouldn't put it past her.

"Charles Braz is dead. He fell from the cliffs. At Pointe du Grouin, just north of Cancale. We're presuming it was murder."

"Charles?"

There was clear horror in her voice now.

"It only just happened. Where are you right now, Madame Briard?"

"I'm at home." She seemed to be finding it hard to speak. "I drove home after our lunch. I've been here ever since."

So much for an alibi.

"Are there witnesses?"

"No. Does that mean I should come to the station?"

"For that, and other reasons."

"You really suspect me?" She seemed genuinely surprised.

"Of course, Madame Briard. Back to Charles Braz: How did he seem when you saw him earlier? What did you talk about? What were his plans after your lunch?"

"I can't believe it. Charles—he's really dead?"

It sounded as though she was crying.

Dupin didn't answer. There was a pause.

He had arrived at the spot where Nedellec had left the coastal path and—he had to look closely—followed a lightly trodden path through the bushy grass, which led downward in narrow, treacherous serpentines.

Dupin embarked on the descent.

"Are you still there, Madame Briard?"

"Yes, yes." She hesitated. "Charles barely said anything at lunch. He seemed distraught, even worse than yesterday and the day before. He kept saying he couldn't take it much longer."

Dupin had to clamber down a section of the path, and clamped the phone between his shoulder and ear.

"Couldn't take what much longer?"

"The thing with Lucille, but everything else too. He seemed broken."

Braz hadn't seemed in all that bad a state to him yesterday, but naturally that didn't mean anything. The most intense of emotions sometimes took a while to come out. And he had surely tried to keep his composure while talking to Dupin.

"I tried to cheer him up. But there wasn't much I could say. He's right, this is all terrible and so hard to cope with. I was really worried about him."

It was a difficult phone call. If Briard was lying to him, lying to all of them, and it really was another murder and she the perpetrator, then she was exceptionally cunning. The thought sent a shiver down Dupin's spine. First, she would have murdered Charles in cold blood, and then brought his supposed emotional devastation into play to suggest suicide. They would never be able to verify what state of mind Braz had really been in. But of course, what she was saying could also be true. As things stood, they couldn't rule out suicide. The only question was: How reasonable was the supposition that Braz had taken his life due to the events of the last few days? Why would he do that?

Dupin had to concentrate on the path; he had almost tripped on a root.

"Did you talk about anything else?"

"No."

"Where did he go after you saw him?"

"He . . ." Briard broke off, then, after quite a long pause, continued. "He wanted to—walk a little. He needed some fresh air, he said."

"He said that? That he was going for a walk?"

"Yes."

"That'll be all for now, Madame Briard. We'll see each other at the station."

Dupin put his phone away and climbed down the last, risky section of path. He couldn't afford to make any wrong moves.

Soon he was standing on the rocks at the bottom, just above the water.

There was no sign of Nedellec. Or of anyone, for that matter. To his left was the protruding cliff they had just circumnavigated on the coastal path. Down here, there was barely half a meter's breadth to squeeze around the cliff wall—and only when the waves had just retreated.

Then Dupin saw it—the scene of the gruesome occurrence. Nedellec, Huppert, and four police officers were standing around the spot.

Dupin had seen many mangled, deformed corpses in his time, but never one as horrifically maimed as this. The sight was hard to take. Charles Braz had fallen sideways on his shoulder onto a sharp rock, to which skin and blood now clung. His head had almost been severed, he lay at an impossible angle; his spine must have broken in multiple places. There were deep, gaping wounds on his neck, and his lilac polo shirt was in tatters. On his upper arms, which were also visibly broken, bare flesh bulged out, his skin having been torn away in strips.

The head and shoulders had slipped down onto a flatter rock after the collision, and his abdomen and legs into a crevice, where the blood had pooled and now stood several centimeters in height. His entire body seemed slack and shrunken, as though all the blood had drained out of it.

Dupin approached, feeling queasy for a moment.

"It won't be easy to identify signs on his body of his having been pushed—if indeed there are any." Huppert's voice was quieter than usual.

"I don't think it was suicide." Nedellec was pale; he too was clearly impacted by the horrific sight.

"I . . ." It hit Dupin like a thunderbolt.

Something had just occurred to him. It hadn't given any forewarning—usually he had at least a vague sense when something was occupying his subconscious, even if it took a long while to identify exactly what it was. But this thought had suddenly appeared in his mind. It daringly connected the things he had seen and heard over the last two days. It was, admittedly, a bold thought. But that had never stopped Dupin from pursuing an idea before.

"Is something wrong, Dupin?" Huppert had noticed his sudden silence and looked concerned. "Do you want to sit down for a moment?"

Dupin's brain was racing, searching feverishly for connections, creating links. It tried to make sense of it all, but couldn't just yet.

"I . . . something's just come to me. It might be too far-fetched, but . . ." Dupin instantly set into motion. "But I think I should follow it up."

"What is it? Where are you going?" Huppert's tone was strict.

Dupin was already a few meters away.

"I'll call later," he shouted out without turning around. Then he concentrated on the difficult ascent—and his thoughts.

It was still far too speculative. One of Riwal's comments during their last phone call had suddenly come to mind and made him think. But if Dupin was right, there had already been clues before then. It could be the key to solving the whole story. It wouldn't only give them the murderer, but perhaps, at long last, the motive.

Dupin clambered up the slope as quickly as he could.

Breathless, he reached his car.

His phone rang.

Huppert. For the third time already since he had set off. And once again he ignored it. He flung the door open and jumped in. It wasn't far. Five minutes.

The engine roared into life; the tires screeched.

It wouldn't be easy to develop this rash thought into an iron-clad theory, but he had an idea. Which, like the entire notion, might well be insane, but that didn't matter. He needed at least an initial clue as swiftly as possible—preferably, of course, a genuine piece of evidence—so that he could then go for broke.

He left the car in the same place he'd parked it the day before and walked the rest of the way.

It was impossible to predict how this conversation would go.

Dupin rang the doorbell. An old-fashioned bell, but no less powerful for it.

He waited. He waited a long while.

Then—without any sounds having made their way outside beforehand—the door opened.

"*Bonjour*, Madame Lezu, I have to speak with Madame Allanic." Dupin caught the housekeeper off guard.

"She—she's not prepared for visitors. I don't know whether . . ."

"I'm terribly sorry, madame," he stepped in, "but I'm afraid there's no option. It's an incredibly urgent police matter."

She paled and stepped to the side.

"Madame is in the living room."

Dupin knew the way.

"I'd like you to be there too, Madame Lezu. You could be of help to me."

Every sentence he spoke seemed to further overwhelm the housekeeper, who was dressed like before in a black skirt and white ruffled blouse.

"I don't think Madame will approve of that in the slightest."

Dupin had already reached the door to the living room. "Come along, Madame Lezu!"

The housekeeper's face displayed pure horror.

He knocked distinctly and immediately went in.

Madame Allanic was lying on a chaise longue, facing away from the door. Her multi-toned woolen jacket was now done up. A television was on, but without any sound; it was completely quiet.

"She can't hear you," whispered the housekeeper, "she's wearing headphones."

All of a sudden, Madame Allanic turned round. Strangely

she didn't seem surprised to see Dupin standing in her living room.

"Good, good"—she removed her headphones with fumbling movements—"there you are at last. It's bitterly urgent."

Only now did she seem to notice the housekeeper.

"I've asked Madame Lezu to stay in the room," Dupin explained.

"Is my husband back? He's back, isn't he? Didn't I tell you."

Dupin knew this would be complicated. But Madame Allanic was his only hope.

"This is about something else. I'd like to know whether you own any valuable jewelry, madame?"

Deep bewilderment appeared in the old woman's gaze.

"They stole everything." She looked around as she spoke, as though she feared unwanted guests. "All our treasure."

Dupin's phone vibrated. He had just put it on silent. It was sure to be Huppert. He ignored it once again.

"That's exactly what I want to know, madame, about your treasure—was it valuable jewelry? Precious stones?"

"It is," she lowered her voice, "a legendary treasure trove."

Dupin tried his question once again; it was decisive. "What kind of treasure is it, madame? I think you're talking about jewelry, right?"

Perhaps he just needed to plunge into her world along with her. Madame Allanic had been talking about treasure from the start. Repeatedly. The housekeeper had even told Dupin when she'd called on Tuesday that Madame Allanic had mentioned gold and precious stones. At the time, he hadn't reacted, thinking it was just insane rambling. But maybe it wasn't. Maybe—as crazy as she might seem—Madame Allanic had been talking about something real the entire time. At least in this respect. In her own way, in the peculiarly mysterious way that her brain now functioned. Maybe there really was a hoard of treasure. Not in the form of centuries-old wooden trunks with fabled gold and silver, but jewelry. Which could be set with valuable gemstones.

This was the thought that had darted into Dupin's mind earlier. Prompted by Riwal's tale of the treasure on the frigate, the wreckage of which had recently been discovered on the ocean floor not far from Saint-Malo. It too had contained jewels— Riwal had expressly mentioned diamonds, emeralds, and rubies. In this light, Madame's speech about her treasure suddenly sounded entirely different. She had spoken yesterday and this morning about thieves, of how she had been robbed, and Dupin, like everyone else, had taken it as the figment of a dementia sufferer's imagination. But what if it was true? What if she really had been robbed? If Madame Allanic really was somehow related to the corsair clan of the Duguay-Trouin family, it would be even more plausible. Perhaps she owned the extraordinary heirlooms?

Madame Allanic had been silent for a while, her eyes wide. "They came and took everything!"

Dupin turned to the housekeeper.

"I must be right, surely, with the assumption that Madame owns valuable jewelry?"

Madame Lezu looked at Dupin fearfully.

"You won't tell anyone, Madame Lezu. Not ever." Madame Allanic seemed deeply agitated, and was now trying to get up.

"Stay lying down, Madame Allanic." Dupin tried to calm her down.

He felt guilty; the conversation was clearly taking a great deal out of her. But he didn't know any other way. He had to try.

The housekeeper came closer to Dupin and whispered:

"Of course Madame owns jewelry. But I don't know how valuable it is. It's in"—now her voice was barely audible—"a small safe, in her bedroom, that hasn't been locked in years. Behind a painting."

Dupin nodded and moved toward Madame Allanic, who was still trying to stand up. He helped her as best he could. She looked at him with gratitude and bewilderment.

"Madame Lezu, could you leave us for a moment, after all?"

The housekeeper looked confused.

"But you . . ."

"It would be very kind of you."

Dupin's cell vibrated yet again. Huppert clearly wasn't giving up.

"Fine, then." With a slightly offended expression, the housekeeper left the living room.

"Now that we're alone, Madame Allanic. Which jewelry is missing?"

Madame Allanic was trembling. Dupin helped to steady her.

"I won't say a word." All her muscles had tensed; she stood as upright as she could, a small, angry protest.

"Then we'll never get the treasure back, madame. I'm here to help you."

Dupin meant it in all seriousness.

"It's gone."

"I know, madame. And I'll get it back. Like your husband would have done."

A shiver went through her.

"He's back, isn't he?" Her eyes lit up.

Madame Allanic wanted to go back to the chaise longue. Dupin helped her.

"Who stole the jewelry from you, madame?"

An oddly impassioned gaze.

"You were robbed, madame. Thieves."

"I know who it was."

Dupin paused. Her sentence had sounded clear and rational.

"Do you want to tell me, madame?"

By now she was lying down again, with a hint of a smile on her face. In the next moment, it disappeared.

"I'm going to Canada, monsieur. And I'm taking everything with me. I won't say a word."

Her wrinkled hands balled into fists, like the reaction of a small child, a gesture that Dupin found strangely moving.

"Beforehand, please help me to find the treasure again, Madame Allanic."

She leaned her head back and turned her face away, after which her gaze became lost again. Perhaps she was back in her inner world.

"I'm begging you, madame. Talk to me. Who was the thief? What did they steal?"

Hélène Allanic showed no more reaction.

Dupin waited, but with every minute that passed, his hopes dwindled that the conversation would continue.

He decided to bring it to a close.

"Thank you, madame. I have to go now. If you want to help me get the treasure back—your housekeeper has my number. You can reach me any time, night or day."

Once again, there was no response.

"*Bonsoir*, Madame Allanic."

He left the room.

The housekeeper was waiting for Dupin right outside the door.

"I hope Madame isn't unhappy with me that I—"

"Madame Lezu, do you know exactly what was stolen from her? I beg of you, tell me if you know. Otherwise you'd be guilty of obstructing a police investigation."

"I . . ." Her face had suddenly lost all color. "But Monsieur le Commissaire! I don't know anything at all. I . . ." She tried to stay composed. "Do you really think something was stolen? Madame has been saying for some time that there were thieves in the house. But so far I've not noticed anything, I . . ."

"So you don't know about any item of value that has disappeared? A piece of jewelry, for example?"

Now she was indignant. "I would have told you immediately if I'd noticed anything like that. Madame tends to misplace things—"

"Show me the safe in the bedroom, Madame Lezu," Dupin interrupted her once again. It was an order, not a request.

Dupin looked questioningly at the other doors that led off from the corridor.

"Madame wouldn't like that at all . . ."

"Unfortunately, I must insist on it."

Dupin knew he had no authority to do this. It could bring him all kinds of trouble.

"Madame would immediately dismiss me from my post and—"

"I'll take full responsibility."

Dupin steered decisively toward the first door.

"I think you need a warrant for that!" She tried to give her tone authority.

"Madame Lezu, do you want to help the police find a serial murderer or not?"

The housekeeper put on an afflicted expression, but began to move nonetheless. She went toward the door at the end of the corridor.

"This way."

Dupin followed her. They entered the bedroom. A sprawling space with its own terrace. Unlike the living room, it was furnished sparsely. A commode with an oil painting hanging above—a harbor scene in an Impressionist style—a wardrobe, and a bed.

The housekeeper went over to the picture.

"If you move the painting to the side a little, you can see the safe." She blushed briefly. "It sometimes happens to me when I'm dusting. You'll see that it's slightly ajar."

Dupin promptly took the painting off the wall; it was surprisingly light.

A square recess in the wall came into view, roughly forty by forty centimeters, and inside it was an old-fashioned safe made of solid metal. As she'd said, the door really was slightly ajar. Dupin was familiar with this kind of safe from his mother's house; thirty or forty years before they had been considered appropriate for securing valuable items.

"Madame couldn't remember the code anymore, nor where she'd noted it down. That's why it's open."

The housekeeper seemed to know a lot about it—without, as she claimed, having ever discussed it with Madame.

Dupin opened the safe door. And found himself staring—a light had switched on inside—at a cluttered, glittering heap.

Dozens of pieces of jewelry, all jumbled together; some seemed inextricably entangled. Long necklaces, short necklaces, bracelets, earrings, brooches, clasps, rings, two watches. All of it looked very old. Some of the rings, brooches, and earrings were set with gemstones in every color imaginable.

Dupin couldn't even hazard a guess at how much it was all worth. For that, they'd need to consult an expert—for which they would need Madame Allanic's express permission. In addition, and this made the idea of an appraisal seem absurd: the jewelry was here. Secure in the safe. Only a few individual pieces could have been stolen at most.

"Madame Lezu, do you know Madame's jewelry well enough to be able to say whether anything's missing?"

She seemed downright incensed. "How should I be able to do that? Madame never wears much jewelry. I've never seen most of it. I don't even know whether Madame herself would be able to say what's here and whether anything's gone."

Dupin wasn't sure whether to believe her. Naturally she wouldn't admit it if she had snooped around in here from time to time.

"Nowadays she only wears two rings," Madame Lezu stated more precisely. "Her wedding ring and family signet ring. Some days she also wears a necklace with an opal, which she loves, and always this one brooch. That's all the jewelry I know."

"Can you see the necklace with the opal anywhere?"

He hadn't noticed it on Madame Allanic.

"At the front, there." She pointed at one of the longer chains. "That's it."

"Does Madame have any close friends who might know anything about her jewelry?"

The housekeeper looked at Dupin with consternation.

"She would never disclose something like that. Madame is very private about her possessions. She has two friends, but only sees them rarely now."

"Have you ever overheard Madame Allanic talking to her nieces about the jewelry? Or do you remember whether she was here at the safe with one of them?"

"No. When her nieces came to visit, I usually stayed in the kitchen. And on my days off, I of course have no idea."

Dupin ran his hand through his hair in frustration.

"Damn it."

Where could he go from here?

He sighed, moved the door of the safe back into its previous position, and hung the picture back on the wall.

"I'm heading off now, Madame Lezu. Thank you for your assistance." Dupin spoke in the most formal tone he could muster. "This little jewelry inspection stays between us for the time being."

The housekeeper nodded, looking a little scared.

Dupin went into the hallway, then paused. Something else had just occurred to him.

He hurried toward the front door. "I'll be back in touch soon, Madame Lezu."

"And what should I do now?"

"Just act as you always do." Dupin had already opened the front door and was stepping outside. "Look after Madame Allanic."

He dashed down the steps.

The address was already saved in the GPS. Saint-Suliac.

Dupin had reached a bigger road heading south. He dialed Huppert's number.

She picked up before it had even begun to ring properly.

"Dupin! What the hell was that?" There was no trace of her characteristic objectivity. "I'm going to ask the prefect to take you off—"

"I think I've solved it. The whole case."

He had to lay it on thick. Go all in. It was the only way to placate her.

"Where are you? What are you up to?"

"Meet me at Walig Richard's antiques store. As quickly as you can. Tell Nedellec to summon the pianist friend there. And also the employee who was there this morning."

"I'm not going anywhere till you tell me—"

"Saint-Suliac, in fifteen minutes. I'll tell you then. I'm sorry."

He meant it.

"I . . ." She seemed torn. "If you don't present us with the solution, you're going to be in serious trouble, Dupin!"

"Trust me, Huppert."

Dupin knew he was taking a massive risk. But his gut told him that he was on the right track.

She seemed to wrangle with herself a little longer, but her cooperative side won out.

"Okay, see you shortly in Saint-Suliac. We're still at Pointe du Grouin."

"Has the medical examiner said anything yet?"

"Only that he's not able to tell us much for the time being. Apart from that Charles Braz hadn't been there long." Dupin could hear that Huppert was walking back already. "And that given the state of the body, the autopsy could take some time. Due to the severity of the injuries, he's very doubtful he'll be able to find clear indications of a struggle or push."

"Has anyone gone to check out Braz's house?"

"Four officers have been there awhile already. Nothing of note. No suicide letter, either. Right, I'll see you shortly, Dupin. And this better be good!"

Dupin stepped on the gas.

Precisely twelve minutes later, he pulled up in front of Walig Richard's shop.

It was just before eight o'clock; the sun was already a little lower in the sky. It would set over the low hills of the opposite shore and was sure to be a spectacular sight; the colors already seemed to be intensifying. A peaceful calm lay over the neighborhood. Only the Bistro de la Grève, where Dupin had drunk his coffee this morning, was bustling with early-summer activity.

Dupin stepped into the courtyard of blossoming artichokes. He realized he didn't have a key for the shop, so he would have to wait. But Huppert and Nedellec would be there soon.

An opportunity to give Nolwenn a quick call.

He headed out onto the narrow pier that stretched far out into the small bay of Saint-Suliac. It was still low tide; immense expanses of sand lay exposed to the evening sun.

"*Bonsoir*, Monsieur le Commissaire. We heard about the latest body." Nolwenn spoke at high speed. "It's all getting a bit out of hand, don't you think? These Malouins . . ."

"I think I know what's happening, Nolwenn. I think I've found the key to the whole story."

"What? Wait a moment."

Dupin heard the irritating on-hold jingle. By now he had almost reached the end of the pier.

"Right, everyone's here. I've put you on speaker. Tell us everything."

All at once, he heard cars racing at far too high a speed toward the *port de plaisance*. Dupin turned to look.

"I'm sorry, Nolwenn. I have to go. I'll call as soon as I can."

"Call us soon!" The call was ended.

Huppert and Nedellec stopped directly behind Dupin's car; the doors were flung open.

A man was hurrying on foot along the coastal road. Dupin recognized him: Richard's employee. Good.

"There you are!" cried Huppert. Dupin had reached the courtyard again. "We're all ears, Dupin."

"Come on, tell us!" Nedellec was impatient. He had the key to the shop in his hand.

"I came as quickly as I could." Richard's employee came over to them.

"Thank you." Dupin took over. "We have a few more important questions for you."

"Of course." The man nodded almost subserviently. "How can I help?"

They stepped into the semi-darkness of the shop.

Dupin flipped on the light and went straight to the glass cabinet containing the old jewelry. Even this morning the jewels had called his attention—then, like in other moments since Monday, he had been really close.

"Catch us up first, Dupin!" Huppert had followed him, pacing swiftly.

"In a moment." Dupin promptly turned to the employee. "You said this morning that over recent years Monsieur Richard had become a kind of jewelry expert."

"Yes, absolutely."

"For stones, too? Gemstones?"

"Of course. The stones define the value."

All four of them were now standing in front of the display cabinet.

"Meaning that Monsieur Richard was capable of valuing pieces of jewelry?"

"Absolutely."

"Do you remember whether he had examined any special pieces of jewelry over the last few weeks? One, or even several, extraordinary pieces?" Dupin specified.

Richard may potentially have gotten involved in this way, and ultimately become a victim. Even if this theory was still very vague, it was the first that would connect Richard with everything that had happened. The first that made some kind of sense.

"I don't know of any. But that doesn't mean anything. Walig often took pieces home for examination. Or stayed later in the evenings than us, at least two times over the past week for sure. He could have been looking at anything. And at the weekends too."

Dupin turned to Nedellec. "Could you ask Monsieur Richard's other employees and friends the same question?"

"Can you explain to us first why—"

"It's incredibly urgent, Nedellec. This might be the crucial detail."

Nedellec frowned, mulling it over.

"What exactly am I asking them?"

"Whether they're aware of Walig Richard having been occupied with one or more special items of jewelry. Perhaps a webpage left open, a telephone call, a conversation, an email, anything."

It was only a faint hope, but they had to try everything.

"As I said, it could be the vital clue." Dupin loaded his tone with pathos.

"Understood."

Commissaire Nedellec headed for the stairs to the first floor and pulled his cell phone from his pocket.

Dupin turned his attention back to the employee.

"Is there jewelry in Monsieur Richard's second store too?"

"No, only here."

"Is there a safe here?"

"No. Only the lockable glass cabinet. But we don't have any really expensive jewelry."

"Richard's home was documented by the forensics team." Huppert spoke up. "I got an inventory of all the valuable items. There was no jewelry on it."

Dupin began to pace up and down in front of the glass cabinet.

"Do you still need me?" The employee was visibly uneasy.

"You can go, but make sure we can contact you. And get in touch immediately if you remember anything else."

Looking relieved, the man retreated.

Before he had even left the shop, Huppert issued her command: "And now you're going to tell me everything that's going on in your mind, Dupin. And by everything, I mean everything."

There was no getting around it: Dupin had to come out with it.

"I suspect that jewelry was stolen from Madame Allanic—one piece or even multiple pieces, of exceptionally high value." He hesitated. "And that one of the sisters did it."

Dupin was still walking up and down in front of the cabinet.

"Hmm." Huppert crossed her arms in front of her chest. "And then what?"

"I'm not sure yet."

What he had formulated was essentially the basis of his theory; all the rest was just random speculation for now.

"It had to have been Lucille—as we all know, she really needs the money. But why would she then kill Blanche? At the market, in front of everyone? Perhaps Blanche found out about Lucille stealing it, and Lucille killed her because of that. Perhaps Blanche had the jewelry that Lucille wanted? Was she the thief first?"

For now, that seemed more logical. But the problem was: there were countless other possible scenarios. Far too many. And they were so different that you couldn't really even use the term "logical." Dupin had already played through many of the variations in his mind.

"But why would Kilian Morel and Walig Richard also have to die?" Huppert joined in the speculation. At least she didn't seem to regard the basic hypothesis as utter nonsense.

"Perhaps because they knew about the jewelry—the jewelry and the theft. Or, because the jewelry, after Blanche's death, was with them or one of them. Probably with Kilian Morel. That would explain his house being ransacked, which his murderer—whoever it is—really put some effort into. They were looking for the jewelry."

The fact that their house, Kilian's office, and Blanche's test kitchen had been searched made the theory that Blanche could have been in possession of the jewelry more convincing than others. But countless questions remained unanswered. Including whether the perpetrator had actually found the jewelry in Blanche Trouin and Kilian Morel's house.

"Maybe Blanche asked Walig Richard to value the jewelry. And so it was with him, at least for a while. Perhaps that's how Richard was involved and why he was killed."

Dupin paused in front of the cabinet.

"But why would Blanche have done that?" Huppert's arms were still crossed. "Steal from her own aunt? They were apparently very close. And Blanche was doing well financially, she wouldn't even have needed the money."

"I don't know."

"And if it was her, how does Lucille come into it?"

Questions with arrow-like precision. And still a blind spot. Dupin began to pace again.

"She must somehow have found out that Blanche had the jewelry."

"And the murder of Lucille's life partner, Charles Braz? How does that fit into the theory?"

"*Ex*-life partner. And we still don't know whether that might have been suicide, after all."

"And if it was—how does that fit together? It doesn't make any sense, it . . ." Huppert paused, something flashed in her eyes. "Unless Charles Braz . . ."

She didn't even need to finish the sentence—it had occurred to Dupin himself on the drive over here.

"It's entirely possible."

"But why would he kill himself now? Guilt? If he was cold-blooded enough to kill Blanche's husband and her friend Walig Richard over the jewelry, why would he suddenly feel so guilty a day later that he takes his own life? Plus the fact that, following your hypothesis, he would've been in possession of the ominous jewelry that everything had revolved around from the start."

Dupin was starting to detect a fundamental skepticism in Huppert's words.

"Perhaps the jewelry is valuable enough to make all of Lucille's financial problems disappear." Dupin knew himself that this wasn't an answer. "I don't know." It was the only honest answer.

"And Lucille Trouin? What role does she play in this scenario? If Charles Braz is the perpetrator—do you think it was all her plan? That she put him up to it? Or that she at least knew what he was planning?"

"I have no idea."

The commissaire's brows knit together. "What proof do you have for this whole jewelry theory?" Huppert became pragmatic. "Some circumstantial evidence, at least?"

"Just Madame Allanic. As confused as she may be."

He was aware that she provided neither proof nor circumstantial evidence, but for the moment, she was all he had.

"The old lady with Alzheimer's?"

Dupin told her about his visit.

"It would fit perfectly," he concluded. "It's possible that Madame Allanic has told us everything already, just in a jumbled-up way. It's entirely plausible that she owns some incredibly valuable pieces of jewelry, presumably from this old corsair clan, the Duguay-Trouins. It would be a very Breton story, and above all"—this might be a key point psychologically, in order to convince Huppert—"your discovery yesterday would be integral to this scenario. Lucille needed money, and very, very urgently."

"Any judge would consider Madame Allanic mentally

incompetent. And she didn't even really confirm it with you—insofar as she would even be able to. I'm doubtful."

Dupin couldn't contradict her.

"We need evidence, Dupin. Solid evidence. And pretty quickly some clear proof."

That was the problem.

"Do you have any idea where the jewelry might be?"

"No."

Everyone who, according to his theory, had been in possession of the jewelry—and who could have attested to its existence—was now dead. Apart from Lucille Trouin.

"Does Lucille even know about Charles Braz's death yet?" The question had occurred to Dupin a few times already.

"I called her from the scene. I wanted her to hear it directly from us. And also, to hear her reaction."

"And?"

"She only listened. And didn't say anything."

"What did you say in terms of whether it was murder or suicide?"

"The truth. That we don't know yet."

"Flore Briard could be conspiring with Lucille Trouin." Huppert returned to the possible scenarios. "She doesn't have an alibi for either yesterday or today. And she needs money herself, if we've been correctly informed. So by now she would be free of anyone who could pose a problem for her. She wouldn't have anything more to fear. And we would only have one chance of convicting her: we'd have to find her in possession of the jewelry."

Precisely.

"Which applies to all three of the remaining suspects," Huppert said, completing the picture. "And even Charles Braz. There were no surprises in his phone records, by the way. Only the calls with Flore Briard, which we already knew about."

Dupin's brain was freewheeling in an overheated way. Without pause and at top speed, he ran through the possible event progressions, but without reaching a conclusion.

"Briard, Clément, and Joe Morel have been at the station for a good while now," Huppert reminded him, something Dupin had almost forgotten. "We . . ."

"Nothing." Nedellec came down the stairs. "Neither his friend nor his employees were aware of any special piece of jewelry or valuation."

It was depressing. They urgently needed a stroke of luck.

"So, Dupin, out with it—what exactly is your theory?"

Huppert pulled out her phone and moved toward the exit. "I'll arrange the interrogations of the three suspects."

Dupin groaned. He didn't feel like repeating it all. But he didn't have a choice.

"Right, okay," was Nedellec's conclusion. Dupin's summary had taken a few minutes. "It all sounds quite fanciful—but right now it's all we've got."

He didn't sound convinced, admittedly, but Dupin had expected more resistance.

"If I've understood you correctly, it could mean that Lucille Trouin orchestrated the whole thing."

Dupin hadn't expressly worded it like that, but it was a possibility. One of many.

"Which means that . . ."

"Briard, Clément, and Morel are waiting for us in the interrogation room. We have to go," Huppert interrupted, having finished her call and rejoined them. Dupin was relieved; all further speculation felt futile right now.

Huppert was already heading for the door. Nedellec and Dupin followed.

Dupin had probably never spent so much time at a police station during an investigation before, not even in Concarneau. This was the third time today he had entered the Saint-Malo commissariat.

He hadn't driven quite so quickly as usual, and so had arrived last. From the car, he had called Nolwenn to tell her about his theory and bring her up to date. They hadn't had time for a proper conversation, but at least she now knew the latest.

The three commissaires walked along the corridor to the interrogation room.

"I've instructed forensics to search the homes of Lucille Trouin and Charles Braz one more time," Huppert informed them. "The only problem is that the new search order isn't exactly very specific. *Exceptionally valuable-looking jewelry, one-piece or multiple?*"

And yet the order was a good one, Dupin felt.

"We don't have sufficient grounds to get search warrants for the homes of Briard, Morel, and Clément," the commissaire admitted. "And Briard will, of course, have her own jewelry, probably from her inheritance too. She could always claim it belongs to her."

"How are we going to approach our conversation with the three of them?" Nedellec brought them back to the most pressing question.

"Head-on confrontation, I'd suggest. Everything on the table.

We'll work with Dupin's hypothesis. And let them tell us their alibis for this afternoon."

"Okay." Nedellec was in agreement. Dupin too.

"Then let's get this started."

Huppert opened the door and they stepped in, one after the other.

Flore Briard was sitting in the middle, Joe Morel and Colomb Clément to her left and right. The small group formed an odd picture.

"*Bonjour,* madame, messieurs." Huppert pulled a chair to the opposite side of the table. Dupin and Nedellec sat alongside her.

"Would you be so kind as to explain . . ." Flore Briard immediately spoke up in a sharp tone.

"We're not here to waste our time on trivial banter, Madame Briard." Huppert fixed her with her gaze. "Among the three of you is a serial murderer who has come into the possession of valuable jewelry. It belongs to the aunt of the Trouin sisters. We know everything."

Huppert let the sentence take effect.

There were distinct reactions on all three faces, even Joe Morel's.

"Jewelry? From Lucille's aunt?" Briard was the first to react, attempting a smile that ended up involuntarily crooked. "That's grotesque. You think everyone was murdered over some jewelry? Jewels, or what? I for one know nothing about it."

As always with her, it was impossible to say whether her indignation was genuine or feigned.

"You of all people could have known about the jewelry, madame. You're Lucille's closest confidante, you work with her, have no alibis for the times in question, and you could certainly use the money," Huppert established drily.

"As I said: it's grotesque! And disgraceful," repeated Briard in agitation.

"What about you, Monsieur Clément?" asked Nedellec combatively. "What do you have to say? You work with Lucille Trouin too, so far, at least. Did she involve you in her plans? Or did you find out about the jewelry by chance and act independently?"

Given that Nedellec had only just been clued in on the theory, he was playing his part very well, thought Dupin.

"Me? No!" The young star chef was clearly rattled; Nedellec's offensive was having an effect, and interestingly a stronger one than Dupin had expected. "I've got nothing to do with it. And I don't find out things like that from Madame Trouin either. She's just my boss. I'm innocent, I swear!"

He made a nervous gesture.

"You were recently in contact with Blanche Trouin too. So with both sisters," Nedellec continued, as nondescript as he was merciless. "You must have seen or heard something."

Beads of sweat formed on Clément's forehead.

"Nothing at all. I've not seen or heard anything."

Dupin intervened: "So why are you so nervous, Monsieur Clément?"

He hesitated. "I'm not nervous."

"You are, and very."

A brief pause, then Clément stammered: "Does my boss know about Blanche's offer now? That I've already signed? Then—that means I no longer have a job."

So that was the source of his anxiety. From his perspective—presuming he was innocent—it was understandable.

"Don't worry, monsieur." Huppert remained as matter-of-fact as ever. "Madame Trouin will soon have such big problems that this disappointment will barely register. Where were you today between three and four o'clock in the afternoon?"

"I was in the restaurant, until just before three maybe. And then I drove home to sleep for a while."

"Can anyone attest to that?"

"No."

"Then you don't have an alibi for today either," summarized Nedellec with a hint of satisfaction.

Dupin, on the other hand, felt frustration rising within him. This conversation was coming to nothing.

Huppert turned to Joe Morel, who was sitting there in his black T-shirt and washed-out jeans.

"You and Lucille Trouin have become closer again recently, Monsieur Morel, and you're also inheriting everything from your brother and his wife, which could now include the stolen jewelry. It's quite conceivable that you're involved."

The commissaire had spoken in an energetic tone, but phrased the content carefully.

Morel leaned back before he answered.

"What can I say." He shrugged, looking entirely unfazed. "I don't know anything about it. And I don't have a verifiable alibi for this afternoon either."

Dupin ran his hands through his hair. The problem was that Huppert, Nedellec, and he didn't have anything with which they could push at least one of the three to talk.

Huppert, too, seemed to be reaching the limits of her patience. "Then we'll just have to take a different approach. I'm going to immediately arrange search warrants for your homes."

"You won't get them." Flore Briard was overtly aggressive.

Joe Morel remained indifferent, as though none of this had anything to do with him, and Clément merely said: "You won't find anything at my place."

Dupin shot to his feet. He was fed up, and couldn't take it anymore.

His annoyance had turned to anger, because what they'd wanted to avoid, at all costs, was happening: they were losing the momentum that had only just come into the investigation, the forward momentum.

"It's no use, we have to speak to Lucille Trouin again." Dupin spoke as though the three suspects weren't even there, and went to the door. "We have to try to get something out of her. She has to realize we know about the jewelry and the theft."

It was infuriating. The whole time they were struggling here, Lucille Trouin was in the very same building, so close to them it was like a relentless provocation. First, she had given Dupin the runaround with her silence, mocking him, and then through her outrageous confession: "It was just a crime of passion." The emotions really may have run high at that fateful moment in the market, but Dupin was nonetheless convinced she was a cold-blooded murderer who had ruthlessly pursued her motive: getting the jewelry in order to make money.

"Dupin, wait!" called Huppert.

It was too late; he was already outside.

Huppert turned to Briard, Morel, and Clément: "We're done here."

The commissaire hurried after Dupin.

Just before she reached the door, she turned around briefly. "Nedellec, please accompany these three out."

Huppert caught up with Dupin. "Trouin will want her attorney present."

The commissaire seemed in agreement with his plan.

They reached the elevator.

"I'll take care of it, Dupin. Meet me here in half an hour."

"See you soon."

Dupin was in dire need of some fresh air. Some contact with the world and reality. He had to stretch his legs, breathe in a little salt and iodine.

He had left the station and walked to the big city beach again, even though he didn't have much time. He continued right up to the water's edge.

The sky had been clear on the drive here from Saint-Suliac—the sun had already sunk down close to the horizon—and now it had darkened. Large, dark, menacing clouds, like earlier this afternoon, but this time even more so. There were bizarrely shaped holes in the clouds, through which the setting sun fell, seeming to display every shade of red, lilac, orange, rose, pink, and yellow in existence. A highly dramatic sight.

The ocean had already darkened, the emerald green dying away in a somber green-black—only where the last rays of evening sun met the surface of the water was it still illuminated. Blindingly so. The strong gusts of wind from the day before yesterday were back too, as were the waves, driving the sea spray into the air.

Dupin had to concentrate on one single question to the exclusion of all others, as important as they may be: Where was the jewelry now?

That was it. That was the question.

After he had stood there for a while, he checked the time. The interrogation with Lucille Trouin was imminent. Their second one.

Although it had been just a short walk, it had done him good.

Ten minutes later, he reached the interrogation room where, not long before, they had sat with Briard, Morel, and Clément. Room 318.

Huppert arrived almost simultaneously, a little out of breath.

"They're both in there. I'm next door with Nedellec again."

"Good."

Dupin went in, without any haste, and calmly closed the door behind him.

Lucille Trouin looked composed, self-assured, and even now, still in possession of an unyielding pride. No sign of uncertainty or sadness—although she had only recently found out about Charles Braz's death. She seemed to have touched up her makeup for the interrogation: her eyebrows looked even darker, more defined than in the afternoon, her skin tone more matte. In the absence of daylight, the reddish shimmer in her hair was no longer discernible.

"We meet again so soon." Dupin made his way toward the chair, but then walked past it and paused in front of the table, on the opposite side to where Trouin and her attorney were sitting.

"Just a moment . . ." The attorney—dressed this evening in a striking, dusky pink polo shirt—seemed to have remembered something, because he shifted closer to Trouin and whispered something to her. She responded. They went back and forth a few times.

"Okay. Madame Trouin is ready. What's this about at such a late hour? It would be better—"

"We know now what's going on." Dupin fixed his gaze on Lucille, speaking slowly and not very loudly. "You killed your sister in order to get to your aunt's valuable jewelry. It was more than a crime of passion."

Dupin paused.

He was sure he saw Lucille's eyes widen a little. It was the only visible reaction. Her self-control was extreme, and must demand enormous focus. It was impossible to make out what was going on in her mind.

With her left hand, she brushed a strand of hair off her face, and Dupin noticed how slender her hands and wrists were.

Dupin stepped closer to the table and leaned forward, propping himself on his hands. He took up the thread again.

"That's the crux of the story. It's that simple. You wanted the jewelry. By selling it you could have warded off bankruptcy and secured the fruits of your lifelong labor. It would have saved you. Perhaps the sum would even have helped you make your ambitious new plans a reality. Either way, what mattered most to you was not losing the bitter contest with your sister. For that, you were willing to do anything. And you still are."

It was eerie. Lucille Trouin sat there steadily, like a wax doll. No blink of the eyelids, no twitch of the lips, not even a discernible rise and fall in her rib cage. Nothing.

"In terms of how things played out in detail," Dupin raised his voice, "whether someone murdered for you or did it of their own accord, and who it was—Flore Briard, Joe Morel, or Colomb Clément—we'll find that out soon. Including what role your ex-partner Charles Braz played and what happened to him."

"I'm intrigued to find out."

She'd spoken so quietly that the sentence was barely audible.

"Your theory is ridiculous, monsieur. Everything about it."

She stood up.

"My client has nothing more to say to your accusations." The attorney strove for a formal tone. "I consider this the end to the interrogation."

Dupin briefly pondered whether he should insist on its continuation, but decided against it.

The attorney followed Lucille, who was already standing by the door and had pressed the bell.

"*Bonsoir,* Monsieur le Commissaire," said Monsieur Giscard.

With that, the two of them left the room.

Dupin remained behind alone.

Suddenly, there was an almighty crash. It came from outside. Thunder.

It had happened quicker than expected; a storm had gathered.

"Well, that was another washout."

Nedellec entered the interrogation room with Huppert behind him. His observation wasn't even meant mockingly.

"I'm not so sure about that," commented Huppert, before immediately changing the subject: "The team from Braz's house have been in touch. They didn't find any jewelry. By the way—"

A booming clap of thunder interrupted the commissaire, swiftly followed by a second. She waited patiently until it faded away.

"By the way, I asked the medical examiner to search the clothing on the corpse again. He didn't find anything."

"We should have Charles Braz's shops, Lucille Trouin's restaurant, and her cheese shop in Rue de l'Orme searched too.

And in principle also the homes and businesses of the other suspects."

"This is getting a little out of hand," muttered Nedellec.

"Let's start with Charles's and Lucille's business premises." Huppert was firm. "And then go from there."

"Whoever is in possession of the jewelry, and murdered to get their hands on it," Nedellec furrowed his brow, "will have hidden it well. How are we supposed to find it without a lead? We don't even know exactly what kind of jewelry it is. A ring, a necklace, a brooch? Several different pieces?"

That was the dilemma.

"They could also have hidden the jewelry somewhere else, outside their homes or workplaces. That would actually be much smarter." Nedellec was excelling himself: one objection after the other.

"Also"—Huppert spoke with an unusually grim expression— "I've arranged for Briard, Morel, and Clément to be under constant surveillance. They won't be able to take a single step without us knowing about it."

"Excellent."

Dupin went across to the window.

"And what if it's not even about jewelry?" Nedellec looked thoughtful. "If we're barking up the wrong tree? Perhaps we're chasing a ghost."

He was certainly right on one point: it felt as though they kept reaching a dead end through pursuing this theory. Objectively, the skepticism was justified. Dupin could be wrong, he could have picked up the wrong scent—one that he was now following with increasing doggedness. It had happened to him before. And yet his instinct was telling him they should stick with it. In desperate situations like this, when he began to get pessimistic, Nolwenn would usually boost him with an old saying which, to non-Breton ears, might sound macabre: *Sometimes you have to die a few times in order to prove you're ill.* Strange in that uniquely Breton way, but true.

"It's the best hypothesis we have right now. The only one. I say we follow it until it leads us to the solution. Or until we have a better one," declared Huppert with her resolutely down-to-earth logic.

Dupin felt happy with that. It was a more solid argument than simply trusting his gut.

"And what do you suggest we do now?" Fortunately, Nedellec didn't seem to want to launch into a fundamental debate about the theory.

"The search of Trouin's home is under way, the surveillance of the suspects has started, and I'll pass through the new orders in a moment—for now we can only wait and keep thinking." Huppert came over to Dupin at the window as she spoke.

Heavy rain had set in. Fat drops smacked against the windowpanes. The hefty gusts of wind were threatening to turn into a serious storm. It was loud even through the closed, well-insulated windows, sounding like crashing waves. A rattling and clattering came from all around. As the light from a flickering streetlamp fell on Huppert's face, Dupin noticed how worn down she looked; these intense days had left their mark. On them all.

"I agree," confirmed Dupin, who had understood Huppert's words as a signal it was time to go.

He desperately needed some time alone; the last few hours had been a breathless gallop. And a lot of "team." Continuing to pull their hair out here wouldn't get them anywhere. More than anything, Dupin needed caffeine. To be anywhere near capable of engaging with his thoughts again.

Huppert glanced at the clock.

"We all need some downtime, so we'll meet again tomorrow morning. The prefects have summoned us to the police school for eight. Dinner's already over." Dupin thought he heard a sigh. "The three of us should meet at half past seven."

Collective nodding.

"Café du Théâtre, Saint-Servan." The commissaire was already en route to the door. "You already know it, Dupin."

Nobody objected. Nedellec and Dupin followed the commissaire.

This time Huppert sighed audibly. "I had to promise the prefects we'd be coming with a hot lead."

Outside, loud thunder boomed once again.

"The usual? The J.M. rum?"

The amiable landlord of the Bistro de Solidor had appeared alongside Dupin's table.

The commissaire had only just taken a seat, having gotten soaking wet on the few meters between the parking lot and bistro. His jeans and polo shirt clung to his skin.

The restaurant was almost empty already, only two tables were still occupied.

"A double, please. And a *café*. Is the kitchen still open?"

They had unfortunately missed out on the famous restaurant in Cancale this evening. And he urgently needed to eat something.

"We still have one portion remaining of today's special.

Pluma de porc avec purée de pommes de terre. The pork comes from a local organic farm, black pigs, much better than Ibérico. With a honey-and-balsamic glaze. And the potato puree is from *vitelottes,* the little lilac potatoes. A velvety Languedoc to accompany it?"

"Definitely."

The owner smiled contentedly. "Just the ticket after a day like today."

He had heard what had happened, of course. The regional radio, TV, and online newspapers were reporting of nothing else. Dupin was relieved when the landlord left it at that and disappeared into the kitchen.

He had pulled out his notebook.

Where could the jewelry be? Who had it?

Dupin stared at the scribbled pages. He leafed through them randomly.

The sound of his cell phone pulled Dupin away from his disconnected thoughts.

Huppert.

"Nedellec's on the call too, Dupin. During the renewed search of Lucille's house, eighteen pieces of jewelry were seized—rings, including ones set with stones, necklaces, and earrings. Which, of course, isn't surprising—it could be her own jewelry. It was stored in a wooden box in her bedroom, which was already noted in Monday's protocol. The team took it all with them. None of the pieces look exceptionally valuable or particularly old, but of course, only an expert can say for sure. Who knows—maybe Lucille was hiding the stolen jewelry in with her own. There's no better way of making something invisible than hiding it in the most obvious place. It's usually the last place people look."

"Without Madame Allanic's help, there's no way of finding out whether the stolen jewelry is in with Lucille's," Nedellec pointed out.

"We should still get everything valued. Then we'll know whether there's anything especially valuable in there or not."

Huppert was right, it was a first step.

"The expert should get to work right away." Dupin felt the productive, jittery restlessness returning.

"Good. Then till later."

Huppert ended the midnight telephone conference.

Dupin reached for the rum glass on the small tray that the landlord had set down during the phone call.

He took a long sip. He liked how smooth it was, with a veiled sharpness. Subtly sweet and simultaneously spicy. Dupin loved contrasts, unusual combinations. The *café* also tasted wonderful together with the rum.

The rain was still pelting down furiously, driven by the ferocious squally wind. Lightning flashed at regular intervals, chased by powerful thunder.

"*Et voilà!*"

Once again, the owner of the bistro appeared as though out of nowhere. This time with a large plate.

The Breton pork tasted exquisite: the honey-and-balsamic marinade wasn't too sweet, and the meat was melt-in-the-mouth tender. But the best element was the potato puree. Dupin could taste a hint of curry and nutmeg. Heavenly; even the aroma alone made him feel happy.

All at once, it hit him.

Dupin almost dropped his fork.

That could be it. Of course!

What had Huppert just said? "There's no better way of making something invisible than hiding it in the most obvious place."

There was a place that was even more obvious than the rest, even more so than Lucille Trouin's jewelry box.

And if he was right with the idea that had just shot into his mind, then he had already seen it. Already seen both, the hiding place—and the jewelry too. *The* piece of jewelry. A very particular one.

He jumped up.

It was utterly insane. The thoughts flashed wildly through his mind.

He laid a few bank notes on the table and hurried over to the door.

As soon as he was outside, he reached for his cell phone. Dialed the number and sprinted to his car.

"What is it?"

"Come to the station at once, Huppert. I . . ."

"Hello? I can't hear you."

Of course, it was the storm. It was drowning everything out.

"Just a minute," he yelled into the telephone. Soon he would be in the car.

"Hello?" Huppert was shouting now too.

He swiftly opened the car door. A gust of wind lashed the apocalyptic rains in.

"Come to the station right away!" Dupin still needed to shout; it wasn't much quieter even in the car. "I'll see you there, I'm already on my way, I'll be there in three minutes."

"What's happened, Dupin?"

"I'll tell you there."

He hung up.

The wheels spun momentarily on the wet asphalt, then the car lurched forward.

The sliding door at the police station entrance was deactivated; for nighttime hours, there was a side entrance.

Dupin rang the bell. As the door opened, he rushed in.

"I'm expecting Commissaire Huppert." He addressed the two startled-looking police officers on night watch. "She should be here in a moment."

"Do you want to wait upstairs in her office? Room 212, second floor."

"Thank you."

Dupin had already hurried past them. He knew the way.

Arriving in Huppert's office, he turned on the light, went over to the window, and stared out into the furious stormy night. Once again, he was drenched to the skin; his clothing clung to him even more than before. He was leaving little puddles of water behind him on the floor.

"I'm here."

Dupin almost jumped—Huppert was standing in the doorway. A dark blue rain jacket hung over her arm.

That was quick. Dupin realized he didn't even know where she lived. Clearly close by. Or she had still been out and about.

"What is it, Dupin?"

"We have to speak with Trouin again, right now."

The commissaire hung up her coat calmly.

"First explain to me what—"

A dim light coursed through the room. Lightning. Then came the explosion of a particularly loud clap of thunder. The storm was refusing to abate.

"Damn it." Dupin had completely forgotten about it in his agitation. "Call Trouin's attorney and tell him to come at once."

For a while, Huppert didn't seem to know how to react.

"I'll explain everything, Huppert, I promise. Like before."

She studied him closely.

"Another idea?"

"Another idea." Dupin nodded.

"Okay." She had made her decision, and took control: "Wait here. I'll organize everything and let you know. Don't go anywhere."

Dupin had no idea what she feared, but if that was the only condition . . .

"Understood. But we have to have the conversation in her cell."

"For now, I'm not going to ask why."

She had already gone.

Dupin began to pace restlessly up and down. The wind gusts slapped the rain against the windowpane, again and again, bringing small, broken-off branches along. Probably from the two trees not far from the window. Their black-green silhouettes swayed wildly to and fro, wrenched around by invisible forces.

Dupin was incapable of forming a clear thought—he just wanted to know. That was all that mattered: finding out if he was right.

It took a full twenty-four minutes until Huppert reappeared, an eternity. It was a quarter to one.

"Okay. We're ready. The attorney is here. I'm coming in too."

That was fine by Dupin.

They made their way to the staircase.

"I can't get hold of Nedellec," said Huppert as they walked down the steps. "I left a message on his voicemail."

They had reached the first floor. The interrogation cell was at the far end of the corridor.

"Here we are."

Huppert opened the door without knocking.

A sterile, rectangular room came into view. A relatively in-conspicuous, barred window, a small table, and two chairs in a somber green tone. Cool white walls, a bed, a nightstand. A narrow cupboard for clothing and personal items. Cold, clinical light.

Lucille Trouin and her attorney were sitting at the small table.

The attorney jumped up.

"This really is the limit!"

His almost conciliatory tone contradicted the intended drama of his performance. It came across as a dutiful show.

"My client doesn't have to put up with this, she was asleep and—"

"Save it."

Dupin went straight toward Lucille and stopped directly in front of her. Huppert had leaned against the wall by the door.

Dupin studied Lucille overtly. Her upper body, her neck.

But she had already gotten changed for bed, he realized. She was wearing a long-sleeved blue T-shirt and wide black cotton pants. Her jet-black hair was tousled, which actually made her even more attractive. As did the fact that she wasn't wearing makeup.

"What's this about, Commissaire?" The attorney tried to lend emphasis to his words.

Dupin turned away from Trouin and moved toward the narrow cupboard.

"What are you doing, Commissaire?" persisted the attorney.

Instead of answering, Dupin calmly began to open the cupboard.

"What's this about?" Notable agitation lay in Trouin's voice. "Stop that! Is he allowed to do that?"

She turned frantically to her attorney.

"Hmm. Difficult to say. If the circumstances demand it." He hesitated. "I . . ."

"He's allowed," Huppert intervened ruthlessly.

The cupboard now stood wide open.

Inside it, at half height, was a clothing rail. Above that were various compartments containing clothes. Clothes that Charles Braz and Flore Briard had brought here.

Dupin's gaze moved painstakingly through the interior of the cupboard.

Hangers hung from the clothing rail. A jacket, a pair of pants, two blouses, and a black pullover, presumably the one she had been wearing at lunchtime.

"We have to take everything out of the cupboard," explained Dupin.

Huppert and the attorney stared at him in silence. Lucille fidgeted nervously on her chair.

"We have to look at every item . . ."

Dupin didn't finish his sentence.

He had seen something. He reached for the hanger with the black pullover.

Hanging from it, only just visible, was something else. Something shimmered from beneath the neckline.

A chain.

A silver chain.

The necklace that Lucille had been wearing at lunchtime and this evening. Dupin remembered it well.

He swiftly took it out from beneath the pullover.

An involuntary smile spread out on his face.

The necklace was set with a stone.

A striking blue gemstone.

"Leave the necklace alone. It's a keepsake from my mother." Lucille jumped up.

Huppert seemed to have been expecting this. She blocked her path.

At that moment the door opened, and Nedellec came in, gasping for air. He must have been running.

"What's going on?" he blurted out.

"In a moment, Nedellec," Huppert assured him. "We have everything under control."

Dupin strode without haste over to Lucille, who seemed frozen to the spot, her eyes fixed on the necklace.

"This is what it was about—only this." Dupin spoke coolly. "This gemstone. This is it. The necklace belongs to your aunt. I'm presuming it's an incredibly valuable stone."

Lucille Trouin remained silent, her face expressionless.

"Here? In her cell?" Nedellec approached. "She had the jewelry here?"

He spoke as though Lucille wasn't even there.

"A perfect hiding place. Almost." Huppert too was staring at the necklace and gemstone.

"People were murdered for this stone." Dupin held it in his hand, the chain swaying beneath. "It's the center of the entire story"—he cast Lucille Trouin a penetrating glance—"that I'm sure we're about to hear in all its detail."

Trouin had seemingly regained her composure. "As I said, it's an old heirloom from my mother."

It was so incredibly cynical. She knew they couldn't check—and therefore neither refute—her claim. Only Madame Allanic could, theoretically.

"I hadn't worn the necklace in a long time, I'd almost forgotten about it, but for the last few months I've been wearing it regularly again. Including on Monday, when—"

Huppert cut in: "Someone must have brought it to the police station. I didn't see it on the evening of the arrest, I'm sure of it. She was wearing it today, I remember. But definitely not the day before yesterday."

She took a deep breath, an unusually emotive gesture for the otherwise prosaic commissaire.

"And that someone was either Charles Braz or Flore Briard. After he or she killed Morel and Richard in order to get the necklace. Thereby eliminating the only people who knew about it."

That was exactly what had gone through Dupin's mind earlier in the bistro, when he'd had the idea about the necklace. Both of them, Briard and Braz, had brought things into the police station for Lucille. Somehow one of the two had managed to smuggle in the necklace. Charles, perhaps, when they'd hugged, or Flore Briard with the things that she'd handed in.

"I'll get the jewelry expert we engaged to come to the station right away." Huppert's tone turned pragmatic. "And send someone to get Flore Briard. I'll have her taken into temporary custody."

"It's better we drive out to Briard ourselves and take her by surprise. So she won't have time to think." Dupin didn't want to take any more risks.

"Good idea. Let's pay her a visit!"

Dupin handed Huppert the necklace.

The attorney, who had watched the scene unfold in silence, now found his words again. "You can't just take my client's personal possessions with you."

"Yes I can. I think this gathering here has fulfilled its purpose, Monsieur Giscard, and I'm bringing it to an end. Unless"—Huppert now spoke directly to Lucille Trouin—"there's something else you want to say, and by that I mean: make a confession. Is that perhaps the case?"

"As I said"—Trouin's voice was firm—"it's a piece of jewelry I've owned for twenty years. I was already wearing the necklace the day before yesterday, no matter what you say."

"Then it should be listed with the things you were wearing at the time of your arrest. All of that was logged, as required by law. So it can easily be checked."

Without waiting for a reaction, the commissaire went over to the door. Then she turned around one more time.

"You can spend a moment longer with your client if you'd like, Monsieur Giscard. I'll close the door. If you want to come out, press the bell next to the door, two of my colleagues will be outside."

Nedellec and Dupin left the room with her.

The storm was finally relenting. There was only the occasional clap of thunder, and the rain had become less insistent.

Commissaire Huppert was sitting at her desk, Nedellec and Dupin opposite, and she looked content. The necklace lay before her on the desk. In her hands was the list that had been drawn up the night before last, after Lucille Trouin's arrest.

"There's no necklace on here. I think that was pretty obvious. Nor with the things that Charles Braz and Flore Briard brought in for her."

"She'll keep insisting regardless. And that it's an heirloom from her mother. She'll claim it was sloppiness on the part of the officials that the necklace wasn't listed, and continue her brazen spiel." Unfortunately, Nedellec was right. "We need foolproof evidence. First of all, we need to establish that the gemstone really is incredibly valuable—and then we need to prove, without a doubt, that it was stolen from Madame Allanic."

"Our colleagues doing the surveillance have confirmed that Flore Briard is at home, by the way." Huppert was already one step further. "But first the jewelry expert. He should be here soon. He's bringing his mobile equipment with him. We probably won't be able to get a definitive evaluation tonight, but an initial appraisal will be enough."

"Shouldn't we perhaps show the stone to Madame Allanic and see how she reacts? She might be able to identify it in spite of her mental state."

Nedellec voiced what had already occurred to Dupin. It would certainly be the simplest way. But he had immediately dismissed the idea again.

"I'm afraid it would be futile." Based on his experience with Madame Allanic, Dupin couldn't imagine it working.

Huppert spoke up. "She's not in the position to give a reliable statement. And she would also need to prove ownership of the necklace with documentation. The statement alone of a ninety-three-year-old with dementia won't help us."

"Perhaps there's some insurance paperwork," commented Nedellec.

"If it's even insured at all." Particularly in families with old money, Dupin knew, this was frequently not the case. "And in order to get to the documents, we would have to speak to Madame Allanic."

"I suggest we wait to see what the expert has to say on the necklace's value—then go from there. Perhaps the housekeeper knows whether the jewelry is insured and where the documents are," Huppert suggested.

At that moment, Dupin's phone rang. He glanced quickly at the display. Claire. He rejected the call, as much as he hated to, but he couldn't talk right now.

Dupin stood up and reached for the necklace.

He studied the stone.

It was almost circular and immaculately cut, set within a delicate silver clasp. Dupin estimated its diameter at one and a half centimeters, perhaps a little more. The most striking feature was its extraordinary shade of blue. A sparkling, constantly changing magical blue that became more intense toward the center—from a light blue shimmer to a deep blue gleam. Endless nuances that changed with every movement and every minimal shift in the direction of the gaze. Looking closer, Dupin got lost in endlessly mirroring and overlapping triangles, all of them in different shades of blue. More and more surfaces and facets opened up—until he felt dizzy.

"A diamond. A blue one."

Nedellec, who was now standing next to Dupin, played the expert. Nonetheless, Dupin wouldn't even have been able to name the type of stone.

"Just a moment." Dupin put the stone back down on the table as an idea came to mind, got out his cell phone, and activated the speaker.

It took a little while for the call to be picked up—understandably; it was a quarter to two in the morning.

"Boss? What is it?" A sleepy voice. At least the inspector wasn't out on a badger hunt.

"Riwal, a large blue diamond—possibly a Trouin family heirloom, the old corsair clan. Does that say anything to you?"

Possibly, it had just occurred to Dupin, it might be a famous stone.

"You found a blue diamond? At the Trouin sisters' aunt's place?"

Riwal's tiredness seemed to have disappeared instantaneously.

"We found it on Lucille Trouin, but it could belong to the aunt, yes."

There was a short pause, as though Riwal needed time to take in what he had just heard.

"Blue diamonds are the rarest and most valuable of all diamonds. What's the diameter?"

"Between one and a half and two centimeters."

"Send me a photo, boss, I'll research it. Off the top of my head, I can't think of anything. But there are a number of famous diamonds that are considered lost."

"Call me when you have anything."

"I will. Is this what the whole case was about? This one stone?"

"I think so."

"Not bad. And do you know who it was?"

"Not yet, but I'm sure we will soon."

"Understood. I'll let everyone know, boss. Talk soon."

The call was ended.

"My first inspector," explained Dupin, seeing the questioning looks of his colleagues. "A little verbose at times, but a universal genius. Specializing in Brittany and Breton history."

"You think this could be a legendary stone?" Nedellec seemed impressed.

"No idea, but—"

A loud knock at the door interrupted Dupin.

"Come in," called Huppert.

A stocky, bald gentleman of around sixty years of age came in. He was wearing a tired-looking gray suit and carrying a leather suitcase in his left hand.

"Monsieur Malguen—I'm the jewelry expert."

He sounded remarkably timid.

"Oh yes—*bonsoir.*" Huppert stood up. "Do come in. Have a seat."

Huppert pointed toward one of the chairs.

"This is the stone in question." Huppert laid the necklace directly in front of Monsieur Malguen on the desk. "We just need an approximate value."

"Then I'll get straight to work."

The expert opened his briefcase and took out several instruments. Then he took the stone between the thumb and index finger of his left hand and reached for a device that looked like a wide electronic thermometer, with a row of LED lights. It seemed to form some kind of scale; the first four were green, followed by four orange and four red.

"A diamond verifier," he remarked succinctly.

A tiny prong emerged from the tip of the device, like the lead in a protracting pencil.

The expert pressed the prong carefully against the stone and activated a small button on the side of the device.

There was a loud beeping sound, and all of the LEDs lit up.

"Okay." The expert raised his eyebrows. "So that means it's not a fake. It could have been a simulant, like zirconia. But it's not."

Now he reached for a compact, rectangular lens—"Microscope 75X" was written on it, presumably a professional magnifying glass—turned on a lamp that was mounted on the side of it, and put the lens to his right eye.

He inspected the stone carefully, moving and turning it expertly from time to time.

"This color is incredibly rare."

He paused for a long while.

"VVS1 Clarity, I presume, the highest clarity, purity, and color intensity."

Another pause. He took his time, turning the stone again.

"No extraneous colors that would compromise the blue. Excellent cut—excellent luster—excellent symmetry."

With these final words, he laid the stone and necklace back on the table.

"So?" Dupin blurted out.

"I'm almost certain it's an incredibly exquisite, extremely rare fancy blue diamond."

"And?"

"Just a moment."

He laid the stone and chain on a third instrument: a black, compact scale with a small silver weighing pan.

"What do you think?" Dupin's impatience increased further.

"I'd estimate it as four hundred to five hundred points." He raised his eyebrows even higher than before. "In other words, four to five carats. I can only say for sure once it's taken out of the setting."

"And what does that mean?" This time it was Huppert probing for more information.

"You mean, how much could it be worth?"

"Exactly."

"Well, it's not that easy to say. Unique pieces like this are usually sold at auction, and the value there is volatile at times, according to the current state of the market and participating collectors. There isn't a fixed price."

"A minimum—what would you say?" This was getting too complicated for Dupin.

"Hmm." The expert cocked his head to the side. "Hmm. I would say—it should fetch five or six million." He spoke with utter calm. "An incredibly delicate stone, no doubt of that— perhaps even a little more, but as I said, it depends whether—"

"Six million?" cried Nedellec in disbelief. "That's madness."

It was. Madness—and it exceeded all their imaginations. Even Huppert looked amazed.

This really would explain everything. *Everything*.

A sum like that would save Lucille Trouin. More than that, it would allow her to put her ambitious business plans into action. Any expansion of her gastronomic activities she could dream of. She would have been able to achieve great things, and in the process, trump her sister.

"Do you still need me?" The expert interrupted the commissaire's long silence. He had already begun to pack his tools back into his briefcase.

"We're almost done here, monsieur," Huppert confirmed. "How difficult is it to sell a stone like that?"

"There are fanatical collectors for whom money isn't a factor. Some of them don't even care where a stone comes from. For five million, it would go pretty quickly, I think. Within a few days. With a bit of research, you can find the people who know how to approach something like that. It's usually easier than one might think."

"Could it be a famous stone?"

"I'd say it's not one of the few legendary missing stones we know about today. But perhaps it was well-known a long time ago."

"Thank you, Monsieur Malguen. For the moment, that's everything. We'll be in touch if we have more questions."

It was much more than they'd hoped. Dupin had feared a considerably more vague appraisal.

Huppert accompanied Monsieur Malguen to the door with his briefcase.

"Many thanks again, monsieur. And—*bonne nuit*."

"My pleasure, Madame le Commissaire. My pleasure."

"Just one more thing, monsieur." The man was already halfway out of the door. "If you could keep this in strict confidence?"

"That goes without saying, madame. *Au revoir*." The expert went to the elevator.

"And now it's time to pay Flore Briard a visit." Dupin got up too.

Huppert picked up the necklace.

"I'll just take this to my safe in the weapons room. We'll meet outside."

On the entire drive they had encountered only two cars; Saint-Malo and Dinard seemed deserted, the streets swept empty. The sky too had been swept empty; it was unbelievable, just a short while before, the apocalypse had raged, and now the night was starry clear. The mountainous clouds had disappeared as quickly as they'd come, the whole storm had been like a ghost, the only lingering reminder the particularly large puddles.

They had taken Dupin's car; it was directly in front of the police station. Driving at a significant speed, they had reached the white gate of Flore Briard's magnificent villa within fifteen minutes.

The moon had risen at the other end of the bay, right over Saint-Malo. A wanly glowing crescent moon, whose sparing light was enough to give the villa an atmospheric appearance. The sharp gables towered up into the night sky.

The sea was in view, a captivating sight even now—admittedly without its emerald green, but in its place was the monochrome magic of a bluish-gray tone. The boats were still pitching back and forth, a final after-effect of the storm.

Dupin rang the doorbell. Three, four times.

They waited. Presumably Flore Briard was sound asleep.

He rang once again.

Now they heard a crackle in the intercom system at the gate.

"Who is it?" A sleepy voice.

"The police. Huppert, Nedellec, and Dupin. We have to speak to you, Madame Briard."

A brief silence.

"What about?"

"Let us in, Madame Briard!" intervened Huppert.

The gate began to move.

Dupin knew the way through the garden.

They entered the villa, hurried through the immense reception hall, and were soon standing in front of the door to Briard's actual apartment.

Two minutes later, Flore Briard appeared. She was wearing leggings and a blue sweatshirt. Her face was bare of makeup, her hair entirely disheveled, giving her a wild appearance.

"And what's so urgent you have to drag me out of bed in the middle of the night?"

She turned and walked along the corridor toward the large living room with the fantastic view.

"We've come to take you into temporary custody, Madame Briard."

Huppert had said it without any trace of drama.

"You're under suspicion of two, possibly three counts of murder. And of grand theft."

Flore Briard stopped. She seemed composed.

"So in your desperation you've all decided that I'm the murderer? I thought that was just a threat, in order to—"

"We are in possession of the stone—the blue diamond, Madame Briard," Nedellec interrupted her.

Briard shrugged lightly. "What diamond? What are you talking about?"

"We're talking about an exceptional gemstone that's worth at least five million euros, which was stolen from your best friend's aunt."

Nedellec dispensed with phrases like "presumably" or "highly likely."

"The stone you murdered Kilian Morel and Walig Richard to get to. Then you took it to Lucille Trouin in investigative detainment. And perhaps you even pushed Charles Braz off the cliffs today."

"That sounds like some wild corsair legend, Commissaire." Flore Briard looked unimpressed. "I have nothing to do with any of it. And I don't know about any diamond either."

Dupin looked her directly in the eyes. "You were in on it with Lucille Trouin from the start. Probably she put you up to it, but that's irrelevant. She promised you a significant share of the profits. You wouldn't have to sell your villa, and could extend your business."

He noticed that he'd lost the renewed energy that he had felt earlier, before their arrival here in Dinard. It was strange.

"You and Charles Braz were the only ones who dropped items off for Lucille Trouin in custody." Nedellec completed the argument. "We were able to seize the diamond in Trouin's cell this evening. Madame Trouin wasn't wearing the necklace when she was arrested, otherwise it would have been registered at the station."

"Not to mention," concluded Huppert, "that you don't have an alibi for yesterday morning—nor for this afternoon."

Flore Briard still looked mostly unfazed.

"So, putting aside for a moment that I don't have any financial difficulties whatsoever—why do you think it's me and not Charles?"

Of course, she would take this tack.

"Investigative detainment as a measure is designed for exactly this kind of situation," deflected Huppert, not having an answer prepared for Briard's question. "So that where there's valid suspicion and an acute flight risk, we can investigate the remaining evidence for the conclusive arrest of a suspect. The law gives us twenty-four hours in which to do that. So let's go, Madame Briard."

Huppert had reached the limits of her patience, and Dupin could understand why.

"You're making a serious mistake, Commissaire." Madame Briard's eyes had narrowed, her voice sounded strangely hissing, and her self-assurance had now evaporated. "I'm warning you. There will be consequences."

She made a sudden movement toward the sofa.

Huppert's hand darted to her gun, and Dupin's muscles tensed.

"My cell phone's on the sofa. I want to call my lawyer."

"You do that!" Huppert kept Flore Briard in her gaze. "Tell him to come to the police station. We'll be there in fifteen."

The journey through the night to the police station had been eerie; no one had said a word.

This was due in part to their immense tiredness. It was three hours already since they had ended their very long day for the first time, having been on their feet for over twenty hours. And a lot more had happened in the meantime. A huge amount. Albeit not enough. Not enough to finally bring light into the dark.

Arriving at the station, they had briefly spoken with Briard's attorney, who had then spoken with Briard alone for a while. She had protested vehemently at first, of course, but then acquiesced. Due to the extreme circumstances, even though the attorney did his best to object, they had the right to demand investigative custody.

Huppert had scheduled a thorough interrogation for the morning. In the presence of the attorney, she had taken Flore Briard to the second cell in the police station. It was directly next to Lucille Trouin's.

The three commissaires were now on the first-floor landing.

"What now?" asked Nedellec.

"Now we get some sleep," replied Huppert firmly.

For a moment, an objection danced on Dupin's tongue— they risked losing the momentum, they might be on the brink of definitively resolving the remaining questions—but he swallowed it down. He felt dizzy and exhausted. Utterly depleted.

"We'll stick to our plan," Huppert continued. "Half past seven in the morning at Café du Théâtre."

Nedellec and Dupin nodded briefly.

Then all three of them left the station, each heading in a different direction.

The Fourth Day

Dupin had arrived at Villa Saint Raphaël shortly after half past three in the morning, and three minutes later he was in bed. Despite his tiredness, it took him another torturous twenty minutes to fall asleep—the miraculous rum was now too long ago. There was too much running through his mind. Once sleep finally came, it was incredibly restless.

When his alarm went off at ten to seven, it took a good while to get his bearings. Only once he'd showered did he regain some of his energy.

He had arrived at the Café du Théâtre a little early and had already drunk two *cafés* in order to get his brain into gear.

Nedellec and Huppert had appeared at half past seven.

They sat in a quiet corner, the café already filling with early-morning hustle and bustle.

Huppert brought them up to date:

"Flore Briard's attorney is about to submit a complaint over his client's alleged unlawful detainment. He's demanding her immediate release. I've spoken with the prefect and she fully supports us and our decision. I've set the interrogation with Briard for nine-thirty."

Dupin was occupied with his *pain au chocolat*. And his fourth *petit café*. From time to time, one of the other customers looked over at them curiously. Dupin thought he heard the words "Britt Team" a few times. He had consistently ignored the newspapers, with their sensational headlines, which lay scattered over many of the tables in the café.

"What are we telling the pre—"

The ringing of Dupin's cell phone interrupted Nedellec.

Dupin saw Riwal's number.

"My inspector."

He took the call.

"Riwal?"

"Morning, boss, is there any news on the rock? Unfortunately, we haven't been able to find anything on a large blue diamond that played a role in Breton history."

Dupin summarized what the expert had told them last night.

"Not bad! Four hundred to five hundred points. Unbelievable." Riwal was highly impressed.

"Was there anything else, Riwal?"

"Success, boss! Mission accomplished."

"What do you mean?"

"Gasoline! That was it! I poured gasoline along the edge of the garden last night. No more sign of a badger, it's unbelievable."

It seemed like a desperately harsh measure, but if it helped. . . .

"Now's not a good time, Riwal, I'm sitting here with Commissaire Huppert and . . ."

"Understood, boss."

"Speak later, Riwal."

"Sorry." Dupin turned back to Nedellec. "What were you saying?"

"I'm just wondering what we should tell the prefects. We're in possession of the stone now, sure, and therefore the probable motive, but we still don't know who the murderer is. If Flore Briard doesn't make a confession and we don't soon find something with which we can prove the murders and the theft, we'll have to release her. Charles Braz, our second suspect, is dead. And we don't even know whether it was murder or suicide."

It was infuriating. They had come so far, so close—and it could still end up a complete failure. The more awake Dupin became, the more intensely he was aware of it. The worst thing was: they wouldn't be able to pin anything else on Lucille Trouin either. She could simply wait it out and stubbornly claim that her sister's murder was purely a crime of passion.

"I'm going to stop in on Madame Allanic again." Dupin had eaten his last bite and was standing up.

"Yes, do that." Huppert was pale; you could see how little she'd slept. "It's worth a try."

A pleasant side effect of going to see Madame Allanic was that it would mean missing part of the meeting with the prefects.

"See you shortly."

And with that he was out of the door.

It was still early; the drive—along Avenue John Kennedy, which ran parallel to the beach—would take less than ten minutes. He knew the route by now.

The cloudless night sky had given way to a cloudless morning sky. An intense, brilliant blue, as though it had been freshly painted.

Shortly before eight, Dupin reached the first roundabout in Rothéneuf and braked abruptly. A now-familiar formation of cars moving at a blithely leisurely pace entered the roundabout ahead of him; the Journées Nationales des Véhicules d'Époque was clearly still ongoing. Dupin spotted an old dark blue Peugeot 404—his father had driven one, the first car that Dupin could remember. Predominantly recognizable by its spherical headlamps, which always looked as though they were observing the world curiously. This time, too, several of the drivers and passengers waved at him. Of course! He finally caught on. He had read it in the paper just recently: his XM-model Citroën was celebrating its thirtieth birthday, officially making it a classic. So he was one of them.

A short while later, he parked the car at the edge of the road in the small cul-de-sac where Madame Allanic's villa sat enthroned. To the right, the marvelous little inland sea, half water, half sand.

Dupin climbed the stone steps to the entrance of the villa and pressed the old-fashioned doorbell.

A second time. A third and fourth.

No one came.

Perhaps Madame Allanic was still asleep. Given her partial deafness, she wouldn't hear the doorbell. And maybe the housekeeper didn't start until later. At half past eight, nine? He should have thought of that. But like always during an investigation, Dupin forgot there was a factual reality outside the case, one which, as banal as it may be, simply continued as normal.

Dupin pulled out his phone and searched for Madame Lezu's number.

"Hello?"

"This is Commissaire Dupin. Are you still at home, Madame Lezu?"

"Yes, monsieur, but I'm just about to leave, yesterday evening I was—"

"I have a question regarding a very specific piece of jewelry, madame." It occurred to Dupin that it would have been better if he'd brought it along, but at least he had the photos he had sent Riwal on his cell. "I'm in front of the villa."

"You're—what?" She sounded shocked.

"I'm in front of Madame Allanic's villa."

"Did you wake her?" the housekeeper asked worriedly.

"I don't think so."

"I'll come immediately, Monsieur le Commissaire. Right this minute."

"I'll wait."

A good fifteen minutes passed before Madame Lezu's arrival. Dupin had used the time to walk down the path that ran alongside the villa to the cliffs, enjoying the wonderful fresh morning air. He could feel the lack of sleep too, despite the huge quantities of caffeine he'd imbibed.

Madame Lezu hurried up on foot.

"Here I am." She already held the front door key in her hand. "I hope you didn't ring the bell again, because—"

Dupin's cell phone interrupted her hasty flow of words.

Huppert.

Dupin stepped to the side.

"Yes?"

"A letter addressed to Lucille Trouin has just arrived here at the station. A letter from Charles Braz. His name is on the envelope as the sender. Handwritten."

"What?"

"It seems Braz wrote Trouin a letter and posted it yesterday."

A message from a dead man.

"Have you opened it yet?"

"You know we can't do that. In investigative detainment, there's unrestricted privacy of correspondence. We would need a court order, which means an intensification of custody. For that we'd need to show there's an acute danger of suppression of evidence. Which is far from easy, and it would take a while. And another thing: if we just open the letter, it won't be permitted as evidence in trial."

"Damn it!" This couldn't be happening.

The contents of the letter could potentially bring the entire truth to light—clear up all the remaining questions.

"This is infuriating."

"Who knows, maybe its contents are irrelevant to the investigation. A declaration of love. Consolation. Or a suicide note. Which means we would at least finally get some clarity on that point."

"I'll be there right away, Huppert."

The letter was now much more urgent than waiting for Madame Allanic. They had to find a way to read it, no matter what, even if it seemed impossible. He could visit Madame Allanic later.

"Good. Nedellec is with the prefects, giving them a report. I'll wait in my office. And I'll see to the intensification of custody, even if it's complicated."

Huppert had already hung up.

Dupin turned to the housekeeper, who was still standing there with the key in her hand and looking at him with a mixture of curiosity and anxiety.

"I'm afraid I'm urgently needed elsewhere, Madame Lezu. But I'll come back later. Just one thing: Has Madame Allanic insured her jewelry?"

"I . . ." The situation seemed to overwhelm Madame Lezu. "Insurance? No!" Her face showed indignation. "For Madame, jewelry is something completely private. These are very old, personal pieces from the family inheritance, no one ever insured them. Someone from the insurance company could get the idea of stealing them." She shook her head adamantly. "She would never risk that."

She was starting to sound like Madame Allanic herself, thought Dupin.

"Do you know anything about a special blue diamond? On a silver chain?"

She thought for a moment. "No. Nothing at all."

"Then thank you, Madame Lezu. And until later."

Dupin was already dashing back to his car.

Twelve minutes later, Commissaire Dupin rushed into his colleague's office.

"And?"

Huppert was sitting at her desk. "I asked two colleagues to compare the handwritten address on the envelope with other documents from Charles Braz."

"And?"

"The handwriting seems identical."

She held the letter out toward Dupin.

"I made the application for intensified custody and surveillance of correspondence. But actually we have no other choice but to give her the letter soon."

Dupin studied it closely. The handwriting looked a little erratic.

Madame Lucille Trouin / Commissariat Central Police Nationale / 22, Rue du Calvaire / 35400 Saint-Malo. Sender: Charles Braz / 12, Quai Solidor / 35400 Saint-Malo.

The envelope was pasted shut.

"I have an idea. Of how we could do it."

Huppert raised her eyebrows. "How?"

"It's a little unorthodox—but it could work."

Dupin had racked his brains on the drive over, and the idea had come to him just before he reached the station.

"Out with it."

The plan wasn't complicated—within two minutes, he had explained it.

Huppert leaned back; she seemed at a loss. "I don't know, it sounds a bit outlandish."

She was silent for a good while.

Then she sighed.

"We'll give it a go. I'll tell the janitor, the restroom is directly next to the interrogation room. Then I'll call Trouin's attorney. As soon as he arrives, I'll fetch Trouin and bring both of them into the interrogation room. Officially, this discussion is connected to new findings. I'll ask a few questions, and at the end I'll hand her the letter, as casually as possible. I'll give you a call beforehand. After that, only text messages. Oh yes," something else occurred to her, "and I'll let Nedellec know. He has to be there. It's a good excuse to free him from the prefects."

"Perfect!" Dupin was already on his way to the door. "I'll take a look at everything."

It was hard to say what the chances were—but perhaps they would get lucky.

The commissaire then stepped into the restroom next to the interrogation room.

A unisex restroom. Perhaps fifteen square meters. Four cubicles. A washbasin directly behind the door, on the wall to the right-hand side. Over it, a mirror, a paper-towel holder. It smelled strongly of cleaning fluids.

He looked around.

The first toilet cubicle looked the most probable. He went in, activated the flush, and then went out again.

To play it safe, he would hide in the farthermost cubicle.

He played through the entire plan once more in his mind.

With a satisfied look on his face, he left the washroom. Only to pace impatiently up and down in the corridor on the third floor. The time dragged and dragged, until eventually his phone rang.

"We're ready, the janitor too. Everything's sorted. The attorney is here. We're going into the interrogation room now. Nedellec isn't here yet, but we'll start regardless."

"Okay."

Dupin put his phone on silent.

He retreated back into the restroom. The fourth cubicle. He left the door just slightly ajar—in such a way that it wouldn't draw attention—and positioned himself on the toilet lid. Then he waited.

Long minutes passed. At times, it felt like hours. He stared fixedly at his phone, so he could see at once if a message from Huppert arrived.

Nothing.

Five minutes.

Seven.

Ten minutes.

It surely couldn't take this long. The situation in the interrogation room must be going differently than expected.

He was just about to send Huppert a text message when the door suddenly opened.

He froze.

Someone stepped into the room.

They paused. In front of the washbasin, presumably. They walked—Dupin held his breath—past the four cubicles. Then stopped again and returned to the washbasin.

Dupin's muscles were completely tensed. But there was only one thing he could do: wait. And hope.

For a while, he didn't hear anything. It was completely quiet.

Then, all at once, a noise made its way to Dupin's ears, one that he immediately recognized. This was exactly the sound he had been hoping for.

And again.

The sound of paper being torn.

Then he heard steps again, the door to one of the toilet cubicles being opened.

Now. This was the moment.

He sprang into action.

In one leap, he was out and lurching to the right.

The door to the first cubicle stood open; she hadn't yet had time to pull it shut. Inside it was Lucille Trouin. She jumped, her face showing both bewilderment and panic. Everything happened at lightning speed. Dupin was just a meter away from her. In a few fractions of a second, she leaned forward and threw the scraps of paper she was holding in her right hand into the toilet.

The torn-up letter.

Everything seemed to have played out exactly as Dupin had imagined. At the end of the interrogation, as planned, Huppert had given Trouin the letter from Charles Braz, had perhaps even had one of the officers do it. Either way: with the receipt of the letter, Lucille Trouin had found herself in a very tight spot. Presuming, of course, that the letter contained something controversial, something incriminating—which Lucille would have known or at least feared. She must have immediately run through all the possible scenarios in her mind. In order to avoid the police getting their hands on the letter, she had decided to destroy it on the spot. There would be only one safe option in the vicinity: the toilet. And just one point in time: immediately.

"You're too late, Commissaire."

Lucille Trouin spoke with a triumphant smile, her right hand on the flush, which she pushed down. Then, in confusion, she pushed it again.

No water had appeared. And nor did it on her next attempt. She stared at the toilet in disbelief.

Dupin seized the moment and pushed his way into the cubicle, knocking her a little to the side in the process.

"You can flush it as often as you like, Madame Trouin. The janitor turned off the water. And if the letter was written in ink, we'll be able to read every word perfectly."

Dupin had already checked; none of the paper scraps had fallen into the U-bend.

"What are you thinking, following me into the toilet, that's—" she began, only to be interrupted by a loud bang.

The door had been flung open and slammed against the wall.

Huppert. With two police officers right behind her.

"Well?" she addressed Dupin, all the while staring at Lucille Trouin.

"We've got it!" Dupin nodded his head toward the toilet bowl. "As expected, she was planning to destroy it."

Huppert took a step toward the cubicle.

"Come out, Madame Trouin," ordered Huppert.

"You set me up!" Lucille Trouin balled her fists and stepped out of the cubicle. "You've no power to—"

"We absolutely do," Huppert retorted, now standing just a few centimeters away from Lucille. "We're responsible for your safety. And we had reason to fear you were planning to hurt yourself. It was our responsibility to check on you."

"Hurt myself?" Lucille was shouting now, she was beside herself.

Dupin leaned over the toilet, unmoved by her reaction, and reached for the scraps of paper.

They'd gotten lucky.

"There it is. Written in ballpoint. Wet, torn, but we'll be able to decipher it."

They would reassemble it right away.

"You've clearly disposed of the letter, Madame Trouin."

Huppert had returned to her rigorous practicality. "That terminates the privacy of correspondence."

That was the showstopper to their plan.

Dupin could see Lucille's derailed expression in the mirror above the washbasin.

"It's over, Madame Trouin." Dupin's voice was calm.

They had brought Lucille to the moment of truth. For the first time, she was backed into a corner, and she knew it—now they had to continue, bring the situation to a head, use every tool they had to force her hand.

"Your aunt and Madame Lezu have just confirmed with me that the blue diamond belongs to your aunt. It isn't an heirloom from your mother."

As he spoke, Lucille had turned around to him as though in slow motion, then paused.

Now she stood there motionless, her gaze fixed on Dupin, empty, soulless. Otherworldly.

It took a while, but eventually she began to speak. Or rather, to whisper.

"Charles thought, or maybe I should say hoped, that he'd be able to win me back by doing this. By—committing these barbaric acts." She spoke earnestly, sadly, pausing between individual words. In Dupin's ears it sounded completely contrived. "He—he's the murderer. He murdered my brother-in-law and Walig Richard." Now a few tears ran down her cheeks, and she made a dramatic gesture with her hand. "It's tragic."

It was brazen. Brazen beyond all measure. Just like her "confession" yesterday. She didn't even try to present her spurious emotions in a moderately credible way. Dupin struggled to control himself—but he let her talk; they had waited long enough.

"That's precisely what the letter says," she continued. "That Charles wanted me back. Couldn't live without me. That he did all of it for me, for us. And that he could no longer bear it and was therefore putting an end to his life."

All the same, if it really did say that in the letter, it was an incredibly important piece of information. And there would be no point in Lucille Trouin lying. They would be able to read the letter soon anyway and discover its contents—regardless of how Lucille's interpretations might look.

"I wanted to protect him. Charles. For many years, I really did love him, I . . ." She stopped and covered her face with her hands. "Poor Charles! How ill he must have been the whole time, I should have noticed it sooner. I feel so guilty. In his fury he even claimed I put him up to it all—that I'd said we could start afresh with the money, after the whole land purchase fiasco—and our relationship crisis. That I'd promised him that. He concocted it all in his mind so it reflected his innermost hopes. He," a sigh, "confessed everything to me when he visited. He said he'd gotten the diamond back for me, murdered Kilian Morel and Walig Richard and . . ."

"The necklace was with Monsieur Richard?"

"No. It was at my sister's house. Charles found it there. Walig Richard had valued it at my sister's request, she wanted to know how much it was really worth."

This part of Lucille Trouin's theatrical statement corresponded pretty much with their suspicions.

"Walig Richard," she continued, "knew about the stone and so, according to Charles's ill logic, he had to die. He wanted to get rid of everyone who knew about it."

She took a deep breath in and out, then closed her eyes.

"He told you all of that when he visited the station?" Huppert didn't seem to want to allow her any pause.

"He hugged me. He whispered it in my ear. The policeman wouldn't have been able to hear. And during the hug Charles also pressed the necklace into my hand. And"—her tears flowed again—"told me it was his pledge of love."

"And? How did you react?"

"I said he had to turn himself in at once. That I condemned everything he'd done. That he was ill. The situation didn't allow me to say much more. And of course I was completely shocked."

No one in the room moved; the two police officers also stood there as though rooted to the spot.

"Read his letter! He writes that he couldn't get past my reaction. That he only did it all for me—and that I've now suddenly turned my back on his love. Instead of declaring my love to him once again . . . Do you get how extreme his mental illness was?"

She wiped the tears away with the back of her hand. Her hair fell into her face, and she made no move to brush it back.

"But he didn't turn himself in—he made a different choice. It's terrible."

Dupin had now realized why she wasn't making much of an effort with her performance. Her aim wasn't to sound convincing, but merely to establish her strategic position for everything that was to come. An interpretive perspective. Initially, of course, in reference to the letter. She had read it, she knew what was in it, and now intended to incorporate each and every word into her argument. Before Huppert and Dupin could read the letter themselves. She was fully aware that Huppert and Dupin wouldn't be taken in by her attempt to drag herself out of the affair and pin everything on Charles Braz. But—she would follow a clear line from the beginning on. It didn't get more perfidious than that.

Dupin had no doubt she had used Charles Braz like a puppet on a string. Abetted him in an abhorrently subtle and brutal way. People who were desperately in love were capable of anything; even more so when they were cruelly rejected. In all probability she had given him exactly what he'd claimed in the letter: a promise. The promise that they would get back together. That they would make a fresh start. Only to then drop him coldly, once he had done everything for her. He must have been so heartbroken.

"I don't believe a word you're saying, Madame Trouin."

Huppert was clearly in complete agreement with Dupin.

"The fact alone that you tried to destroy the letter shows you wanted to avoid our discovering its contents no matter what. But now you can't prevent that, given the failure of your little mission here, you're trying everything to twist it to the shape of your own story. But you won't succeed." There were surprising signs of emotion in Huppert's tone. "As far as your sister's murder is concerned . . ."

"What's happened? I came as quickly as I could."

Commissaire Nedellec stood in the doorway. His gaze flitted cluelessly back and forth.

"Later, Nedellec, later!" Huppert was firm.

Nedellec obediently positioned himself next to the washbasin.

"So, Madame Trouin, do continue!"

Lucille Trouin took another theatrical deep breath. "I lost my composure, in a terrible way, for several fatal moments, just like I already told you. I think there had just been too much hurt, and—"

"We know this old story, Madame Trouin. Tell us how the story with the diamond began in the first place."

"Blanche stole it from my aunt, who years ago, when we were little, sometimes told us about her jewelry, about a legendary blue diamond. But back then I thought it was just a myth and . . ."

"Why would your sister have done that?"

"Oh—for numerous reasons. It would have allowed her to expand her restaurant and businesses however she wanted, her husband's too. And, more than anything, to put me in her shadow even more."

In a way it was tragic, and probably she really felt that deep down: she was the victim, the eternal victim, and had only been defending herself. The complicated truth was that probably both were somehow correct. Nonetheless, Dupin felt no sympathy for her.

"It was greed. Blanche was greedy, she always was, even though she was great at passing herself off as generous. As someone who didn't care about money, possessions, and all that. She—"

"*You* were the one who bankrupted yourself." Huppert seemed to have had enough. "*You* had the ambitious plans to expand. I don't believe that your sister stole the diamond."

"She did, it was her!"

"And how and when did you find out about it?"

"I looked at the jewelry from time to time when I visited my aunt, and there was always this big blue stone. It was completely irresponsible of her to store it so carelessly. It wasn't even insured. I always told her. Just think of her housekeeper, Madame Lezu. Naturally she could have decided that she deserved an extra something, after all her devoted years of service to my aunt, before everything goes to the sister in Canada."

"You haven't answered my question."

"I was at my aunt's on Monday morning, visiting—and the necklace with the stone was gone. I immediately realized what must have happened. I was furious. And remember what I'd just found out—about Blanche stealing my sous-chef and publishing my father's recipes in her own name. It was too much for me. I stormed out of the villa, got in the car, and drove to the market. To Blanche's stall. I confronted her, told her to her face that I knew about the theft. When she denied it point-blank," she lowered her gaze, "I lost my head. My control. It just took hold of me. Any psychiatrist will be able to tell you about the toxic impact of all those wounds."

In an exaggeratedly melancholic pose, she ran her hands through her hair.

"And that's it. That's absolutely everything there is to say. I don't have anything to do with the terrible events after that. And no one can expect me to turn in someone I loved for a long time, and in a certain way still do. I would never have been able to betray him."

Dupin had experienced a lot over the course of his career, had convicted unscrupulous, calculating murderers—but Lucille Trouin's cold-bloodedness seemed to surpass them all. Of course, there was a reason she was like that, but nonetheless, after a certain point—he *had* to see it like that, otherwise he lost all hold—a person was entirely responsible for their own actions.

Not for the cards they'd been dealt, but certainly for what you made of them. That was Dupin's deepest conviction.

"The only reason you didn't turn him in is because he would have told the truth"—Huppert was justifiably refusing to let Lucille Trouin's claim stand—"thereby destroying your chances of getting away with the diamond. You almost managed it. You had the stone in your possession, and no one would have found out about it. You would have claimed a crime of passion, and got a reduced sentence. Instead of doing life for murder, you would have been convicted for manslaughter, and free within one or two years. On parole, perhaps even earlier. As a millionaire."

It really was that dramatic.

Lucille's pupils had narrowed. "I've said what I have to say. The truth and nothing but the truth." She began to move, heading toward the door.

The police officers, who so far had remained silent, glanced at Huppert, who gave a minimal nod.

"Accompany Madame Trouin. Her attorney is still next door in the interrogation room. After that, take her to her cell. We'll have the opportunity soon enough to continue this conversation."

Lucille Trouin raised her head—it was intended to be a gesture of pride, but looked grotesque—and left the restroom, accompanied by the police officers.

The three commissaires had retreated to Huppert's office and reassembled the wet scraps of Charles Braz's letter as best they could.

The message was short.

Lucille,

I gave everything I had, did everything you wanted. I knew it was wrong, that I was committing terrible, unforgivable acts.

I did it for us, for our love. You know that.

You said we would have a fresh start.

Now you've torn the ground out from under all of it. From me.

I can't go on, Lucille, I don't want to go on.

I love you, now and forever.

Charles

"The letter confirms everything we thought." Huppert was the first to speak.

The three commissaires huddled over the desk, just as they had the night before when studying the diamond.

"That's the proof. It was cold, premeditated murder. Lucille Trouin used Charles Braz to carry out her malicious plan. Presumably she called him on Monday when she was on the run, despite what he said in his statement. Perhaps from some café. Or maybe they even met somewhere, they would have had enough time. We'll get it out of her." Huppert had long since returned to her objective mode. "It won't be easy for her to convince anyone of her claims."

"So Briard, Joe Morel, and Clément have nothing to do with the whole thing, they're innocent. As was Walig Richard," Nedellec summarized, Huppert having caught him up on the events on the way back to her office. "Charles Braz was the murderer, incited by Lucille Trouin. Kilian Morel may have known about the stone, and probably also where Blanche was keeping it, but presumably that was all he was guilty of. If that. As things stand, there are only a few unanswered questions."

"Speaking of Flore Briard"—it seemed to have just occurred to Huppert—"we should release her at once." She reached for the phone. "And then quickly meet with the prefects and inform them about the latest developments."

"Some of it they already know," clarified Nedellec. "I just sent them a message . . ."

Dupin's phone. He had turned the volume up again.

The number looked familiar.

"Yes?"

"Monsieur le Commissaire?" A frail, female voice.

"Speaking."

"This is Madame Lezu."

The housekeeper. She sounded scared. "You said you'd be back soon."

It had actually resolved itself, at least the question regarding the diamond.

"We've since found out that it really is about a necklace belonging to Madame Allanic. A necklace with a very valuable stone, the blue diamond I asked you about earlier. It was stolen from her. In that sense, it's no longer urgent. I'll come by between eleven and twelve."

He would have to tell Madame Allanic everything, regardless of how much her confused mind would be able to process. And soon. Before the story in which her diamond played a key role reached the press. Above all, he would have to reassure her, tell her that the stone had been returned, that she would soon have it back. But he would also have to tell her that one of her nieces—Blanche? Was it really true?—had stolen the gem. One thing was certain, the whole thing would be incredibly upsetting for her.

"Really? Has someone confirmed that to you? That it's about the blue diamond? That all those people were murdered because of it?"

The anxiety in Madame Lezu's voice had been joined by something else. He detected a strong sense of discomfort.

"That's exactly right, Madame Lezu. Lucille Trouin has just confirmed it."

"I—I understand . . . I think I need to speak with you, Monsieur le Commissaire. I don't have anything to do with all of this, nothing at all, but still. There's this one thing."

"What's this about, Madame Lezu?"

"I'd prefer to tell you in person."

Dupin had an ominous feeling.

"I'll be there shortly, madame. In ten minutes."

"I'll wait in front of the house for you."

Dupin hung up.

"What does she want to talk to you about? Any ideas?" Nedellec probed.

"I have no idea."

"Get round there!" Huppert instructed him. "We'll give your apologies to the prefects again."

"I'll be in touch."

He had already left the office.

Madame Lezu was waiting impatiently for Dupin, standing on the solitary street that led to the villa.

Dupin parked the Citroën at the side of the road, and the housekeeper immediately came up to the car door.

"I'd prefer to speak with you here outside." She glanced an apprehensive glance back at the house. "It's—it's about me. In a way."

Dupin was still getting out of the car.

"What's bothering you so much, madame?"

"I . . ." She paused. Dupin noticed that she was trembling slightly.

"Tell me, Madame Lezu, there's no need to be afraid."

She seemed to get a grip on herself.

"I saw something. Without intending to, of course." She seemed to grow more uneasy by the second. "During Lucille's last visit here, about three weeks ago, I saw her looking at Madame's jewelry. Madame was sitting on the terrace, like she always does when the weather allows. I was working. Her niece crept into Madame's bedroom, the door was open just a little, I was about to clean the hallway—I—" She almost tripped over her words. "I swear to you I wasn't spying on Lucille, it was just a coincidence."

She fell silent, as though she'd used up all her strength. Of course, Dupin doubted her assertion a little. She probably *had* been spying on Lucille. But that wasn't important.

"Do go on, Madame Lezu."

"She had the blue diamond in her hand. I saw it with my own eyes."

"What did she do with it?"

"She looked at it and took photos with her cell phone. Then she put it back again."

"And you're completely sure about this? Including the fact that she put it back? That's very important for us, Madame Lezu."

"I'm completely sure."

"And Lucille didn't notice you?"

"Oh no, definitely not."

Three weeks ago, therefore, the diamond had still been in the safe in the villa. And Lucille had shown unequivocal interest in it. It fit with the chronology of the land fiasco—that she had received the catastrophic news shortly before that.

"I then called Madame Blanche to tell her. I . . ."

"You did what?"

"I didn't want to tell Madame Allanic, she would only have gotten really upset. She would have misunderstood, she . . ."

"You called Blanche Trouin? And told her her sister had been looking at the blue diamond?"

Sheer panic lay in Madame Lezu's gaze.

"I . . . I thought Blanche should know. I didn't know what to do, please understand me, Monsieur le Commissaire. Who was I supposed to speak to? Madame Blanche was such a nice, honest person. This is incredibly unpleasant for me, I didn't want anything to do with the whole thing. I . . ." Her face had lost all color. "I'm so incredibly sorry."

So that was one of the calls itemized on Blanche Trouin's cell phone bill. Dupin remembered Huppert having told him about it. It fit perfectly.

"Why didn't you mention this sooner?"

"I . . . I wanted to, but I—I was afraid. Do you think I . . ."

Her voice failed her.

"What did Blanche say when you told her?"

"She just thanked me, that was all. Then she hung up."

"And then she came by and picked up the necklace with the diamond?"

"I don't know. I didn't pay any more attention to the matter. It wasn't my business, after all." She slowly seemed to be regaining her composure.

"Do you know whether Blanche was here at any point after your call?"

"Not on the days I was working, no, definitely not. But perhaps on my day off, I can't say about that."

"And you didn't happen to check to see whether the necklace was missing?"

"Of course not. I don't have the authority to look at Madame's jewelry, it would be a breach of trust and cause for dismissal. As I said," she was trembling again, "I discovered the safe by accident only, but I didn't open it myself, not ever."

Dupin believed her.

"But you would still have helped the police enormously, if . . ."

He let it be. It was futile, and in the end would only lead to Madame Lezu feeling devastated. It was what it was.

"Did I do something wrong, I mean, will I be prosecuted?"

"No one will prosecute you, Madame Lezu. What you've just told me is incredibly significant for our investigation." Dupin ran a hand through his hair, struggling to take it all in. "It's good that you decided to confide in me."

Madame Lezu had most probably handed them the last piece of the puzzle: that it really had been Blanche who had taken the diamond. Even if, as things looked, they would only ever be able to speculate over her reasons. Perhaps one could put it like this: Blanche had wanted to secure the necklace because she suspected Lucille was intending to steal it.

On closer consideration, it was chilling: in actual fact, Lucille's plan had been perfect. She had had every reason to presume that, given her aunt's confused state, no one would ever find out about the theft. If Madame Allanic's sister in Canada had inherited her estate, it would no longer even have been possible to reconstruct everything.

"And you're sure nothing can happen to me?" There was something pleading to the housekeeper's tone.

"Completely sure, Madame Lezu."

Faced with thinking about the answer he should actually have given Madame Lezu, Dupin felt dizzy. It was extreme. If Madame Lezu had not, with the best of intentions, called Blanche, then the entire sequence of events would never have been set in motion. And even before that: if she had come into the hallway a few minutes later and not seen Lucille with the stone . . . Blanche wouldn't have taken the diamond herself, Lucille wouldn't have realized this on Monday morning—and nobody at all would have died. Nothing would have happened apart from the theft, which presumably no one would ever have discovered.

A shudder ran down Dupin's spine, giving him goose bumps.

"I'd like to have another quick word with Madame Allanic."

Ten minutes later, during which Dupin had waited on the terrace, the housekeeper accompanied Madame Allanic— dressed in a dark green suit—to her wicker armchair next to the little table in the sun.

Madame Allanic looked overwhelmed.

"*Bonjour*, Madame Allanic." Dupin sat down on one of the cast-iron chairs and came straight to the point, not wanting to make it complicated. "I have good news. We found your necklace with the blue diamond. It's back. We just need it for a little longer, then we'll return it to you."

Astonishment and disbelief crept into the old woman's features. All of a sudden, she smiled.

"My husband—I told you. He'll find the thieves. He'll bring everything back. And he'll come back himself. He'll put everything straight again, everything."

She had incorporated Dupin's news into her own world. Into her own fantastical world, which seemed bizarre to outsiders. Dupin felt deeply moved. The news had reached her deep within. And had taken away her anguish. He wouldn't bother her with anything more. This reaction was enough for Dupin; he had fulfilled his role. In a certain way, as strange as it might sound, this moment here was the end of the case—at least for him.

"Good." He got up. "Then I'll leave you to the sunshine and your beautiful view, Madame Allanic."

She seemed to have retreated back within herself, and had lowered her head. It was a peaceful sight.

"*Au revoir*, Madame Allanic," he said to the old woman, then turned to the housekeeper. "*Au revoir*, Madame Lezu. It was a pleasure."

Dupin was overcome by what was actually an entirely inappropriate exhilaration. He let it be.

He left the terrace, light-footed, and a few moments later, the villa.

Before he even got back to the car, he got out his phone. Huppert and Nedellec were presumably sitting with the prefects now.

Huppert picked up at once.

"And?"

"There's news . . ."

Dupin swiftly and succinctly summarized the important details.

"This is completely insane," said the commissaire, "but conclusive. We're almost done here. I'll just pass on this part of the story, and then that's that."

This meant, or at least Dupin understood it in this sense, something along the lines of: "Everything's sorted, we no longer need you here."

"Good." Dupin pondered for a moment. "I'll come by the station later."

"Do that. The prefects have called a press conference for twelve-fifteen. I'm sure this will be of national interest. You should at least briefly—"

"I'll try."

It was the last thing Dupin wanted to think about right now. He didn't have the energy left. Nor the enthusiasm.

"Really, do try. And this evening there's the big good-bye dinner. Until then, Dupin."

Dupin put his cell phone away, and walked along the narrow path that led down to the inland sea.

He had time for a little walk. Time to stretch out on a particularly beautiful, welcoming spot on the fine, white sand for a while. He would do nothing but stare up at the endlessly vast, endlessly blue sky. And think about nothing. Nothing at all.

The short walk by the inland sea had turned into one and a half hours.

It had done him good. Dupin had walked along the beach

for a quarter of an hour, then found just the spot he was looking for.

Comfortable in the sand, with the sun on his face, he had
almost nodded off a few times, but was thwarted by a few loudly
screeching gulls. A deep tiredness had descended over him.

There was no trace of the previous night's storm. The world
had long since dried out again, and the sun reigned in all its
glory over the vast, endless sky. A wonderful early summer's day
on the Atlantic coast—on days like this, you could breathe more
deeply and freely.

On the way back, Dupin had called the Concarneau office
and reported back to Nolwenn. Just the most important details;
the more comprehensive report would follow. She had been very
content.

He hadn't reached his car again until just before twelve. Unequivocally too late for the press conference. Wanting to spare
himself the discussion with Huppert, he had sent a text message.
Astonishingly, the response was merely: *All fine. See you at 1:30
in my office*. She didn't seem to take offense. Completely unlike
Locmariaquer. Shortly after twelve he had tried to reach Dupin
three times in quick succession. Dupin had ignored it. He knew
him, and his annoyance would be short-lived; by the time of his
grand appearance in front of the press, at the latest, all would be
forgotten.

Just to be on the safe side, Dupin had driven straight from
Rothéneuf to Saint-Sevan; he didn't want to be anywhere near
the police school before his meeting with Huppert. He had
parked his car close to the market, and was planning to have
another coffee in the Café du Théâtre—as a good-bye. He had
passed the market halls where it had all begun three days before.

In spite of the coffee and his doze on the beach, he had almost fallen asleep on the barstool. His strength was completely used up, and it was only getting worse, not better. On the radio he had heard snippets of the latest report on the case, and was glad that, amidst the café hubbub, he couldn't fully make it out.

In a peaceful side street—on the way back to his Citroën—he had tried to reach Claire. He'd actually wanted to do it this morning; she hadn't tried to reach him again since he'd rejected her call the night before. But once again it went to voicemail. He couldn't help feeling a little uneasy.

Shortly after half past one, Dupin had arrived in the police station as planned.

Nedellec was still in conversation with his prefect, so Dupin had been alone with Huppert. The strain of the last days could be seen on her too.

Huppert had given him an account of the press conference. Dozens of reporters and numerous camera teams had been there. Her boss, the host prefect, had presented an overview of the case and its resolution, then each of the three other prefects had added a commentary, and finally the "Britt Team" had been thanked profusely.

They had showed the press both the letter from Charles Braz and the diamond—Dupin didn't want to imagine the headlines that would arise from even just the "legendary blue diamond from a corsair treasure trove." And perhaps it really had originated from a corsair. For a moment, Dupin had chuckled to himself, thinking back to the eager town historian who had told them about the adventurous René Duguay-Trouin. The entire story couldn't have been better suited to Saint-Malo.

The prefect had omitted from her summary the exact details

of how they had gotten access to the letter—the scene in the restroom. Huppert had finished her report with a contented remark: "Everyone's in agreement that Lucille Trouin won't get away with it." Dupin had remained silent the whole time.

He was out of the station again by 2:05, and had driven straight back to his hotel. He laid down for a nap, and only woke up again at half past six. But that didn't matter. The case was solved, it was over.

He showered and changed into a fresh, dark blue polo shirt and his last clean pair of jeans. Tomorrow morning he'd be going back to Concarneau.

The restaurant was only a stone's throw away, so Dupin walked there through the balmy summer air.

At exactly seven thirty, he entered Saint Placide—the final stop of their epicurean program—more punctually than on any of the recent days.

As soon as he walked in, Dupin felt a sense of peace. The restaurant was spacious, and had round tables with long white tablecloths; it was like a meditation on simplicity. Stone-gray chairs with elegantly curved backs, an oak floor, the walls painted in white and terra-cotta, lamps hanging over the tables in differing geometric shapes, gold inside, bathing everything in a warm light. A wooden counter bearing dozens of different wine decanters.

Smiling, Dupin reached the table at the far end of the restaurant. In spite of his punctuality, he was the last to arrive.

"Ah—there he is! Mon Commissaire!" called Locmariaquer. "So he does still exist."

Dupin resolved not to let the prefect affect him and his good mood this evening, no matter what he said.

Dupin greeted the group.

The "Britt Team" was sitting together, with Huppert in the middle, which Dupin was happy to see. Really happy, he noted—almost a little sentimental.

"And to you too, Commissaire Dupin." The host prefect stood up ceremoniously and everyone followed her lead. "Congratulations! Excellent work! Finistère has really done its bit!"

She nodded approvingly.

"We were a good team." Dupin looked at Huppert and Nedellec. "A very good team."

They really were.

The prefect reached for her champagne glass—there was already one at Dupin's place setting too—and lifted it into the air with a flourish. "I think we should now make a toast to the three commissaires. To your exceptional investigation skills! To the Britt Team!"

The others picked up their glasses too.

"Hear hear!" the red-haired prefect from Morbihan agreed emphatically.

Even the surly expression of the prefect from the Côtes d'Armor brightened. "Absolutely!"

"What a triumph!" Locmariaquer, of course, couldn't leave it at a simple toast. "I would say the four Breton *départements* have proven their combined clout impressively. And much more spectacularly than could ever have been the case in a seminar or training exercise—let's be happy it happened like this. What a wonderful opportunity!"

Locmariaquer's comment was so abstruse that the prefect didn't even respond to it.

"To all of us! To the Breton police force! To Brittany!"

Everyone drank.

"Not to forget, of course, the incredible results," Locmari-aquer continued, "which we prefects were able to achieve in our intensive consultations and which we—"

"Many thanks, my esteemed colleague. Let's proceed to our reward for the efforts of the last few days." The host prefect's eyes gleamed. "Let's turn our attention to the heavenly creations of Luc Mobihan, the famous chef of Saint Placide, one of our greats, bestowed with a Michelin star. It's also the celebratory conclusion of our culinary roundelay."

Everyone took their seats.

"I'll hand over to Isabelle Mobihan, our hostess and wonderful *sommelière*."

A friendly looking woman in a colorfully patterned dress had appeared at their table.

"*Bonsoir*, mesdames, messieurs. Perhaps you're already familiar with the motto of our kitchen: *Voyages et aventures*."

It had been the motto of the entire case—a perfect conclusion.

"Luc's immense curiosity drives him to continually search for extraordinary taste experiences. He's always bringing new ideas back from our travels all over the world, frequently from Mauritius or the Seychelles. Imagine Saint Placide as a *cabinet gourmand des curiosités*, we don't concern ourselves with gastronomic trends. It's said that the most complicated thing of all is to achieve simplicity, and that's precisely what we try to do."

She gave the group a warmhearted smile and pointed toward the plain white cards that lay at every place setting.

"We've decided to offer you the menu *Choisir, c'est se priver du reste*—to choose is to deprive yourself of everything else. It consists of nine courses. You'll find them listed on the little menu cards."

A wonderful concept and a heavenly promise. Dupin felt his excitement building. He was hungry, yes, but it was more than that: pure Lucullan lust.

"Each course will be accompanied by selected wines. We wish you a wonderful evening."

Within seconds, a silently captivated study of the menus commenced. Everything sounded like pure poetry. In moments like these, Dupin felt very aware of how much he loved French culture, a culture that ranked a masterful menu composition alongside a great opera, painting, or novel. An event.

The menu read like a collection of Dupin's most delicious dreams: from wild oysters with shallots and red wine ice cream, and abalone mussels with garlic foam, via hand-gathered scallops with citrus fruits and Madagascar pepper, to pan-fried pigeon with café jus and young vegetables from Mont Garrot. Not to mention the desserts.

Over the next few hours, they would explore a sensual epicurean wonderland even more delicious than the land of milk and honey.

Among the prefects, delighted discussions had begun about what the menu held in store for them.

Huppert reached for her glass, which held the last sip of champagne, and spoke under her breath so only the two commissaires could hear:

"To the three of us."

She smiled.

They toasted.

Dupin hadn't thought it possible, but it looked set to be an enjoyable evening. They all seemed to need it.

The Fifth Day

It had turned into a late night. And it had actually been pretty lively, almost boisterous. Even Locmariaquer had been bearable.

Dupin hadn't got back to his hotel until almost one in the morning. Huppert had stayed until the end too, despite the day ahead holding several thoroughly unpleasant, challenging tasks for her. In particular, yet another interview with Lucille Trouin, in which she had to confront her, amongst other things, with Madame Lezu's statement and once again with Charles Braz's letter. It would be the last interrogation in Saint-Malo; afterward Lucille would be transferred to Rennes. It was highly likely that even now she would try to find some way of twisting the facts. But nothing could help her now; in the end she would be sentenced to life imprisonment.

Shortly before half past eight, Dupin had been woken by the rays of sunlight heralding the new day.

He had slept with the windows wide open, and the wonderful morning freshness had filled the room.

As he woke up, the entire case—the two rival sisters, the murders, all the inconceivable events of the last few days—seemed like a dark chimera, a somber, nebulous nightmare.

Dupin had survived the week, he was a free man. The weekend lay before him, starting with this Friday morning. In a few hours he would be back home. And Claire would be back tomorrow night; the two weeks without her were finally over.

Dupin had enjoyed an unhurried breakfast, and the wonderful hotel owner Madame Delanoë had sat down with him for a while. They had only briefly mentioned the case, talking mainly about the beauty of the Emerald Coast, which was Madame Delanoë's home, and of which Dupin had seen a fair bit over the past few days.

Afterward he had packed and thrown everything in the car, which he had driven right up to the open gate of the Villa Saint Raphaël.

Dupin took one last sentimental look around him before getting in the car. It was a stunning estate, a real find. Grand, elegant, but not intimidating. A forecourt with white gravel and a tall, picture-postcard palm tree. But the most wonderful thing was the magnificent exotic garden behind the house. A little oasis.

Madame Delanoë stood by the gate. *"Au revoir,* Monsieur Dupin, it was such a pleasure to host you. I hope you'll come back again soon. But perhaps without any murders—just for enjoyment."

"I will. Claire will love it here."

Dupin had already been thinking about doing so over the

last few days. He had to admit that he'd fallen a little in love with the Emerald Coast. He would surprise Claire with a little Saint-Malo trip. It was only a two-hour drive, and the Villa Saint Raphaël was fantastic for a weekend break. What's more, he now knew so many excellent restaurants.

Madame Delanoë handed Dupin a large paper bag. "A driver dropped this off for you earlier."

He took the bag. There was a card attached to it: *A memento of Saint-Malo—best wishes from Rue de l'Orme. Yours, Louane Huppert.*

Dupin couldn't help but grin.

Curious, he glanced into the bag.

It was astonishing: A bottle of Rhum J.M., buckwheat cookies, buckwheat honey, two jars of *babas au rhum,* a pretty little spice jar with an orange label—*"Curry Corsaire"*—and of course, butter from Yves Bordier, a *demi-sel* and one with Roscoff onions.

"Amazing!"

Dupin's exclamation was heartfelt. But how did the commissaire know about the rum?

He packed the bag into the car and said good-bye to Madame Delanoë a second time.

After ten minutes, he reached the Route Nationale heading westward, then immediately turned off into the deserted inland, and made his way from the northeast back to the southwest of Brittany.

Two hours and seventeen minutes later, having made good time, Dupin parked his Citroën on the spacious lot in front of the

Amiral, a stone's throw from the harbor and the Ville Close, Concarneau's legendary old town.

It was just before half past twelve. The perfect time for a light lunch. Something simple.

Perhaps his regular table would still be free.

He stepped into the Amiral, his home away from home, off Avenue Pierre Guéguin.

All at once, he came to a halt.

Where his regular table should have been, three of the tables for two had been put together, as though for a small party.

One single chair was still empty; all the others were occupied.

He couldn't believe his eyes.

The whole group. Nolwenn, Riwal, Kadeg—and even their colleagues Le Menn and Nevou.

They were immersed in the daily papers, which, as the headlines showed, were reporting nothing but the case.

Dupin couldn't help but feel moved. They must have gathered here on the off chance; no one had known he was coming here. Although the probability that the Amiral would be his first stop in Concarneau was admittedly exceptionally high.

Dupin went over to the table.

"Monsieur le Commissaire!"

Nolwenn was the first to notice him. She jumped up and seemed overcome, almost as though she was happy to even see him alive again.

"There you are! Welcome home. Finistère is so proud of you! Although we must admit," she gave a conciliatory smile, "that Saint-Malo did a good job too."

They really had.

"It's about time you came back, boss!" Riwal had also stood up.

Kadeg got up now too, it almost looked choreographed. "Good to have you back."

The second inspector also made it sound as though Dupin had been away for weeks, months even, and for a moment it looked like he was about to hug the commissaire, but then he quickly sat down again.

Then the two policewomen made a move to stand up—Dupin preempted them.

"Please, don't get up!"

He emphasized the request by sitting down himself.

"Well, finally!"

Paul Girard had appeared as though out of nowhere, the taciturn owner of the Amiral and Dupin's longtime friend. They gave one another a firm hug.

"I've got a few extra-large entrecôtes for you all. Spectacular pieces."

"Perfect!" Dupin exclaimed.

That was just the thing, it couldn't be better. Something simple . . .

Nolwenn reached for her glass—Dupin had already seen the bottle, one of his favorite red wines, Lagarde, an everyday Bordeaux—and began to speak:

"Taol da bouez' ta!"

One of the most beautiful Breton expressions, it meant: Cast off your worries!

"On Monday you'll have to explain everything to us in minute detail. But not now. Now we eat!"

Dupin picked up his glass too.

Nolwenn gave the celebratory toast. *"Yec'hed mad!"*

Translated literally, it meant something like "good health," but actually the magical saying expressed much more:

The best of luck, the best of everything.

Acknowledgments

My heartfelt thanks to my friend Harald Schulte for his expertise. For this volume, and all the others.

About the Author

International bestselling author JEAN-LUC BANNALEC lives in Germany and the southerly region of the French department of Finistère. In 2016 he was given the award Mécène de Bretagne. Since 2018 he has been an honorary member of the Académie Littéraire de Bretagne. He is also the author of *Death in Brittany, Murder on Brittany Shores, The Fleur de Sel Murders, The Missing Corpse, The Killing Tide, The Granite Coast Murders, The King Arthur Case,* and *The Body by the Sea.*